W9-AGE-834

SIMON BLOOM:

THE
OCTOPUS EFFECT

SIMON BLOOM:

THE
OCTOPUS
EFFECT

MICHAEL REISMAN

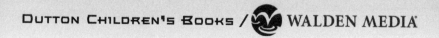
DUTTON CHILDREN'S BOOKS / WALDEN MEDIA

*Whether you love to read or not, whether you like science or not,
and whether you're a boy or a girl, this book is for you . . .
because everybody wishes they could fly.*

*This book is especially dedicated to my dear friend Alison,
who believed in me even when I forgot to*

DUTTON CHILDREN'S BOOKS
A division of Penguin Young Readers Group

Published by the Penguin Group • Penguin Group (USA) Inc., 375 Hudson Street, New York, New York 10014,
U.S.A. • Penguin Group (Canada), 90 Eglinton Avenue East, Suite 700, Toronto, Ontario M4P 2Y3, Canada
(a division of Pearson Penguin Canada Inc.) • Penguin Books Ltd, 80 Strand, London WC2R 0RL, England •
Penguin Ireland, 25 St Stephen's Green, Dublin 2, Ireland (a division of Penguin Books Ltd) • Penguin Group
(Australia), 250 Camberwell Road, Camberwell, Victoria 3124, Australia (a division of Pearson Australia Group Pty
Ltd) • Penguin Books India Pvt Ltd, 11 Community Centre, Panchsheel Park, New Delhi – 110 017, India • Penguin
Group (NZ), 67 Apollo Drive, Rosedale, North Shore 0632, New Zealand (a division of Pearson New Zealand Ltd) •
Penguin Books (South Africa) (Pty) Ltd, 24 Sturdee Avenue, Rosebank, Johannesburg 2196, South Africa •
Penguin Books Ltd, Registered Offices: 80 Strand, London WC2R 0RL, England

CIP Data is available.

Published in the United States by Dutton Children's Books,
a division of Penguin Young Readers Group
345 Hudson Street, New York, New York 10014
www.penguin.com/youngreaders

Designed by Elizabeth Frances   Printed in USA   First Edition
ISBN 978-0-525-42082-8   10 9 8 7 6 5 4 3 2 1

WHO'S WHO IN THE WORLD OF
THE TEACHER'S EDITIONS

THE KNOWLEDGE UNION

It is a secret organization responsible for making sure the universe runs smoothly. Sometimes the members even succeed. Among them are:

BOARD OF ADMINISTRATION

Janathus Misht • Overseer of the Science Orders
Standrus Presst • Lead Examiner and Chief Executive of the Board
Madda Roobet • Chief Analyst of Keeper Affairs

THE COUNCIL OF SCIENCES

Ralfagon Wintrofline • Keeper of the Order of Physics
Gilio Skidowsa • Keeper of the Order of Biology
Olvero Lombaro • Keeper of the Order of Chemistry
Allobero Foreedaman • Keeper of the Order of Astronomy
Skyrena McSteiner • Keeper of the Math League
Solomonder Smithodrome • Keeper of the Order of Psychology

ORDER OF PHYSICS

Eldonna Pombina • Assistant to Ralfagon. Don't forget your earplugs around her.
Simon Bloom (co-Keeper) • He's a good person to name a book after.
Owen Walters • He controls direction and speed, but nothing's as fast as how he talks.
Alysha Davis • The electricity she absorbs/discharges is almost as jolting as her attitude.

Loisana Belane • She shifts solids, liquids, and gases; useful with melted ice cream.

Willoughby Wanderby • He'll spin you like a merry-go-round set to ultra-scary-fast.

Mermon Veenie • He's big, he's bad, and he throws a mean bolt of lightning.

Robertitus Charlsus • He'll make the ground—and you—shake.

Myarina Myashah • Get on her bad side and it'll be worse than seven years of bad luck.

ORDER OF BIOLOGY

Flangelo Squicconi • It's a bird, it's a plane . . . no, wait, it's a bird.

Kender • He may look like a big bug, but it's *he* that might squash *you.*

Targa • She's basically a human espresso machine that also works in reverse.

Cassaro • He attacks with a cloud of fungus, which is just as disgusting as it sounds.

Grawley • Sure, he's fuzzy, but his bear hugs could really ruin your day. Or your life.

Kushwindro • Jungles are filled with life, but he makes them try to end yours.

Preto • Part man, part fish . . . all bad.

Kostaglos • Never get into a spitting contest with this venomous fellow.

Zillafer • She may be full of hot air, but her spikes make her nastier than any balloon.

Baharess • Trust me, her belch is worse than her bite.

Trurya • Now you see her, now you don't . . . see anything!

Najolo • Alone he's a noisy little ape; with hundreds of his friends he's a party—a bad one.

Demara • You'd better have more than insect repellent if she sends her swarms after you.

Jaynu • Just because she glows doesn't mean she's very bright.

Cubec • He can find you wherever you go, but that's about all he can do.

Branto • His control over hibernation even puts him to sleep.

ORDER OF CHEMISTRY

Krissantha • She can make you go to pieces. Literally.

LaCurru • Not your usual mad scientist–type; he's madder.

HISTORICAL SOCIETY

Miss Fanstrom (Keeper) • Watches over history and the present (the hair and now).

Greygor Geryson • Narrator for Order of Physics (and this book); quite a snappy dresser.

Sirabetta • Her colorful tattoos are as pretty as a picture—a violent, deadly picture.

OUTSIDERS

Everybody who's not in the Union. Yes, that includes you. And him. And her. Not sure about that one over there, though. . . .

SIMON BLOOM:

THE
OCTOPUS
EFFECT

YES, IT'S TIME FOR ANOTHER CHRONICLE . . .

You know that universe you're living in? It's a pretty old place. Every religious group, philosopher, or scientist has a different explanation for when—and how—everything got started. But, at the very least, it's clear the universe is no spring chicken.

After all that time, you'd think it would have learned to take care of itself. Unfortunately, that's not true. The universe is a messy, danger-filled place in need of constant watching after, like an infant playing around electrical outlets, a busy road, or a gang of hungry alligators. That's one of the reasons the Knowledge Union was formed. The members use the immensely powerful Books, each one allowing access to the secrets of the universe, so they can keep reality from winking out, or everything turning purple, or whatever other catastrophe might occur.

With the Union around, you'd think existence would be fine, right? Wrong! Accidents often happen in spite of—or even because of—their work.

My job in the Union is Narrator—I chronicle history as it unfolds. It used to be a dull job; I rarely got to watch any fun changes or exciting mistakes. Then, five months ago, Simon Bloom entered my Chronicle and prevented a disaster.

By finding and becoming Keeper of one of those incredible Books—the *Teacher's Edition of Physics*—Simon gained control over all the laws of physics. Aided by his friends Owen and Alysha, he used the Book to stop the terrible Sirabetta from using her terrible powers in her terrible scheme to take over the universe. (Which would have been really bad.)

Pretty impressive for an eleven-year-old. I even helped in my own way; it was a great day for Narrators everywhere!

You'd think that would have been it. The Union should have gotten everything on track and put it all back in neat working order. Sure, Simon still had command of three physics laws, but his friends and he should have been able to return to their normal lives of friends, family, and school.

Only five months later, however, the universe we worked so hard to save was about to get in more trouble than ever. And Simon Bloom, now twelve years old, was going to find himself in an enormous amount of danger.

As before, it began on a Sunday. . . .

CHAPTER 1

ALL BOOKS GREAT AND SMALL

It was Sunday morning in the quiet town of Lawnville, New Jersey. The time was eleven o'clock, part of that long, getting-hungry stretch between breakfast and lunch.

Simon Bloom was spending it doing his favorite thing: reading. He'd loved it since he'd first learned how, and the ability to control a few laws of physics hadn't changed that.

Of course, he could enjoy his powers, too. Simon was sitting above his bed . . . eight feet above. On the ceiling. His butt was firmly planted there as he sat, cross-legged, with his head hanging down toward his bed. He had used his control over the law of gravitation, changing it on himself so he was pulled up instead of down like everything else on the planet. For Simon, the ceiling *was* the ground. To him, the rest of his bedroom—his bed, his desk, his bookcases, the dirty laundry he'd not quite gotten around to tossing into the hamper—appeared to be on the ceiling.

He preferred to sit that way whenever his parents weren't home and thus couldn't walk in on him. This was often, since his mother, Sylvia Bloom, was working on a new advertising campaign that had her putting in long hours in her office. His father, Steven Bloom, was focused on his own lab work as an astrophysicist, studying gravitational relationships between certain star systems.

Now, Simon was deep into one of his favorite books, about children in the future training in zero-gravity for an alien war. One brilliant boy gets stuck with terrible responsibility and pressure, but he just wants to be a kid.

Simon was distracted from his reading by a twisting sensation inside his stomach and his head. He wasn't sure what it was, but it made him feel something strange was happening. Something he should be prepared for.

He spoke a series of words that were complete gibberish to me; only a Keeper of the Book of Physics could understand them. Fortunately, Narrators can often read the surface thoughts of our Chronicle-subjects, so I knew he was using his second formula. This gave him control over friction, which he used to make the pages of his book stick in place: it worked much better than a bookmark. He then increased the book's friction to make it adhere next to him on the ceiling. Now his hands were free, if needed.

Simon looked up (down, really) and frowned at a blurry patch forming in the air above (er, beneath) him. Something was making a hole in the middle of his bedroom.

The hole was accompanied by the jarring sound of air ripping. It was a noise Simon knew well; it was about as pleasant as taking a swarm of bees, teaching them how to use maracas and finger cymbals, and putting them inside your ears for a music recital.

Simon's frown turned to a smile as he saw who his visitor was. The *Teacher's Edition of Physics* appeared, bursting out of the hole like a jack-in-the-box. Though it looked like an ordinary textbook, it was far more. It was a Book: one of those links to the endless power of the universe. It was also a dear friend of Simon's.

You see, Simon knew what every Keeper and Narrator did: the Books are more than just tomes filled with powerful formulas. They might not be alive, exactly, but they were aware. They could think. And, most importantly, they could act on their own. Simon Bloom found and was able to use the Book of Physics because *it* had chosen *him*.

"Hello, Book," Simon said aloud. He tried to be calm, but his heart started beating faster. He hadn't seen the Book on its own since it was returned to its previous owner, Ralfagon Wintrofline. Ralfagon, the Keeper and leader of the Order of Physics, was careful to keep the Book by his side.

"What are you doing here?" he asked it. "Is Ralfagon okay?"

The Book ignored his questions and floated over to him. Simon took hold of it in one hand (despite being the size of a huge textbook, the Book weighed about the same as a small paperback). He stroked its spine, and it glowed bright blue and vibrated in response. The scene was rather like a boy and his pet dog, although this dog was blue, hairless, rectangular, and could destroy the universe. Plus, it was house-trained.

You must get ready, Keeper, it said, using the mental link they'd developed.

"Ready for what?" If Simon's heart was racing before, it was sprinting now.

Ready for the end of things as you know it. For the next stage. And all the dangers that will bring.

What? Simon thought back to it. *What do you mean?*

Once again, the Book ignored his question. *Make sure Owen Walters and Alysha Davis are prepared, too.* It made a mental noise that was surely the Book version of a sigh. *The end is coming. You must make sure there will be a new beginning.*

The Book hovered silently for a moment more and then vanished with a noisy tearing of air and a *poof*. Simon stared with confusion and more than a little fear at the space the Book had been occupying. What had it meant? End? Next stage? Dangers? He remembered well the problems his friends and he had faced when he first found the Book. Some were a lot of fun, but some had been of the almost-certain-doom variety.

Simon glanced at his clock. Though it was upside down to him, the big, red digital numbers were easy to read. He was late!

I have to figure this out, Simon thought. *But I've also got to go.*

Simon stood up on the ceiling, bringing his head a few feet closer to his bed. He jumped, twisted in midair, and shifted his personal gravity back to normal. Suddenly the ground was his ground again. Simon landed feetfirst on his bed and bounced to the floor. After gathering a few items into his backpack, he went to his window.

He was halfway outside when he remembered the book he'd been reading; it was on the ceiling, still stuck by friction. With a snap of his fingers, Simon made the book drop down to his bed; it remained open to the right page.

Simon hopped outside his second-floor bedroom window, using his friction control to let him scramble up the side of his house like a much shorter, less-colorfully-dressed Spider-Man. He climbed onto the roof and glanced at the trees in his backyard. The beautiful autumn leaves were turning from lush green to vibrant reds, oranges, and yellows. They also hid him from neighbors or passersby who might glance up.

From the roof he gazed at the low clouds hanging sheetlike across the October sky. *Perfect. All the cover I'll need.* He rubbed his hands together, licked one finger, and held it up to test the wind (mild, southerly). He reached out with his mind and sensed the twists and curves of gravity along his intended route, noting every falling leaf, strolling person, flapping bird, zooming plane, and suborbital satellite. He smiled. There was no danger of being spotted or, worse, getting smeared painfully in a collision.

It was time to fly.

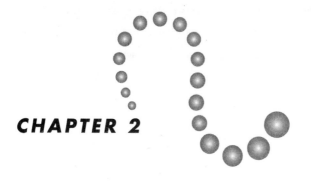

CHAPTER 2

Uᴘ, Uᴘ, ᴀɴᴅ . . . Uᴘ Sᴏᴍᴇ Mᴏʀᴇ

Simon spoke a few more words and, now nearly weightless, jumped into the air. What should have been a regular jump for an average twelve-year-old instead sent him hurtling hundreds of feet above the roof, up to the bottom of the cloud layer. Simon laughed in the thrilling rush of air. He reached the upper limit of his leap and, for a quick moment, peered down through the wispy clouds. It gave him a magnificent view of Lawnville and its surrounding towns.

Then Simon spoke two words that made him zoom across the sky like a human rocket. He'd restored his normal weight, but he'd also changed where he was falling *to*: for him, the ground was now a location in midair, and he gained speed steadily as he was dragged across the sky toward it.

Technically speaking, this wasn't flying—it was more of

a carefully aimed plummet. But when soaring through the air without a helmet, parachute, or even a soft cushion, the not–splatting–part mattered much more than the name of the method. Checking on the weblike network of gravity around him, Simon made the necessary changes to keep on the proper route. After five months of practice, he was able to do this mentally, without words or even gestures.

He fought back the urge to yell, part with delight and part with horror, as he streaked across the sky, zigzagging when needed to adjust his flight path or to avoid a frightened bird. I could sense what he felt—the rush of the passing air, the watering up of his eyes, the shaking in his stomach. No roller-coaster rider, skydiver, or jet pilot had ever felt such exhilaration. At least none that survived.

As exciting as this was, he still couldn't stop thinking about the Book's warning. What did it mean that the end was coming? And when was that supposed to happen? Unfortunately for Simon, this was not the best time to let his mind wander. Despite five months of practice there was a certain . . . trickiness . . . to this type of travel.

Flying by falling means you start by going from zero to about twenty-two miles per hour in the first second. From then on, you're constantly accelerating every second until you reach something called terminal velocity (and doesn't *that* sound charming?), which—if you're flying Superman-style and are Simon's size—is about one hundred forty miles per hour.

That's too fast for anyone to be moving comfortably through the air without any sort of protective suit, jet plane, or Kryptonian heritage. Simon could have changed his personal gravity so he fell—er . . . flew—more slowly, but he was in a hurry. So he had to remember to reverse his gravitational pull every few seconds to slow down. If he got distracted and flew too fast, the rushing air could be blinding. Oh, and he wouldn't be able to breathe very well, either.

Besides keeping his speed in check as he zipped and zoomed, he had to pay attention to his direction. For example, if he went off course and flew too low, he could go down to where there were buildings. Hard, unyielding buildings. That would be bad. And messy. But Simon was quite good at doing many things at once; he was able to watch his speed and stay on the proper path while still thinking about the Book.

When a problem occurred, it was due to something much simpler: someone, somewhere far below, might have been celebrating their birthday. Either that or they just had a thing for multicolored clusters of balloons. Whatever the reason, the person clearly wasn't very good at holding on to those balloons.

Simon was zooming high over Lawnville's Town Square when he got a red balloon full in the face. Even at that speed, a regular, helium-filled round balloon isn't going to hurt much. But it sure can be distracting.

Simon was quickly entangled with a dozen balloons in all the colors of the rainbow, their white strings wrapping around his arms and neck as he flailed. He batted at the balloons and tugged at the strings, which only wrapped him up more. In the midst of his struggles, he accidentally shifted direction and kept falling faster. And faster. Oh, and straight up.

Seconds roared past as Simon struggled with the balloons while moving at around one hundred forty miles per hour. The balloons swiftly burst and stuck to his face and body. By the time Simon got free of the mess, about twenty-five seconds had gone by. That's not too long . . . but it was long enough for him to have flown almost a mile up into the sky.

Okay, that's nowhere near as high up as airplanes fly or many mountains reach, but for a boy without a plane, flight suit, or a pair of goggles, it was not pleasant. And every passing second sent him another three hundred feet higher.

In just a few eyeblinks, Simon was into high altitude—the height at which the atmosphere's oxygen level starts to thin out. There was less wind to sting his face and batter his body, but the temperature was also a lot lower. That kind of cold wasn't much fun, either. Worse, what little air he could suck in was less useful to his horrified brain, and his fear was about to turn to panic. The kind of panic that would keep him from finding a solution and, instead, leave him to keep going up until he passed out.

Simon didn't know if losing consciousness would undo his gravity formula and send him dropping back to the ground, or if he'd keep rising up until he left the Earth's atmosphere, but both were pretty awful scenarios.

Somehow he was able to beat down his rising terror and work the gestures needed to change his direction and speed. He cut through the sky quickly, moving fast enough to get him to safety but not so fast as to give him trouble seeing or breathing. Finally, he reached a reasonable height, back at the bottom of the cloud layer, and he used all his focus to balance out gravity around him.

Simon let several minutes slide by while he floated there in the cloud, taking deep breaths and celebrating how alive he was. Once he felt ready, he continued his flight; this time he stayed focused on control. At last he reached his destination, hundreds of feet above a multistory apartment building across town from his house. He shifted gravity so he fell to the alley next to the building, dropping hard and fast in hopes that nobody glancing in that direction would get a good look at him.

When he was hidden from sight between that apartment building and the one next to it, Simon reversed the pull of gravity to reduce his speed. He then adjusted it so he could float down slowly, his whole body tingling from the gentleness of the motion. Once his feet touched the earth, he restored all laws of physics to normal and sprawled out on the ground.

Simon lay there quietly, gulping air and appreciating how wonderful it felt to not move. After a minute or so, he stood up, adjusted his clothes as best he could, and threw up into the nearest trash can.

He grabbed the nearby brick wall to steady himself, took several deep breaths, wiped his mouth, and then casually strolled out to the sidewalk.

Simon wasn't surprised that nobody was waiting for him; he was *very* late. His friends must have gone inside already. So he popped a piece of gum into his mouth, entered the building, and walked down the hall to apartment number 106.

My apartment.

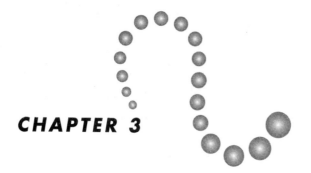

CHAPTER 3

"Rumble" Redux
(and Then Back to Business)

"'Rocket time!'" Owen shouted. He spoke his formula and sent the jungle gym streaking through the air toward the school. Simon returned the jungle gym's gravity so it had its full weight again, and the Order members barely managed to duck before the metal framework slammed into the school's brick wall. It cracked the wall and broke apart.

My apartment shook from the sound, rather like a pile of washing machines crashing down a flight of stairs. Or, to be more accurate, like a bunch of thick metal rods shattering against a big stack of bricks. Inside my living room.

"Kids!" I shouted. "Will you *please* lower that?" I hated to yell; normally, I have the reserve of a true Englishman. But when dealing with such noise, I do as I must.

I tapped a button, and the four adults—those Order

members who ducked under the jungle gym—froze in place. They weren't really in my apartment. Neither was the jungle gym nor the playground where the battle was taking place. (My living room is spacious, but there are limits.)

All those things were displayed on my Viewing Screen: the wall-size, television-like device I use for my work as a Narrator. That battle with the Order members was a replay of past events from a former Chronicle being watched by two twelve-year-olds perched on the edge of my sofa. That is, until I pushed "pause."

With the Screen's replay frozen, Owen, Alysha, and I could hear the sound of knocking at the door. As the kids turned to look, I hastily closed the handheld device I'd been staring at and moved to let my new visitor in.

Simon Bloom glared back at me, his hands folded. "Thanks a lot, Greygor," he said to me as he stomped into my place. "You couldn't have waited fifteen minutes for me before start-ing?" He turned to his young friends. "How much did you watch?"

Alysha Davis burst out laughing, pointing at Simon's head. "Are you okay? Did you get your head stuck in a blender?"

Simon turned to a mirror on my wall and gaped; his short, light brown hair was twisted and tangled around him in a mess of knots and curls. His face was streaked with light gray dirt with trails down his cheeks from where the wind had dragged tears from his eyes. All in all, he didn't make a pretty picture.

"I—" he started to answer. "I don't want to talk about it. Ever." He dashed off to my bathroom to clean himself up and rejoined us a few minutes later.

Owen Walters, the smallest of the three youths, looked at Simon with the expression a dog might have when caught flossing his teeth with your favorite slipper. "Sorry-Simon-but-we-didn't-know-when-you'd-get-here!" He spoke in the rapid-fire, breathless way he reserved for times of extreme anxiety, which, for Owen, was fairly common. Even when only mildly upset, he rarely bothered with punctuation.

"Yeah, sorry; we only just started," Alysha said. "Besides, you know this is Owen's favorite part. He can't get enough of it!"

I frowned at Alysha. On the one hand, they were admiring a Chronicle I had Narrated, and it was lovely to have my work appreciated. Narrators rarely get to meet their Chronicle subjects, while I, Greygor Geryson—Narrator *extraordinaire*—even got to appear in Chronicles with them.

On the other hand, enough was enough; Simon and his friends had come by my apartment many times during the last five months so they could review their exciting exploits. They also tended to empty my fridge and cupboards of all food and drink. Honestly, I've seen swarms of locusts leave more in their wake.

Indeed, Owen used his own physics formula—control over velocity—to snag a doughnut from off my kitchen counter and send it soaring over to Simon. "I saved you a jelly filled," Owen said. His formula let him control the speed and direction of things, though he was most fond of using it on food.

Simon shook his head. "No food. Not yet." He paused. "But thanks."

Owen, taking this as forgiveness, used velocity to send several doughnuts flying from the counter; they zipped across the room and began a fast, if jerky, dance in the air around him. Every time one came close to his mouth, Owen reached out with his mouth and took a bite. Soon his face and shirt were covered in powdered sugar, gooey purple jelly, smeared chocolate sauce, and an assortment of other fillings.

"Hey!" I yelled. "You're getting that all over my couch!" I swear, every visit from these kids taught me new and more wearying methods of stain removal. You'd think entering the seventh grade would have made them act more responsibly.

"Ugh!" Alysha shouted. "And you're getting some on me." She spoke her own formula—capacitance—and generated a bluish white spark of electricity that fried a glob of jelly in midair before it could hit her.

I waved my hand to clear the stink of burned jelly. "Alysha, please," I said. "You'll set off the smoke alarms. I can only imagine what you'll do to my electrical bill." Indeed, Alysha's formula let her absorb huge amounts of electrical energy and discharge it . . . but that electricity had to come from somewhere.

"Don't worry about it, Greygor," Alysha said. She sent an

arc of electricity sizzling back and forth between her fingers, casting a glow on her face. "I'm not getting it from your outlets. There are electrically charged atoms all over, even in the air. I figured out how to absorb some of their charges." She spread her hands apart, creating bigger arcs and sparks.

"Wonderful," I said in a flat tone. "Clearly you have both been practicing since you got your old formulas back." I sighed. "How lucky for me the Order of Physics let you in." Union rules stated that Alysha and Owen had to give up their formulas at the end of my last Chronicle. But once they were officially admitted into the Order . . .

"Would've been sooner if Owen hadn't kept failing the entrance test." Alysha muttered.

"I failed it *once*!" Owen said with a stamp of his foot. "Fine, twice." He shrugged. "I've never been good at tests."

Alysha laughed. "It was multiple choice!" She saw Owen's hurt look. "It doesn't matter; we got in, we got our powers back, and everything's fine. And now it's back to fun and games!" She plucked a doughnut from the air and zapped it with a controlled burst of electricity. "Here, try one that's heated up."

Owen accepted it happily while Simon joined them on the sofa and, at last, felt well enough to eat one of the doughnuts. After a quick bite, he gave a sticky smile and devoured it. Using formulas tended to tire the user, but rest or food restored their strength. With all the gravity control Simon used today, no doughnut was safe.

"Ah yes, you're all very impressive," I said. "But do any of you remember this?" I triggered the remote for my Viewing Screen, focusing my latest, greatest Chronicle on tall, menacing-looking Mermon Veenie, a villain who hurled devastating bolts of lightning. Then I showed them Sirabetta, a beautiful blond woman whose arms and legs were covered in a variety of colored tattoos. Each tattoo gave her command over a different science formula.

I showed the kids a series of images: Sirabetta using one tattoo to fly through the air, as well as resist Simon's gravity and Owen's velocity control. Next, an image of another tattoo melting the street with sizzling heat. Then another to cause explosions with air pressure. And a fourth to launch a glowing, destructive ball of silvery energy.

"Together they put the Keeper of the Order of Physics in the hospital and almost stole the Book of Physics!" I said. "With that, Sirabetta would have stolen the other science Books and done who-knows-what to the entire universe. And she almost killed you all! How is *that* fun and games?"

"Yeah, but Greygor, we beat them," Alysha said. "They've both had their memories wiped and their powers taken away. There's no more threat . . . not even the need for a new Chronicle," she added, gesturing to my Viewing Screen. So far as the kids knew, they'd be on-screen if another Chronicle had begun.

"Plus Simon's officially joining the Council today," Owen said. "I hear there'll be cake!"

Simon frowned. "Actually, something bad might be happening." As Alysha and Owen turned to stare at him, Simon related what the Book said earlier that morning.

"That's got you worried?" Alysha shook her head. "That's the dumbest warning ever! It's like a psychic saying something bad is going to happen soon. Of course something will—that's how life works. But what? And when?"

Simon shrugged. *Maybe Alysha is right*, he thought. *Why worry?*

Owen shook his head. "Doesn't sound good to me. I mean that Book knows things, Simon. If it says we're in danger then we should at least be ready—" He paused and leaned forward. "Wait what's that?" He was pointing to a blinking green light beneath the Viewing Screen.

I tried to act casual. "Oh that, that's nothing. Just an indicator light. To remind me that the Screen's been paused." I moved quickly but calmly until I was standing in front of the Recording Monitor atop my desk.

The device, closely resembling an ordinary computer monitor, could ruin everything if the kids saw it. They'd notice it was filled up with words and might realize that a new Chronicle had started. Fortunately, they had no clue—

"Why are you standing in front of the Recording Monitor?" Owen asked. "Is there something you're not telling us?"

Drat. Before I could think of something to say, the phone on my desk rang. The kids and I stared at it as it rang once, twice, three times.

"Aren't you going to answer that?" Alysha asked.

It was an excellent question; the truth was, it had never rung before. Not in decades of narrating from this apartment. "Of course," I said. "But please hush—it'll be important Narrator business, no doubt."

I picked up the phone. "Hello?" I tried to keep my voice from shaking.

"Mr. Geryson," a woman said in a clipped English accent. "This is unacceptable!"

I cringed. It was Miss Fanstrom, the Keeper of the Historical Society. My boss!

"Do *not* give them any sign that you're speaking to me," Miss Fanstrom said.

"Er," I said. "Why yes, I would like to hear about your apartment cleaning service." I managed a glare at the kids. "It happens I have *quite* a mess to take care of."

"Clever," Miss Fanstrom said. "Now be cleverer and send those three on their way. I'd rather not have them discover a new Chronicle's started . . . not yet, at least. They'll know soon enough."

"Of course. Except . . . how?" I coughed. "How do you get it so clean, I mean?"

"Tut tut, Mr. Geryson," Miss Fanstrom said. I could picture her hair—a two-foot-high black tower—remaining perfectly still as she shook her head. "You are the one who chose to let Mr. Bloom and his friends come over again and again despite our Society's rules on the subject. You must be the one to deal with the problems it causes."

I decided not to remind her that it was *she* who first sent them to visit me in the previous Chronicle. Telling your boss such things wasn't good for job security.

"A wise decision, Mr. Geryson. Now get to it."

The line went dead, leaving me to wonder for a moment whether she'd known what I was thinking. There was no time to worry about that; I had to get rid of these kids. But how do you get three seventh graders to do anything they don't want to do?

I turned to the kids. "My, such interesting cleaning tips." I cleared my throat to buy some time to think. A–ha! "Now that you three are leaving, I can give them a try."

Alysha folded her arms. "Leaving? We've only been here for a little while!"

I smoothed out my comfy brown bathrobe (standard issue for all Historical Society Narrators) and struggled to keep my voice calm. "Oh, you can stay if you want. But I figured you might want to play with your formulas at Dunkerhook Woods before you meet with the Council of Sciences."

Simon, Alysha, and Owen looked at one another. Their glances said it all. Even hyperanxious Owen was tempted by the idea.

"Okay," Simon said. "Maybe we'll come back later, though?"

"Whatever you like, Simon," I said, keeping myself between them and the Recording Monitor as I ushered them to the door. I could only hope that whatever happened next would be enough to keep them busy for the rest of the day.

As I closed my door behind Simon and his friends, I pulled that handheld device out of my bathrobe pocket and flipped a switch on it. Suddenly my Viewing Screen image changed from the previous Chronicle's frozen playground fight-scene to that of the current Chronicle: an image of the three kids rushing down the hall.

With Alysha and Owen reviewing old action on my wall-size Viewing Screen, I'd had to watch Simon's experiences on my mini–Viewing Screen. It wasn't the same, but it did the trick in emergencies.

I sighed and removed my eyeglasses to rub the bridge of my nose. The last time Simon and his friends were featured in a Chronicle, my life and the nature of the Union had been thrown into upheaval. What would happen *this* time?

I settled into my reclining chair. It's not as if I could do anything more than just watch, but with so much at stake, I might as well be comfortable.

CHAPTER 4

There's No Place
Like the Woods

Now that I'm officially narrating once more, I realize some of you might not have read the previous Chronicle. If not, shame on you. I'll continue to toss in a little background as we go, though reading the first Chronicle—*Simon Bloom, the Gravity Keeper*—certainly wouldn't hurt. (You can do that now if you wish.) (I'll wait.)

And now, back to the action! Simon, Owen, and Alysha left my apartment building and entered the same alley Simon had landed in. They put on their backpacks, held hands, and then jumped, with Simon's gravity control letting them leap hundreds of feet. Unlike Simon's solo flight, this time they used Owen's velocity control to move through the air. His formula made for much smoother, safer flying than Simon's did . . . but it was still fast.

Within minutes the trio reached their destination: the dead–end street Van Silas Way. Owen brought them down in the backyard of a house closest to the end so nobody would see them land, and then they walked out to the street.

Thanks to a complex combination of the Knowledge Union's formulas, the people that lived on Van Silas—in fact, most people on Earth—would never be able to go beyond the edge of that dead end. That was because the formulas worked against Outsiders—those not in the Union. Outsiders wouldn't be able to send anything (a Frisbee, a flashlight beam, a bag of squashed grapes) past it, on purpose or by accident. They wouldn't have even thought about it; to them, the street just ended.

Simon, Owen, and Alysha knew exactly what was past Van Silas Way: a forest. But calling it a forest was like saying a mountain range was bumpy ground or an anaconda was a scaly worm. True, these woods took up less land than most normal forests, but what they lacked in acreage they compensated for in height.

The trees were ordinary species (oak, maple, ficus, etc.), but most had grown to redwood size over the years and now stretched hundreds of feet into the sky. Fortunately, the same formulas that kept Outsiders from noticing the woods also kept them from flying planes, hang gliding, or getting catapulted through that airspace.

The forest's name was Dunkerhook Woods, and it was

glad to see the kids. I know, how can a bunch of trees be glad about anything . . . remember, this is no ordinary woods. If it wanted to be happy about something, you'd best not argue. The woods had been a fan of Simon Bloom since it first let him see and enter it five months ago, and the feeling was mutual. Although Simon, Owen, and Alysha had been to Dunkerhook Woods many times since that initial visit, they never grew tired of it.

The woods let loose the Breeze—its equivalent of a welcome mat minus all that foot wiping. The Breeze washed over the trio, filling them with renewed strength and good feeling. That and the energizing Dunkerhook air made naps, caffeinated drinks, and spa visits look bad by comparison.

There were other marvels to the woods. If you explored enough—and believe me, these three had—you could find shrubs that moved from place to place in search of tastier soil, and bushes that changed color and smell just to mess with the insects.

Running down the center of this wondrous mass of vegetation was a wide, smooth dirt path that passed through a clearing. This was the special meeting place of the Order of Physics, who used their own physics formulas and the *Teacher's Edition of Physics* to watch over the universe and help humanity advance their scientific wisdom.

The clearing had numerous tree stumps that served as seats for the Order members. The stumps weren't like those in

Outsider forests. These were quite soft and extremely comfy, provided you didn't try to lean back in them—they had no backrests.

Simon and his friends liked to use that clearing to play with and practice their formulas. As they arrived, however, they found someone waiting.

"Loisana?" Simon exclaimed. "What are you doing here?"

It was Loisana Belane, a willowy, redheaded Order of Physics member. She was one of those four whom the kids fought in their school playground after Simon first got the Book. Of course, back then the Order thought Simon and his friends were thieves who'd attacked their leader and stolen the Book. Now that Simon, Alysha, and Owen were in the Order, too, they were all supposed to be friends.

"I know you guys come here to practice with your formulas," Loisana said. "I figured I'd see if you minded one more."

Simon looked to Owen and Alysha, who shrugged. It might be weird having her there. She was in her twenties or thirties—as old as some of their teachers! Simon and his friends didn't want to have to act differently around her. But she was a fellow Order member . . . these were her woods, too. They couldn't really ask her to leave.

"Sure, why not," Simon said. "You could help us try some new stuff." He stood quietly, thinking. "Okay . . . maybe you could start us off with some water?"

Loisana uttered the words of her formula, and in response, water dropped from the sky over much of the clearing (though not where they were standing). It wasn't rain. Loisana controlled changes in phase: she could make matter (solids, liquids, and gases) turn from one form to another. Now she was taking the moisture in the air and turning it into liquid form.

"Okay," Simon said. "And I'll keep it off the ground." He made the entire water-filled area a gravity-free zone, causing the liquid to drift through the air as tiny globules. "Now, Owen, can you make them bigger?"

"Bigger than you, he means," Alysha said.

"Alysha!" Loisana hissed. "That's not very nice!"

Alysha rolled her eyes and Owen shrugged. "Don't worry about it, Loisana," Owen said. "We're friends—we mess with each other all the time."

Owen spoke his velocity formula to control the speed and direction of several falling water droplets. He caused droplets to collide, making them double-size. He repeated this again and again until there were six enormous floating globes of water, each roughly the size of a small car. He made them swoop and spin through the air.

"It's easy," Owen said. Then he grinned and glanced at Alysha. With a flick of his fingers, he sent a globe hurtling at Alysha. "Now let's see how you handle them!"

Alysha dodged the huge ball of water and flung a handful of coins—each filled to the brim with electricity—at it. The coins exploded upon impact, shattering the globe.

"Ha!" Alysha said. She turned back to Owen as a second

giant water orb slammed into her. She was knocked onto her butt and drenched with water and dirt: mud.

"Owen!" Alysha shrieked. She ran at him and snapped her fingers, sending a small arc of electricity at his legs. He yelped and jumped back.

"Wait a minute!" Loisana said. "You could hurt each other!"

Alysha frowned. "No, it's not like that. We're fine!"

Owen nodded. "This is how we practice, so we can be ready for anything. We have to keep each other alert and come up with new stuff all the time."

Simon nodded. "Now Alysha knows she's got to be ready for multiple attacks, and Owen's got to find a defense against her electrical shocks."

"I suppose that's all right, if it works for you," Loisana said.

"It helped us beat you," Alysha said with arms crossed.

Loisana chuckled. "True. That was quite a fight, wasn't it? I'm still amazed that Willoughby Wanderby overreacted like that; he was positive you were the enemy."

Owen frowned at the mention of his former gym teacher, now fellow Order member, who had led the attack on them in the playground all those months ago. "You know, we've been in the Order with him for months, but he never talks to us."

"Some people don't react as well to getting an electric shock," Alysha said.

"Okay," Simon said. "The reason I wanted Owen to make those water globes was for Alysha to have target practice. I have an idea for her to try. Plasma."

"Like blood on those medical shows?" Owen asked. "Or like plasma TVs?"

"Like the TV but different," Simon said. "Alysha absorbs electricity from the air, right? She does it by moving electrons into and out of atoms, making them ions."

"Atoms with a positive or negative charge," Alysha said.

"So, these ion–atoms become plasma?" Owen asked.

"If there's enough ionized gas, yes," Simon said. "It's in lightning and the sun. But it doesn't *have* to be dangerous. The aurora borealis is plasma, and that's just a pretty light show."

"Oh good," Owen said. "So there's no danger of her blow-ing us up."

Simon chuckled. "Bad news, Owen. I want her to try using plasma as a weapon. Alysha, concentrate on the ions in the air and make more. A lot more. Then see if you can blast the water globes."

Alysha rubbed her palms together, closed her eyes, and started playing with the electrons in the air. She made more and more ions until finally a searing white ball of fiery light formed in front of her. It sizzled and swirled and, a moment later, ruptured with a *boom* that left a huge cloud of dust where Alysha had been standing.

Simon, Owen, and Loisana rushed over to check on her.

"I'm fine, I'm fine," Alysha said, coughing from within the dust cloud. "My clothing's singed, and I'll bet my hair's a mess, but at least I'm dry now."

"I think you're going to need some practice before that

becomes useful," Owen said, pointing at the clearing. Though the water globes had been destroyed, several tree stumps were scorched or reduced to piles of ash, too.

"Oh yeah," Simon said. "I'm pretty sure that the more of the gas you ionize, the hotter the plasma."

"Sorry, woods!" Alysha said. As if accepting her apology, the Breeze blew, clearing the burned smell from the air and refreshing the friends.

"It'll heal itself," Simon said. "We've got time for less . . . explosive . . . practice."

"I think that's it for me today," Loisana said. "This was nice, but I've got things I have to take care of." She smiled. "I'd love to join you guys another time, though."

"Sure," Simon said. Owen and Alysha nodded.

Loisana waved and walked down the path toward Van Silas Way.

"Kind of weird that she was here waiting for us," Simon said. "Don't you think?"

Alysha snorted. "Come on, don't be so paranoid."

Owen shrugged. "The Book did say bad things might happen."

"Nah, she's probably right," Simon said. "Now what do you guys think of this . . ." He started to discuss his next ideas for his friends and him.

Loisana, meanwhile, went around a bend in the path and out of the kids' sight. My Viewing Screen followed her from a distance, though. That's why Simon, Owen, and Alysha didn't see what I saw—a figure stepping out of the trees near the end of the woods.

I squinted but couldn't tell who it was, nor could I hear what they were talking about. But it made me very suspicious of the friendly seeming Loisana Belane and her mysterious appearance at Dunkerhook Woods.

I wished I could warn Simon and his friends about this, but I had no way to contact them. Besides, there was that stupid rule about Narrators not interfering! All I could do was watch and hope that this wouldn't prove a problem for them later on.

CHAPTER 5

THE BEAR OF BAD TIDINGS

My Viewing Screen image shifted, taking me away from Simon Bloom and his friends. It refocused on a dim jungle with only the barest hint of light filtering down through the heavy vegetation. I could sense humidity so thick I was practically sweating from my living room. And I had the air-conditioning on!

I stared in confusion; where was this, and why was it in my Chronicle? Then a slight rumbling sound caught my attention. My first thought was of a mild earthquake, but I soon saw the source: a massive brown shape loping through the foliage.

It was a grizzly bear walking on all fours, growling low in the back of its throat as it lumbered along. The beast rose up on its hind legs. It was huge—almost eight feet tall. Its growl turned into a roar that shook the trees around it.

"Okay, okay, keep your fur on," a voice said. A dusky–

skinned, broad-shouldered man stepped out from a thick patch of greenery.

The grizzly bear's roar cut off abruptly, replaced with a *whuf* of recognition. It shimmered and shook, becoming an average-size man wearing a brown sweater and brown corduroy pants. "Greetings, Kushwindro," he said huskily.

"Yup, good to see you, too, Grawley," Kushwindro said, stretching as he yawned.

Grawley nodded. "Did I wake you?"

"Not a problem," Kushwindro said. "The jungle never sleeps."

"Seriously? You're awake all the time?"

Kushwindro chuckled. "I'm kidding; I just woke from a power nap. What's up?"

"It's finally happening. *She's* on her way."

Kushwindro frowned. "*She's* coming here? *Here* here? I can't hide us all!"

"You don't have to; *she's* going to make a secret place for our forces. At most, you'll have to shift some foliage around."

Kushwindro smiled. "That's not a problem." He gestured, and a tall plant nearby dipped in response, dropping low enough for him to pluck a banana.

"We'll only be hiding for a little while," Grawley said. "Until we're ready for the good stuff." He laughed, a grumbling noise that sounded like construction work.

"You're not going to like it here, pal," Kushwindro said. "Pretty hot and humid."

The man-grizzly, mopping at his sweaty forehead with one hand while tugging at his now-soaked sweater with the other, growled. "Clearly." He shook his head. "*She'll* probably do some sort of climate control, too. *She* can do all sorts of things."

"No doubt. Speaking of incredibly powerful, any word about Sir?"

Grawley shook his head. "I guess it's not time yet. But I'm sure it won't be long. And then, between the strength *she* has and Sir's killer tattoos, we'll be unstoppable." He let out a rumbling laugh.

Kushwindro laughed with him. A moment later, he held out a fruit. "Banana?"

"Thanks, no. I'm a berries, fish, and honey man. And the blood of my enemies."

"Okay, that was gross," Kushwindro said. "All that tooth and claw stuff? No thanks. I prefer to let my friends do the dirty work." Vines and branches around them flexed and grasped the air in response to another of his gestures.

Grawley shrugged. "Either way, as long as we get the job done."

Both men grinned, and the jungle image faded from my Screen.

CHAPTER 6

SHORTEST FIELD TRIP EVER

After Simon and his friends finished their playtime, they went back to Simon's house—around the corner from Dunkerhook Woods—to clean themselves up. At the appointed time they returned to the woods for the big meeting—Simon's official entrance into the Council of Sciences.

The Council was composed of different Keepers from the various Science-based Orders. The Keepers had to obey the rules of the Board of Administration, which was in charge of the entire Union, but the Council got to oversee most of the Science Orders' activities. Being admitted was a big deal for Simon; his friends and he were excited.

The trio waited just within the border of Dunkerhook Woods and took out their hooded raincoats—standard issue for Order members.

"How do you feel, are you nervous, I'd be nervous," Owen said.

"I'm fine," Simon said. Then he shrugged. "But stop asking me that every thirty seconds. You're *making* me nervous."

Owen touched the sleeve of his blue raincoat. "Why do we have to wear these?"

Alysha rolled her eyes. "Owen, remember those Gateways? The big blue door-things that come up out of the ground?"

"Sure," Owen said. "They let Order members teleport to places."

"Right," Alysha continued. "And it always rains before the Gateways appear so Outsiders don't notice." She tapped her blue raincoat. "We need these to stay dry."

"What?" Owen squeaked. "*We're* taking a Gateway?"

"How did you think we were getting to the Council?" Alysha asked.

"I don't know, but I was expecting something with a seat belt! I mean, teleportation? Do you guys know what that can do to you if it goes wrong?"

Before Alysha could respond, the sky outside the woods darkened. Gray clouds quickly covered all of Van Silas Way, and within seconds, the rain started to fall. Drizzle became downpour and then deluge. From where Simon and his friends stood, cozy and dry within Dunkerhook Woods, they could just make out the glowing blue doorway spring up, ten feet wide by ten feet high, nearby on the street.

A moment later, a tall but stooped man stepped out of

the Gateway. This was Ralfagon Wintrofline, the *other* Keeper of the *Teacher's Edition* and the leader of the Order of Physics. Supposedly, he has learned and memorized most of the formulas inside the Book of Physics; he is said to be one of the most powerful men in the universe.

Ralfagon showed his age, leaning heavily on his cane as he limped over to the entrance to the woods, and stuck his head in. He swept back his hood and brushed aside strands of shaggily cut gray hair to peer through his bushy gray eyebrows at the kids.

"Hello there, friends," he said with a smile. "Been waiting long?"

Simon shrugged. "No . . . you're early."

"I am?" Ralfagon asked. "Hmm. Early for what?"

Though cramming all that physics knowledge into his head made Ralfagon mighty, it also made him a *bit* absentminded . . . in much the way that fire is a *bit* warm. He was also a physics professor at nearby Milnes University (where people knew him as Professor Ralph Winter). His students have secretly called him Old Man Winter since one December afternoon when he spent a half hour trying to start up a snow-covered bush with his car keys.

"The ceremony?" Alysha said. "Simon's joining the Council?"

"They haven't changed their minds about letting him in have they?" Owen asked.

"Oh, that!" Ralfagon said. "Of course, of course. Not, that

is. As in no, they haven't changed their minds." He chuckled. "Okay . . . hoods up and follow me."

The three friends walked behind Ralfagon and were almost instantly surrounded by sheets of rain. The raincoats were Union-made especially for this; the hoods let Simon and his friends see fine through the vertical flood.

Simon sloshed through the growing puddles as he went, marveling at how the coat somehow kept his ordinary, store-bought sneakers from getting wet. He felt a little cold and damp from the moisture in the air, but that was a lot better than getting drenched.

As they arrived at the Gateway, Simon realized this was his first time so close to one. He was astonished to notice it was almost two-dimensional . . . maybe as thick as a piece of paper. He was tempted to touch its side but feared it would give him a paper cut or, to be more accurate, a Gateway-cut.

Ralfagon's front leg moved forward, crossing the surface of the Gateway. Simon and his friends gasped: his leg appeared to have been cut off. Simon looked around the other side of the Gateway and saw no sign of the leg on the other side.

"Wait!" Simon shouted. Ralfagon paused in midstride, one leg planted firmly on the rain-coated street and the other . . . gone. "How do we use this?"

"It's as easy as it looks," he said. "Step through, and you'll be at our destination."

Simon glanced over at Alysha and Owen; Alysha's eyes

were wide, but she was poised, ready to follow Ralfagon. Owen, on the other hand, was frowning. Now that he was so close to the Gateway, he probably wanted something more secure than a seat belt. A full-body air bag, at least.

"Where is your leg now?" Simon asked.

Ralfagon pointed to the leg on the street. "It's right here. Oh, this leg?" By the movement of his thigh, it was clear that he was shaking that other leg. Wherever it was. "At our destination. Outside the Board of Administration's headquarters."

"You mean you're here," Owen asked, "but one leg is miles and miles away?"

Ralfagon pulled that leg out and shook it in the air for them. "See? It's fine."

"What if the Gateway shuts off while we were still going through it?" Owen asked.

"Hmm. Interesting question," Ralfagon said. "Let's not find out. Come along, now, the Board likes to keep things on schedule." And with that, he stepped through completely, causing not even a ripple in the blueness.

Alysha and Simon looked at each other. "Me first, or you?" Alysha asked.

Simon noticed how Owen was eyeing the Gateway. "Better idea—all three at once." He took one of Owen's arms and tilted his head to Alysha.

She nodded and took the other arm. Working together, they heaved Owen forward as they passed through the blue wall. Linked as I was to their thoughts, I was able to experience the exact sensation of traveling by Gateway. Words fail to describe it.

That's not to say that the journey went beyond my abilities to narrate; there simply wasn't anything to tell. Their Gateway travel from rain-stricken Van Silas Way was effortless, like stepping out from under a waterfall.

"Okay, that was a letdown," Alysha said.

Simon and his friends were now in a large field of finely ground gravel, facing a group of men and women: the Council of Sciences. The Keepers of some of the most powerful Books in existence. The respected leaders of the various Science Orders. Who were currently pointing at the kids and snickering.

Simon nervously checked to see if something was hanging out of his nose while Alysha ran her hands through her hair, which was matted down under her raincoat hood.

Gilio Skidowsa, Keeper of the Order of Biology, removed his wire spectacles to rub his eyes. "It's nice to see you young science warriors again." He gestured to the ground. "But you've got a man down."

Simon and Alysha looked to the ground in front of them and saw Owen sprawled in the gravel. As they helped him up, he blushed. "I expected a rougher reentry!"

A lanky man stood next to Gilio; he wore glasses with thick lenses that magnified his eyes to look the size of half dollars. "Don't be so hard on him," he said with a smile. "I was nervous the first time I went through a Gateway."

Owen nodded in thanks, and the man grinned. "I'm Olvero Lombaro, hello! I'm the Keeper of the Order of Chemistry." He paused, looking concerned. "You *do* like chemistry, don't you? Why, it's the most fascinating science of all! It's closely related to physics, you know. We get to use beakers and pipettes and we wear goggles . . ."

Allobero Foreedaman, Keeper of the Order of Astronomy, came up next to Olvero and clapped him on the shoulder. "Calm down there, Ollie," he said in a scratchy voice. "I don't think she really cares about that right now. Maybe we should just focus on why we're all here." He gestured to Simon. "That one."

Ralfagon clapped his hands. "Wonderful! Let's make it official for young Simon so we can get on to the best part. I believe we have ice-cream cake!" Ralfagon gestured past the Gateway, which sank into the ground and vanished at that moment.

The Gateway's disappearance revealed a huge structure with angles and curves of various styles that didn't fit well together. It looked as if a bunch of architects had designed separate buildings and merged them into a single one in order to give people the worst possible headache. At the top, hundreds of feet aboveground and arguably the worst fitting in style, was an arch. While most of the building was made of an extremely shiny metallic substance, the arch was so dull it seemed to absorb light rather than reflect it.

Above the metallic entry doors hung a wide placard with various symbols, each of different colors, etched into it. Simon recognized the blue squiggle for the Order of Physics and guessed the other shapes and symbols represented the other groups within the Knowledge Union. Surely this was the Board of Administration's headquarters.

"I think that archway is new," Ralfagon said. "Something odd about it. In any event, once a Board member makes it official, our Council will have another member!"

"It is more complicated than that, Ralfagon," a slow, firm voice said from behind.

Simon and his friends turned to see a very thin man; his crisply pressed slacks, dress shirt, and tie hung loosely off his body. His gaunt face seemed almost impossibly smooth, and his mouth, eyes, and eyebrows looked to be manually attached in a Mr. Potato Head sort of way (without the mustache or glasses) rather than naturally grown.

Something about him made Simon feel like backing away, but he knew that would be rude. This man was clearly someone important.

"Young friends," Ralfagon said, "this is Janathus Misht, an official from the Board of Administration. He oversees the Science Orders and is here to witness Simon's induction into the Council as co-Keeper of the Order of Physics."

"That is incorrect," Janathus said. "This boy will not be a Keeper with you."

Janathus's expression did not change as he spoke. To be more accurate, he hadn't been showing an expression before and gave no indication of starting one up now.

"In fact," he continued, "this boy might not remain a Keeper at all."

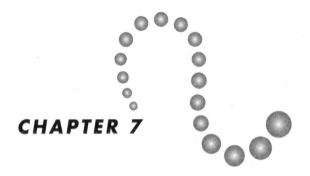

CHAPTER 7

Keeper No More

Janathus's statement drew gasps, grunts, grumbles, groans, and a lot of grousing among the Council members, which just goes to show how versatile the letter *g* is for describing unhappiness.

Alysha made the first coherent comment. "Oh yeah? Try and stop him!"

Janathus stared at her; I noticed that he wasn't blinking, nor had he yet during his entire time in this Chronicle.

Ralfagon cleared his throat and held up a hand. "Forgive the young lady's brashness. I think she simply wants to know why Simon can't be a Keeper with me. I know he's young, but the Book chose him, and he's certainly proven himself."

There was the barest hint of an upturn at the corners of Janathus's mouth. "Two points. One: the Board has decided that two Keepers cannot coexist with the same Book. We want no additional complications brought to this already messy system."

Janathus paused for a moment and then continued. "Two: I did not mean to say that *Simon Bloom* would definitely have to step down as Keeper. You, Ralfagon Wintrofline, may be told to resign from your post. Or perhaps you both might be removed and a new Keeper appointed."

If there had been an outcry before, there was an out-scream now.

Ralfagon waited for his fellow Council members to quiet down. "What's this about?" he asked in a polite but firm voice.

"You are respected throughout the Union, Ralfagon, but you've been at your post for a long time. Perhaps too long. Would a capable Keeper be so easily ambushed and lose possession of his *Teacher's Edition*? Can you still be deemed competent, or despite your ample service and legendary power, are you now unsuitable for the task?"

"I think I—" Ralfagon began.

"We at the Board of Administration intend to determine that," Janathus continued, cutting Ralfagon off. "Right now."

"In two point five minutes, to be precise," said a strong, cold voice. Another man walked from the building toward Janathus. He wore a crisp white dress shirt with thin blue stripes, a red paisley tie, and pressed navy blue slacks held up by navy suspenders. Unlike Janathus, he did have an expression; with lips tightly pressed, eyebrows bent, and nose slightly wrinkled, it was a look of distaste.

"Welcome to the Board of Administration," the man said. "For those who do not know me"—he directed his cold gaze toward Simon, Owen, and Alysha—"I am Standrus Presst, Lead Examiner and Chief Executive of the Board. I will oversee your case today. For your information, Ralfagon, that arch was installed last Saturday. Janathus and Madda requisitioned it four months, three weeks, and two days earlier."

"What's a Madda?" Owen whispered.

"I am Madda," a deep, female voice said. "Madda Roobet." A curly-haired woman of medium height and more than medium girth appeared next to Standrus. She was wearing a well-pressed outfit that reminded Simon of his mother's business suits, only more severe-looking.

"It's getting hard to keep track of all these people," Alysha whispered to Owen. "And the weird names aren't helping."

"As Chief Analyst of Keeper Affairs, I will be conducting your evaluation," Madda continued, fixing Alysha with a frosty look. "I assume the Keepers have brought their respective Books with them?"

The Keepers nodded sourly. I could tell they did not like the way the Board members talked down to them,

Simon was bursting with questions but was far too nervous under the Board members' joyless, pitiless gazes to say or do anything. Alysha had no such reservations. "And just how are you planning on *evaluating* Simon and Ralfagon?"

"Young lady," Standrus said, "you are speaking out of turn. We have a procedure for non–Keeper interrogatives, and you are clearly not following it."

Gilio chuckled. "That's kids for you, Standrus. Minds of their own and everything. It's what makes them humans, instead of dull robots!"

Olvero held up his hands in a calming gesture. "Whoa there! No need to get excited, everyone. Standrus, members of the Board, I think what Gilio is *trying* to say is that Alysha has a valid question. These kids don't know your procedures."

Standrus frowned deeply. "Janathus, you are liaison to the Council. Handle this."

Janathus nodded. "We on the Board are charged with doing our best to maintain the order of things. To keep the universe from getting disturbed, perhaps destroyed, by anyone unworthy of their place in the Union. Keepers face the strictest judgment, since they have the most potential to cause disasters."

Alysha rolled her eyes. "That's great, but you didn't really answer my question."

"There are schedules and procedures, child, and we must keep to them."

"Why?" Alysha asked. "Is asking a question without filling out a form going to destroy the universe?"

Standrus checked a shiny metal pocket watch. "We have wasted enough time," he said with a scowl. "Keepers, follow us." He flicked his eyes over to Alysha. "Non-Keepers must remain outside. Which includes Narrators." He looked up in the sky, somehow gazing into my eyes from the Viewing Screen. "All observing Narrators will put their Chronicles on hold for the duration of our meeting."

Simon's, Owen's, and Alysha's jaws dropped open, as did mine. No Narrator? Outrageous! You cannot put History on hold!

Ralfagon cleared his throat and raised his cane into the air. "Might I have a moment? I am, as Janathus says, elderly. I would love to catch my breath."

Janathus turned to Madda, who frowned. Standrus didn't look up from his watch as he said, "You have exactly fifty-seven seconds before you disrupt our schedule."

Simon turned away from his friends and the Council members. He closed his eyes, feeling as if he'd been dropped into a nightmare. He had to know something.

Book, he thought, contacting the *Teacher's Edition of Physics* through their mental link. *If they make Ralfagon the only Physics Keeper or if they fire both of us, will I have to give up some of my formulas?*

It responded quickly. *Yes.*

Simon frowned. *Will I still be able to talk to you like this?*

There was a slight pause. *No, you would lose that ability, as would Ralfagon if he is removed from his post.*

That hit Simon hard. He hated the idea of being separated from the Book, but he also worried about Ralfagon. The old

Keeper was a bit nutty, but he was a good person and a good friend. If the Book was taken from him, what would he have left?

Simon braced himself and asked one last question. *Will the new Keeper at least let my friends and me stay in the Order? Or could we be kicked out?*

This time, there was a long pause. Finally, the Book responded. *Given your age and the attitude of the Board, it is unlikely you'd be allowed to remain. You'd probably have your minds cleared of all your experiences with the Union, too.*

Simon shuddered at the thought of losing it all—not just his powers and the Order, but his memories, too. Worst of all, he became friends with Owen and Alysha around the time he found the Book. That meant they might lose the memories of their friendship, too!

"Enough time-wasting," Standrus said, jarring Simon from his thoughts.

Janathus gestured to the BOA building. "Council, Simon Bloom, follow me."

Ralfagon's face was tight with concentration, but at Janathus's words, his expression smoothed out, as if he'd found an answer to a pressing question. He cleared his throat. "Actually, Janathus and . . . er . . . others, that won't be necessary."

One of Janathus's eyebrows arched ever so slightly; it was a tiny movement, but for him it was a monumental expression change. "Oh? Why not?"

"Because I've decided to resign my post as Keeper in favor of Simon Bloom."

"What?" everyone shouted at once.

Ralfagon turned to Simon. "I'm old, I'm tired, and I have a lot of television to catch up on. Besides, the Book has been eager to return to Simon's side."

The Book floated out from within Ralfagon's jacket and, after sending a quick flash of blue at Ralfagon, zipped over to Simon. It hovered over him until he put his hand out, and then it descended gently into his grasp.

Simon was too stunned to react. Finally, he found the ability to speak. "But . . . I'm not ready for this!"

Ralfagon smiled warmly. "I believe you are."

"The Board will discuss this," Janathus said. "Everyone go into the building."

Standrus frowned. "That is not possible. We must reschedule everything."

"Surely we can judge the boy's merit now?" Madda said.

Standrus shook his head. "*We* are the Board of Administration. *We* make agendas and *we* follow them. Changing our procedures for simple convenience would make us no better than"—he wrinkled his nose at the kids—"than everyone else."

Standrus turned to Ralfagon. "You've already yielded your Book to Bloom, so he shall be acting Keeper." He reached into his pants pocket and pulled out what looked like a black plastic postage stamp. He tapped it, and a multicolored, three-dimensional display of a calendar appeared in front of his face.

After a moment's examination, Standrus grunted. "I suppose I can move some things around for the good of the Union. We shall reconvene here the same time next Sunday to discuss Simon Bloom's place as Keeper and to decide what knowledge, if any, Ralfagon Wintrofline will be allowed to retain for his retirement. Until then, he will remain in Lawnville and not engage in any excessive formula use."

Janathus's mouth came as close to a frown as it ever had. "But, Standrus, surely—"

"We exist to maintain order, Janathus, not disrupt it any further." Standrus nodded to the assemblage. "I expect you all to be prompt next Sunday."

Standrus turned and walked swiftly to the BOA headquarters.

The Keepers rushed to Ralfagon's side while Simon, Owen, and Alysha stared at one another. That's why none of them noticed what I did: Madda and Janathus turned to face each other and exchanged an unreadable look.

Madda made a subtle gesture and mouthed, *"What now?"* Janathus, stone-faced, nodded once and mouthed the words, *"Not to worry."* Then they hurried after Standrus.

As friends and fellow Keepers raised their voices in confusion and anger, Simon looked down at the Book and sent it a mental message. *I didn't want to give everything up, but I didn't want this to happen! What will Ralfagon do? Will they wipe his memories?* He paused and looked at Owen, Alysha, and the assembled Keepers. *And me?* Simon thought to the Book. *A leader? How can I possibly be ready for this kind of responsibility?*

If the Book had an answer, it chose not to share it.

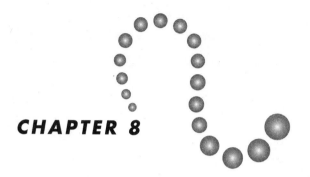

CHAPTER 8

GIRL IN THE HOOD

After a long, grim night thinking about all that had happened, I was happy for morning.

It was Monday: a new day for Simon and his friends. (Obviously it was a new day—otherwise it would be called Sunday Part II.) Instead of showing me how Simon was dealing with the turn of events, my Viewing Screen focused elsewhere.

I briefly stared in confusion at a large building of ivy-covered brick. Part of the advantage of being a Narrator, though, is often being able to understand what's happening on-screen. I realized this was Enrico Fermi Middle School, located in Stoneridge, the next town over from Lawnville.

I almost dropped my breakfast scone. Was my Screen malfunctioning? Was it still covered by warranty?

Then I saw who was coming down the cobblestone path toward the front entrance. A blond girl, barely thirteen years old, shuffled toward the school. She was pretty, with silky blond hair and big blue eyes, but her face and hair were almost completely covered by the hood of her black sweatshirt. She didn't know why, but it felt right to wear it like that; she only took off the hood when her teachers made her.

Her name was Sara Beth, but she didn't know much more about herself—not even her real last name. Her foster parents and the school faculty called her Sara Beth Doe, but she hated that last name. No, she hated the attention it brought her. She walked hunched over, hoping to avoid notice. To shrink into herself; to become invisible.

The closer Sara Beth got to the school entrance, the more aware she became of the students gathered around the front lawn and steps. As she started up the walkway to the building, she noticed the girls wearing short-sleeved shirts and skirts that let them enjoy the lingering warmth of the early fall weather. It was torture for Sara Beth to see them like that. Doing what she could not.

Don't look at them, she said to herself. *Maybe they'll leave me alone this time.*

"Doe a deer!" That was it: the first yell. Next came the avalanche. She sped up.

"A female deer?" There it was; the inevitable follow-up.

"Doesn't look female to me! How can you tell with that hood?"

"C'mon, Doe, let's see that scary face!"

"No, let's see those freaky arms!"

"Yeah, and those creepy legs!"

Sara Beth kept walking, making sure her arms were completely covered by her sweatshirt. Sometimes the sleeves rode up when she walked this fast. Her jeans, at least, would definitely keep her legs covered. Everyone knew about her arms and legs, of course, but if she kept them hidden she had a chance of getting out of this.

The yells drew louder, closer; at least ten kids, maybe a dozen, were ahead of her. They were standing along the edge of the grass and the stone walkway leading to the school. One of them stepped onto the cobblestones and faked an accidental bump. It was all Sara Beth could do to keep moving; her every instinct said to either run off or turn and fight. But she couldn't do either. She had to keep going. She was almost at the entrance and the relative safety of the halls when a hand reached out and grabbed her left sleeve.

"No!" Sara Beth cried as someone yanked the sweatshirt up to reveal her left arm.

There it was, her shame revealed once again for all to see: bizarre tattoos of blue, green, and yellow up and down her arm. They were mostly shapeless, like the work of some crazy artist who'd gotten at her with a permanent paintbrush. But to Sara Beth, they *almost* made sense. They *almost* meant something.

"That's enough, all of you! Leave her alone this instant!"

The voice was cultured yet loud and unyielding. It pierced through the crowd's taunts and scattered the mocking kids. "Are you all right, Miss Doe?" the voice asked gently in a polished British accent.

Sara Beth looked up; this was the one person in the school she was willing to meet eyes with. "It's nothing new, Miss Fanstrom; just another day."

A woman gazed down at Sara Beth, her natural height (almost six feet tall) extended by a nearly two-foot-high tower of black hair that stood motionless atop her head. "Miss Doe, I wish that wasn't the case. I know children can be cruel, especially when you are so vulnerable. No memory of your childhood, no known family, and those markings . . ." She trailed off. "It is vitally important that you keep your chin up and not let their petty taunts get to you. You are more than they say, more than you know. Miss Doe, you have the seeds of greatness in you!"

Sara Beth fought back the urge to shout or sneer; she didn't want to offend her one ally in the school. "You always say that, Miss Fanstrom, but I don't feel it. I don't believe it. I mean, sometimes . . ."

"What, child?" Miss Fanstrom gazed through her thick-lensed, black-framed glasses. One hand, as always, held a slim leather briefcase, but the other rested comfortingly on Sara Beth's shoulder. "Tell me."

Sara Beth sighed and looked around. The other kids were all gone, having rushed into school through the other entrances to avoid their new principal's wrath. This was as private a conversation as Sara Beth could hope for.

"I feel like there's so much inside me. More than the things I can't remember. I feel like I shouldn't have to worry about such jerks. Like I shouldn't have to be scared of them."

As often happened during their talks, the top of Miss Fanstrom's hair bent forward, pointing at Sara Beth. "Please, Miss Doe, continue. You can tell me anything."

Sara Beth rubbed at her left arm, silently cursing the tattoos. Did she dare say what she felt? She had to—she had to say it aloud before it consumed her!

"I feel like I'm better than them. And if I could only remember who I was, if I could only be my true self, they would not dare mock me. They would fear me!" Her voice trembled with building rage. "And I would laugh at them, because they would be right to be afraid!"

Sara Beth winced suddenly, and put a hand to her forehead. "But every time I feel that way, my head starts to hurt, and I stop thinking about fighting. I just take whatever they say and do to me. And I dream of the day I don't have to."

The top of Miss Fanstrom's hair swiveled away. It seemed, to Sara Beth, almost like a sad gesture. Or a disappointed one.

"I know it's hard," Miss Fanstrom said. "But that anger, that thirst for revenge, it won't help you. It will only bring more hurt. Can you not see past it? Rise above it?"

For a moment, Sara Beth ignored that she was talking to her one friend as well as the school principal. For that

61

moment, she let loose all she was feeling. "Rise above? You don't know what it's like! I don't remember anything—*anything*—before five months ago. If the social workers didn't tell me my name was Sara Beth, I wouldn't even have that. No parents, no home, no life. And if that's not bad enough, I have *these*!" She stuck out her arms and then pointed to her legs.

Sara Beth scowled deeply. "I have to take it from them," she said as she gestured to where her schoolmates had been. "Every day. It's all I can do to hold it together in front of them. I hide in a stall in the girls' room and cry between classes so they don't get the satisfaction of seeing it." She sniffed back what was dangerously close to becoming a new round of tears. "I don't know who I was or what I did before, but part of me *knows* I don't deserve this. And that part . . . yeah, *that* part can't wait to get even."

Miss Fanstrom shook her head sadly, her hair not budging from the movement. "My dear, I've only been at this school for as long as you have, but I've had my share of experience. I've seen much cruelty among children and among adults as well. Those who think they're strong pick on those who think they're weak. But the truly strong are those who find a way to break free without being cruel right back. Perhaps one day you'll understand that."

Sara Beth sniffed hard to fight back her running nose and rubbed her eyes with the ends of her sleeves. "I guess. But I doubt it. Anyway, I'd better get to homeroom."

Miss Fanstrom gave Sara Beth one last pat on her shoulder and nodded.

I looked on as Miss Fanstrom watched Sara Beth Doe walk up the stone stairs to the school. Once the girl disappeared into the entrance, Miss Fanstrom turned and gazed up into the sky. Despite being many miles away, she locked eyes with me through my Viewing Screen and exhaled sadly. "I try, Mr. Geryson, truly I do. But I don't know if I can reach that child before it's too late."

She was talking directly to me! "I know you do your best, Keeper," I whispered. I wasn't sure if Miss Fanstrom could hear me, but I felt for her struggle, much as I did for Sara Beth. No matter what that girl did before, I hated to watch her suffer now.

But I felt a chill when I thought of her past. Five months ago, Sara Beth Doe knew her real name: Sara Beth Daly. She preferred her Union name: Sirabetta, or Sir.

Five months ago, those shapeless tattoos had been perfectly formed, each corresponding to a formula stolen from the various Science Orders. And every formula was hand-picked to protect Sirabetta, harm her enemies, or otherwise aid her goals: to let her steal and control the *Teacher's Edition of Physics*, then the other Books of the Science Orders and, ultimately, to take over the entire Knowledge Union.

That pretty, scared, blond thirteen-year-old girl had been in her early thirties until Simon Bloom, in a stroke of luck, used his space–time formula to defeat her by turning her into this younger version of herself.

I shuddered at the thought of her regaining the memories that had been taken from her. What if she found a way to resume her mission of conquest? A way to seek revenge on Simon for having thwarted her, especially now that Simon was reeling from his new position as sole Keeper? Worst of all, what if the vengeful Sirabetta remembered that I chronicled her downfall and helped Simon and his friends bring it about?

Though I felt great pity for her current misery, I wanted nothing but to see Sara Beth's life stay the way it was.

CHAPTER 9

HOW THE COOKIES CRUMBLE

My Viewing Screen shifted images, this time showing the concrete exterior of Lawnville's own Julius Henry Marx Junior High School. As was to be expected from a town called Lawnville, the grass in front of the school was neatly trimmed and a vibrant shade of healthy green. It sprang right back up after the many students stomped their feet across it on their way in. The warning bell had just sounded, and boys and girls aged twelve through fourteen were dashing to get inside and avoid being marked late.

Except for two.

Alysha and Owen shifted nervously as they waited for Simon. He was supposed to meet them before school, their custom since entering junior high. This Monday, for the first time in the almost two months since school had started, Simon was late.

"Anything?" Alysha asked Owen.

Owen, in an uncharacteristic show of quietness, shook his head while keeping his eyes trained on the sky. He was using his ability to sense velocity, seeking any movement in the distance: that of Simon Bloom flying. It was certainly cloudy enough for Simon to travel that way without being spotted, but there was no hint of him.

"Did you talk to him after he went home yesterday?" Alysha asked.

Again, Owen just shook his head no.

"Me neither. I called, but he didn't answer his phone. I've never seen him like that, not even years ago. He'd be really quiet, daydreaming, but never so—"

"Lost," Owen said.

"Yeah," Alysha whispered.

Finally they saw him coming toward them. Walking.

"Hey," Alysha said. "Why didn't you fly or friction-slide over?"

Simon's eyes had bags under them, and his face was pale, as if he hadn't slept much. "You know the rules; we're not supposed to show off our powers."

"Yeah, right," Alysha said with a chuckle. "Really? You do it all the time."

"I'm the only Keeper now," Simon said. "And the Board might be watching."

Owen nodded. "Those creeps are probably going to show up as new teachers or something so they can keep an eye on you."

Simon looked around with a haunted expression on his face. Alysha glared at Owen, who shrugged and mouthed "*Sorry*" to her.

"Come on," Alysha said. "You don't want to be late for homeroom. And we have that quiz today in math." She grabbed Simon's sleeve, and Owen grabbed the other; at their tugging, he followed them into the school.

Though Owen was in a different homeroom than Simon and Alysha, he accompanied them to theirs to make sure Simon was okay. Owen and Alysha kept to either side of him through the halls, with Owen secretly using his formula to prevent the hordes of kids that swarmed past from jostling them. It was a trick Owen had perfected since getting his velocity control back; he was still the smallest kid in his grade (and now, in junior high, the smallest in the school), but subtle pushes here and there had given him the reputation of being tough.

They saw hulking Barry Stern, the biggest kid in the school and a former bully in the sixth grade, hurrying to his own homeroom. Barry spotted the trio and quickly pressed against the row of lockers to give them room to pass. Simon and Alysha barely noticed him, but Owen smiled and nodded to the much larger boy.

Barry's face went pale; he was clearly terrified of Owen.

He used to tell anyone who'd listen how devastating the smaller boy was at dodgeball. Barry didn't have many people willing to chat with him, though. He'd lost most of his friends after the once-popular Marcus Van Ny, Barry's best friend in sixth grade, had annoyed everyone with wild tales of Simon, Owen, and Alysha having magical powers. Marcus moved away when his father—secretly Order of Physics traitor Mermon Veenie—suffered partial amnesia and went to prison for a number of crimes. And Barry, now a social outcast, simply tried to keep his head down and make it through each day.

In homeroom, Alysha kept a close eye on Simon as he stared off absently; she figured his imagination was wandering, as it often did. She saw the problem when their homeroom teacher tugged at her attendance book, which was somehow too heavy to lift.

"Simon," Alysha muttered, leaning over to him, "snap out of it!"

Simon blinked and returned his attention to the class. The teacher almost fell over backward when the notebook, suddenly at normal weight, sprang up in her hands.

Owen and Alysha were both in Simon's first period class, history; a whispered warning from Alysha put Owen on alert, too. Sure enough, classmates murmured and pointed as several crumpled sheets of paper and the teacher's empty Styrofoam coffee cup mysteriously floated up out of the garbage pail in the front of the classroom.

Owen used velocity to tip over the can. The clatter startled Simon; he realized what he was doing, and the drifting objects fell to the floor with the rest of the trash.

In third period math, in the middle of their quiz, various students dropped their pencils; chaos ensued as they chased the unnaturally slippery pencils across the floor. Alysha groaned at this. When she saw the tissue box on the teacher's desk start to slide, she rolled her eyes and took action. She briefly drained the electrical flow from the overhead lights, plunging the room into a full minute of darkness. This gave her time to rush over to Simon's desk, swat him on the shoulder, and hiss, "Knock it off!" into his ear. He did, and things went back to normal.

By lunchtime, most of the seventh grade was buzzing with talk of ghosts. The teachers, on the other hand, were sure that a coordinated prank was being played on them by their students, and they were discussing how to catch the culprits.

Owen and Alysha confronted Simon, pulling him outside for privacy.

"What is going on with you?" Alysha demanded. "Some kids in your second period English class said the teacher's chalk couldn't leave a mark on the blackboard!"

Owen nodded. "And at least three kids walking through the halls smacked into lockers as if they'd jumped, but they swore they were just walking normally!"

"I didn't know I was doing it," Simon moaned. "I can't stop thinking about maybe getting us kicked out of the Union. Or, almost as bad, staying on as boss and having all those Order members—no, the entire universe—relying on me!"

"You've got to stop this before someone gets hurt," Alysha said. "And if you keep making these mistakes, it might convince those Board jerks to kick you off!"

"You know what you need to do?" Owen asked. "Talk to Ralfagon."

Alysha snorted. "What, for crazy lessons? I mean, he's nice, but still . . ."

"He found a way to be Keeper of Physics for a long time," Owen said. "And if anyone can understand what Simon's dealing with, it's him."

"Okay, good call, Speedy," Alysha said. "Simon, you should go after school."

Simon shrugged. "I don't know."

Alysha turned Simon's head to follow a student running out of the cafeteria. He was chasing part of his lunch—a small bag of cookies—as it floated away. "You've got to try something!"

Simon gestured, and the cookies fell to the ground with a crunch. "I guess it couldn't hurt, right?"

Alysha and Owen looked at each nervously, thinking the same thing at the same time: *could it?*

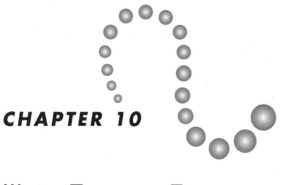

CHAPTER 10

WHEN TROUBLE CALLS . . .

I'd like to say that the rest of that day passed by uneventfully, but that would be a lie. Simon Bloom did manage to get his formulas under control in his classes, but the Viewing Screen changed scenes to show me a bigger danger brewing.

The image on my Screen was of a home in Lawnville. It was a tidy place, with the kind of neatness that shows the owner was far too concerned with straightening up and not enough with actually living there. It was clearly the residence of someone with a rigidly controlling, cruelly forceful type of mind. A torturer, maybe. A dictator, perhaps.

A telephone rang. A middle-aged, unremarkable-looking man stepped into his living room and grabbed the phone in the middle of the first ring. His name was Willoughby

Wanderby, Order of Physics member and grade school gym teacher.

"Wanderby here," he said into the phone. His voice was commanding, unyielding, and basically not much fun to listen to.

"The time has arrived." The voice was distorted, making it impossible for me to get a bead on it. Male, yes; adult, certainly; but other than that, it was indistinct.

Wanderby seemed equally confused. "What are you saying? Who's this?"

"I don't repeat myself. This is the call you've been waiting for. Your mission is about to reach its next stage. Your true duty is upon you."

Wanderby didn't exactly have a pleasant complexion normally, but the words he heard turned him startlingly pale. "I . . . I understand."

"Of course you do," said the voice. "Now be quiet, listen, and understand more."

Wanderby was silent; whoever he was speaking to got all the obedience he wanted.

"It happens tonight. Don't delay and don't fail. Understand?"

Wanderby nodded, then realized he was on the phone and had to say yes.

Before he could say it aloud, the voice responded. "Excellent. You know where to go after that. An instruction packet will arrive for you with additional details. Guard it with your life, because that's exactly what you'll lose if anything happens to it."

Wanderby nodded again, chilled at the threat and the realization that he was being watched. He waited for further instructions or words; a dial tone alerted him that his caller had already hung up.

Wanderby stomped away to another part of his house with an unnerving look of resolve on his face. "It's time, Sir," he whispered. "It's finally time."

My Viewing Screen image faded away, leaving me shaken and confused. What was all that about?

There were too many unknowns going on in this Chronicle. Too many possible dangers. First Loisana's mysterious—maybe dangerous—conversation. Then the bear-man Grawley and his jungle-controlling friend, Kushwindro, who were definitely up to no good. After that, a secret back-and-forth communication between Board members Janathus and Madda . . . what could *they* be up to? And finally, Willoughby Wanderby and his secret phone call.

What did it all mean for Simon, Owen, and Alysha? And for me?

Trouble, no doubt.

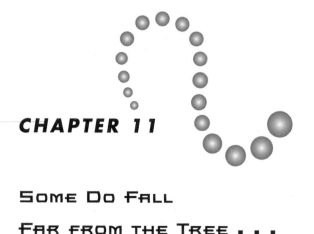

CHAPTER 11

Some Do Fall
Far from the Tree ...

That day after school, while Willoughby Wanderby was making sinister plans, Simon went to Milnes University to see Ralfagon. He'd visited on a few Saturdays during the last five months, mostly to discuss his formulas or to spend quality time with the Book. This time, the Book was with him and was his . . . at least for now.

Simon decided Milnes University, clear across town, was too far to walk to. With heavy clouds and fading daylight on his side, he took Owen's and Alysha's advice and used his gravity control to fly there. This time, Simon paid strict attention and didn't have any run-ins with rogue balloons, so the trip only took minutes.

He dropped down to the ground around the corner from

the Department of Physics building, planning to walk through the main entrance. He marched to the double-glass doors and froze; there, coming right toward him, was his father!

Five months before, Simon's father had confided that he had a secret side project: examining the strange phenomena in and around Lawnville. To that end, Steven Bloom often met with Ralfagon Wintrofline—knowing him as ordinary Professor Ralph Winter—for help with his theories. (Little did Steven know that the phenomena were a result of the Order of Physics's activities, especially those of Simon and his friends.)

There was no mistaking Steven Bloom's gray, frizzy hair; the belly pushing out at the misbuttoned short-sleeve, button-down shirt; or the squat frame. Fortunately, Steven rarely watched where he was going, including now. Simon had time to dash to the side of the building and gravity-leap to the top of the three-story roof.

He peeked over the edge and watched his father head toward the parking lot. Simon scurried across the roof to the corner where Ralfagon's third-floor office was. Seeing one of the windows was open, he increased the friction on his hands and knees and crawled off the roof. Between his extra friction and reduced weight, he easily climbed down the wall and swung himself into the office.

"Nice landing," a woman's deep voice said.

Simon whirled around in a panic but calmed quickly. "Eldonna!"

Eldonna Pombina, the short, stout Order member who acted as Ralfagon's university assistant, smiled warmly. "Ahem . . . you mean Donna, don't you?"

Simon nodded. When around Outsiders, Eldonna went by her non–Union name of Donna Pom. She was always there to greet Simon during his past visits; she usually had to wake Ralfagon up, too.

"Good to see you, Simon. Close call with your father, though."

"How did you know?"

Eldonna gestured to a computer monitor that showed images of the building's outside. "Special formulas let us keep watch; they also help hide any Order activity from Outsiders." She chuckled at Simon's surprised look. "This way, no students or faculty notice when 'Professor Winter' accidentally rearranges a watercooler's molecules into a massage chair." She laughed. "True story."

"Ah, but who got to take that chair home?" Ralfagon limped in, dressed as always in his faded tan overcoat.

The Book of Physics slipped out of Simon's backpack and floated in front of him. It flashed blue at Ralfagon, who smiled and nodded. "Hello, old friend. And welcome, Simon. Eldonna, we'll be in my office."

Simon was expecting to find Ralfagon's office messy. The man often used formulas of motion to rearrange things without noticing, making Simon's mistakes that day seem downright harmless. Today, however, the office was almost neat.

Ralfagon noticed Simon looking around in wonder. "It took a great deal of concentration, but I couldn't have things floating around with your father here."

"That's what I'm here about," Simon said. He explained his troubles from the day. "How do I control it?"

"There's a quick answer and a long one," Ralfagon said. "The quick one is, you just do. The long one . . . is long."

Simon stared. "Um, okay. I've got some time."

Ralfagon shrugged. "Excellent. I've been looking forward to this . . . especially in light of your new position. Which makes you uncomfortable."

Simon paused, unsure if he should say it. Finally, "Yes! Can't you change your mind? Maybe if we go to the Board together and convince them that we can work together, they'll let us be co-Keepers. You can take charge again, but my friends and I can stay in the Order, too!"

Ralfagon shook his head. "I doubt that's an option. Besides, Janathus—though a soulless bureaucrat—may be right. I may be getting old and sloppy." He gestured as he said this, and Simon had to duck as a chair drifted past. "See?"

"But won't you miss it? Being Keeper? The formulas? The Book?"

"I should be fine. Former Keepers usually enjoy a quiet retirement, keeping a few formulas so they can join in Order affairs from time to time. Will I miss my bond with the Book? Yes, very much. But I'll feel better about it with such a worthy successor."

"Me? How am I worthy?"

Ralfagon sighed. "Simon, you may not believe it, but I know you're ready for this. Age doesn't matter; all that matters is who you are and what you're capable of. And you are capable of wonderful things. You saved my life, you stopped terrible villains, you brought your friends such power and joy."

"The Book did it all," Simon protested. "It found me, it gave me the formulas . . . I've been lucky, that's all."

"Oh, really?" Ralfagon said with a chuckle. "The Book and I have had many discussions about you, and neither of us came to that conclusion." He gave Simon a long look. "You're losing control of gravity and friction because they've become a part of you. When you don't keep your mind under control, as I've stopped doing so well, they can slip out. But the real secret to using Union abilities is that your only boundaries are your intellect and your imagination. And you, my boy, are lacking neither."

"What do you mean? There's so much I can't do. I can't even use space–time; I'm terrified of it. It turned Sirabetta into a thirteen–year–old; if I use it wrong, it could do a lot worse to me or my friends or my family."

"Simon, do you trust the Book? Completely?"

"Yes," he said, without hesitation.

"Then trust in yourself, especially with space–time. I never used it because the Book warned me against it. Yet the Book *wanted* you to have it. And using that formula saved you and your friends. And the whole universe."

Simon remembered how hard that battle had been; he couldn't deny that he was a little proud of having pulled it off. "I guess."

"Well, I *know*." Ralfagon tapped his fingers on his desk. "Hmm, let's try something—if you'll forgive a little Newton humor." He waved his hand, and in a flash of light, a bright red apple appeared in the air a few feet above Simon's head.

Simon mentally triggered his gravity formula to gently push and pull the apple in all directions at once—stopping it in midair—and then lower it to the desk.

"Good," Ralfagon said. "Now, I have no idea what you did with space–time to defeat Sirabetta," Ralfagon said. "But there are higher laws than I know. Laws that only the Books know, and they only tell us what they choose. So let's experiment; try doing to the apple what you did to Sirabetta."

Simon frowned. "But you're eating it."

Ralfagon looked down; sure enough, he'd absently picked up the apple and taken a bite. "Oops, sorry," he said, a bit of juice dribbling down his chin. "I skipped lunch."

Ralfagon put the apple down, wiped at his mouth with his sleeve, and nodded to Simon. "Now, focus on the apple, and let's see what happens."

Simon stared at it intently and concentrated as he spoke the formula. The apple vibrated, rippled, and in an instant, was whole again.

Ralfagon leaned forward to examine it. "Amazing! Not only did you restore the bite, but the taste of apple is gone from my mouth!" He looked down at his sleeve. It had been damp from him wiping his mouth, but now it was dry. "I remember eating it, I remember how it tasted; you didn't affect my memory of it. Yet you undid the result of my actions." He checked the clock on the wall. "And you didn't affect the rest of the time–flow; it's a localized time–reverse! Now, try making the apple *older*."

Simon closed his eyes and envisioned what he wanted to do. He repeated the formula and opened his eyes. The apple was still there, with no bite taken out and no apparent change. "See? I told you I'm no good at this."

Ralfagon leaned forward, eyes wide. "Don't be so sure. Look!" He pointed to a spot on the desk several inches away from the apple. There, almost invisible against the beech–colored wood surface, was a tiny puddle of applesauce.

Simon stared in awe. "I did that?"

Ralfagon nodded. "I think you summoned a future version of the apple. Although I don't understand why it would become applesauce . . . I was planning on eating the rest of the apple after you left." He waved his hand. "I'm sure there's some significance to it. In any event, you've done well. Very well."

"But what good is that? To not even know what I did?"

"Simon, all you need is to be patient. And to practice. And to maintain concentration. And to be careful." He paused. "Maybe I should write up a list." He searched his desk for a pen.

"Does it matter?" Simon asked. "I don't even know if I'll be allowed to use the formula after Sunday. Or if I'll even be in the Union anymore. And if I am, I'm sure I'll cause some disaster. If not with space-time, then with gravity or friction or another law."

Ralfagon shook his head. "The Book chose you for a reason. For your ability. Your strength. Your character." He shrugged. "I think it really likes the sound of your name, too. Didn't hurt, anyway." He cleared his throat. "But I fear something bad is afoot in the Union. Something that will only get worse. And you, Simon Bloom, can put it right. Whether you believe it, whether you think you can, I know you will do it. The Book—*your* Book—knows it, too. Once you accept that, you will amaze everyone."

Ralfagon gestured, and the door to his office swung open. Eldonna was waiting outside. "Everything go okay, boys?"

Ralfagon nodded, ignoring Simon's frown and low-hanging head.

Eldonna looked past them and saw the apple on the table. "Why, Professor Winter, you've got an apple. What a coincidence; I was thinking about making my special homemade applesauce. I'll need a few dozen more apples, though; one apple would make barely any."

Simon and Ralfagon looked at each other and then back at the splotch of applesauce on the desk. That explained that.

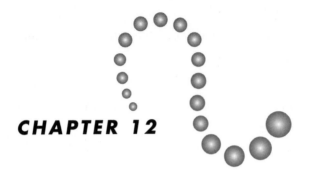

CHAPTER 12

DIAL 51R FOR VILLAIN

That Monday evening, Sara Beth Doe sat quietly in a corner of the Stoneridge Public Library. Simon Bloom would have been interested to know that she was relaxing through reading. She was deep into a book about a girl who defied her world's rules, disguising herself as a man to become a knight of great skill and magical power.

Sara Beth frowned as a shadow fell across her. She looked up and saw a man—average height, middle-aged, nothing special. But there was something about him . . .

"Sara Beth," the man said in a firm, almost commanding tone.

"Do I know you?" He did seem familiar somehow.

"Listen, there's nothing to worry about. I'm a teacher from

an elementary school in Lawnville. I've come to help you. To save you," he added in a hushed voice.

That freaked her out. "Look, buddy, I'm no idiot," she said. "Get out of here before I get a librarian to call the cops."

"Please, Sara Beth. I know who you are. Who you *really* are! I can tell you why you can't remember anything . . . and I can even tell you about your tattoos."

Sara Beth glanced down at her covered arms and legs. Had this nut job been watching her? But what if he really did know something? What if he could help?

"Fine, but get out of the way." She gestured for him to move aside so she had a clear path to run. "And if you act creepy, I'm screaming. Loudly."

"Yes, yes, of course. But I want to help you, Sir."

"Did you call me 'sir'?"

"Sir. Sirabetta. That's who you *really* are. Can't you remember? Formerly Sara Beth Daly, you were a member of the Order of Psychology. You should have been Keeper. You tried to serve the greater good and were punished for it."

Sara Beth stared at him. What was this crazy person saying? "That's it—get out of here." But her voice had no conviction; something was nagging at her.

The man made no move to leave. "The Union couldn't keep you down; you had a way, some secret method of fighting off their memory wiping. A way to remember your true self. You gained tattoos of tremendous power." He pointed to her arms and legs. "You found other people who wanted freedom from the strict rules and injustice in the Union. You were going to overthrow it, starting with Ralfagon Wintrofline."

"Ralph–a–gone?" she asked, numbly.

"The Keeper of the Order of Physics. We put him in the hospital so you could take his Book, the *Teacher's Edition of Physics*. That brat Simon Bloom got to it first."

Sara Beth shivered. That name. "Simon . . . Bloom?"

"Yes! He and his friends stole the Book, took its powers, fought you, fought me, fought that idiot Mermon Veenie. They won. Somehow they defeated you, made you a child instead of your true age. Ruined your tattoos. But I'm here to set things right. Those fools in the Order of Physics never suspected where my loyalty truly lay. And your faithful followers are waiting for you to resume control. To lead us to glory. Now is the time, Sir. It's time to restore your greatness!"

Sara Beth frowned. The man sounded like a babbling psycho, but somehow every word he said almost made sense. It was on the tip of her mind, just out of reach, but so close. So close. "My greatness?"

"Once you're back to your proper age, your tattoos should work again. You'll be able to control all that power and use it to destroy our enemies!"

Sara Beth's heart pounded, and her head throbbed, as if something was pushing, straining to get free. She pulled up her sweatshirt sleeves and stared at the colors. Yellow, green, silver, blue. Were they ever more than just blotches?

"This is it, Sir. We'll take a secret route to the Order of Biology, where allies will restore your proper age. That should also restore all your magnificent power. We'll topple the Council of Sciences, tear apart the Keepers, and destroy Simon Bloom!"

"Order of Biology? Council of Sciences? Keepers?" Part of her was starting to see. To feel how *right* this all was. Whatever was fighting inside her mind was winning . . . breaking free of its chains.

"We won't go by Gateway, of course—the Union would know. We'll use another method, not as fast, but safer. Come on, Sir—remember. Embrace the truth!"

The man's face was bright red from his excitement. He was practically foaming at the mouth. He looked completely bonkers. And yet . . .

"I know you?" she asked, tentative at first. But then, "I *do* know you." She pulled out a small mirror from her bag and stared at her reflection. It had never seemed so artificial. "You have powers? Show me."

"Of course, Sir." He pointed to a nearby cart filled with books. "Keep your eyes on that!" He spoke what sounded like nonsense to Sara Beth and then pointed at the cart. It started to spin around, faster and faster, its wheels squeaking as it rotated on the carpet.

The books went flying in all directions; Sara Beth had to dodge as one soared at her. Finally, the cart smashed into the far wall, clanging loudly.

Sara Beth gaped at him. Her first quick thought was about

the damage to all those books. Then she realized what she'd just seen . . . how was that possible? But deep down, she knew. Whatever barrier there was in her mind was crumbling. She pushed up her sleeves and stared at the colors there. That blue blob on her right arm . . . she associated it with air expanding, making things explode. She patted at a spot on one leg, where her jeans covered another blue mark. It made her think of blazing, all-consuming heat. And that silver tattoo below the knee of her other leg gave her an image of a glowing ball of light that could shatter solid steel.

These thoughts shattered more than steel. Memories that were supposed to have been destroyed were returning, coming back from where they'd been safely stored by an old Order of Psychology trick she'd taught herself years before.

"Yes. YES. Your name . . . you are Willoughby Wanderby!" He nodded eagerly. "And I . . ." There was pain, now. A piece of her, deep inside her head, was disintegrating and beneath it—inside it—was another thing entirely. Her everything. Her self.

"I remember!" she shouted, triumphant. Her hands were clenched into fists, both held above her and shaking. Trembling with rage. "I remember everything." She finally, truly *saw*. The books around her were filled with pathetically limited knowledge. The Outsider librarian rushing over, probably to investigate the noise, was a helpless fool. Her own thirteen-year-old hands were her prison. And the novel in one hand that just minutes ago had offered her such peace was only a distraction from her true purpose, from the blood and pain she'd have to dispense before she was done.

Sara Beth Doe stared at the book in her hand. Then Sira-betta tossed it aside. There was no room for peace for her now. It was time for war. And vengeance.

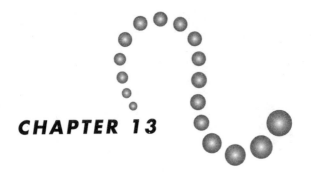

CHAPTER 13

Mission: Really Hard (Should They Choose to Accept It)

On Tuesday morning, Alysha and Owen met outside their school and waited for Simon.

"What's with everyone?" Alysha asked as she gestured toward their schoolmates. There was none of the usual fun or cheeriness in the air outside Julius Henry Marx Junior High School. No boys were riding on skateboards or playing with hacky sacks. No girls giggled together or flirted with the boys. Instead, the students were standing in tense clumps and talking in hushed voices.

"I hope it's not about what Simon did yesterday," Owen said.

"I'm sure it's nothing," Alysha said, but she couldn't hide a frown. She waved to a friend, who came over. "Hey, Jill," she said. "What's the deal?

Jill glanced over her shoulder. "It's really weird; the teachers are freaking out." She nodded to the windows of the cafeteria; Alysha and Owen followed her gaze. Sure enough, the teachers were huddled together inside and whispering. Occasionally, a teacher made a slashing motion with a hand or shook a fist in the air.

"Yup, they're freaking out all right," Alysha said. She turned to Jill. "See you inside; we're going to wait for Simon." Jill waved and walked off while Alysha pulled Owen back to their usual waiting spot.

Alysha saw Owen's mouth open and held up her hand. "Just hold on, Speedy, we don't know the facts yet. Save your strength for Simon–Watch, so we can stop him from accidentally blowing the whole place up or something."

"Hey, *you're* the one with the plasma problems," Simon said from behind them.

Alysha and Owen whirled around. "Simon!" Alysha said. "I was just . . ."

Owen looked at his feet.

"Wow, you two are speechless?" Simon asked.

"We just . . . you know . . ." Alysha said. "So how are you feeling?"

Simon shrugged. "Getting over a stomachache. Indian food for dinner."

"You know what I mean," Alysha said with a roll of her eyes.

Simon smiled. "It's fine. I'm fine. I think. I'm still nervous and all, but talking to Ralfagon helped a little. What's going on?"

Alysha related what Jill said, and Owen stomped his foot. "This can't be a coincidence! Maybe it's something the Board's up to, or it has to do with Ralfagon. We're going to walk in there and find a bunch of new teachers from the Union here to gang up on Simon and us because Ralfagon had to retire."

"Don't be paranoid!" Alysha said. "Remember, Ralfagon *chose* to step down."

"I'm sure it's normal school business," Simon said. "Not some Union invasion."

There was a loud burst of static as the school's public announcement system turned on. After a few loud *thunks* from someone testing the microphone, a voice rang out.

"All students please report to your homerooms immediately. Your teachers will escort you to a special first period assembly so you can meet your new principal."

"Oh, no," Simon and Alysha said at the same time.

"Told you so," Owen said.

Once the assembly ended, hundreds of students and faculty members filed out of the main auditorium. It was a slow process; everyone turned back to stare at the new principal, especially those who remembered her from Martin Van Buren Elementary. Many murmured about the sudden change in school leadership and, of course, that towering column of hair.

Eventually, all but four people were gone. The only ones left in the auditorium were the new principal and the three students she'd asked to stay after. Now that the place was empty, Simon, Alysha, and Owen made their way down the bleachers to the auditorium floor, where Miss Fanstrom waited.

"That was not pleasant," she said in her clipped British accent. "It was hard enough arranging my transfer to Martin Van Buren Elementary last May and to Enrico Fermi Junior High this September. But a third move a month later? I'll be hearing about this from the PTA, I have no doubt."

Miss Fanstrom clapped her hands and smiled warmly at the three friends. "No use weeping and wailing though, is there? Mr. Bloom, Mr. Walters, Miss Davis, it's a pleasure to see you all again. I'm guessing you have questions for me, yes?"

Simon cleared his throat. "Yes. We haven't seen you since you sent us to see our Narrator five months ago."

Alysha folded her arms. "Every time—every single time—we went to your office to talk to you, you were mysteriously off school grounds or in a meeting!"

"Wait-Enrico-Fermi-Junior-High-in-Stoneridge?" Owen asked in a verbal blur.

The top of Miss Fanstrom's hair swiveled toward Owen. "As always, Mr. Walters, your powers of observation are only outshone by your rate of self-expression."

"Are there Union members in Stoneridge coming to get us?"

"Ah, and then there's your capacity for needless worrying. No, Mr. Walters, though you have many dangers to face, that is not one of them. Allow me to explain."

In her calm yet crisp voice, punctuated by the top of her hair periodically shifting its aim from one youth to the next, Miss Fanstrom recapped what they already knew—how, five months ago, the Council of Sciences was unable to remove Sirabetta's ruined tattoos. The Board was unwilling to over-look her crimes, but since she was trapped as a thirteen-year-old girl they found it easiest to try to give her a fresh start.

The Order of Psychology erased her memories, and she was put into foster care, placed in the next town so the Order of Physics could keep an eye on her. Willoughby Wanderby volunteered to be the point person on this. His discipline as a gym teacher made him seem a good choice, especially since his battle with Simon and friends in the previous Chronicle was believed to be a complete misunderstanding.

Miss Fanstrom went on to explain how Sirabetta was treated at school, as well as how the kids' former gym teacher freed her.

"So Mr. Wanderby was really a bad guy all along," Alysha said.

Owen nodded. "That explains all the laps we had to run."

Simon, again without thinking, rested his hand on the flap of his backpack. "Okay, what now? Is the Order of Physics going after them? The whole Union?"

Miss Fanstrom frowned. "I wish it were so simple. Any official Union action requires authorization from the Board of Administration. Ordinarily the Board is slow to do anything—they have so many procedures—but for several months now they've been positively glacial." She paused. "In fact, I've noticed many rather peculiar things about them lately." She shook her head—hair unmoving—as if to dismiss a thought. "Besides, we can't be certain they even know. Or the Council, either."

"What?" shouted Alysha. "Why not?"

"Because Mr. Wanderby is the one who would report such a thing," Miss Fanstrom said. "As far as most know, all is well."

Simon sat down on the nearest bleacher seat. "*You* know. You and Greygor."

Miss Fanstrom nodded sadly. "Yes, we do. But there are rules for these things."

"Forget the rules—our lives are in danger!" Alysha yelled, kicking the bleachers.

Miss Fanstrom wagged her finger. "Tut, tut, Miss Davis. Behave yourself! You are a young lady—I expect better self-control." She looked away, and her tower of hair wobbled. "I understand your fury; I truly do. But everyone, even Keepers and principals, has restrictions."

"It's not just *our* lives at risk," Owen said. "How can you not tell someone?"

Miss Fanstrom nodded solemnly. "I have, Mr. Walters. I have told you three."

Simon locked eyes with her. "And I'm the Keeper, now. It's my responsibility." He looked away and shook his head sadly. An idea struck him, and he straightened, eager; he opened the backpack and put his hand on the Book. "Can I contact the other members of the Council?"

"If you'd like," Miss Fanstrom said.

"Can I have them organize a group to go after Sirabetta and Wanderby?"

"You can ask them to."

Simon smiled. "And, as Keeper of the Order of Physics, I can get the other Physics members to go after them, too, right?"

"Yes."

"Wait," Owen said. "Mr. Wanderby and Mermon Veenie were both secretly in league with Sirabetta. What if there are more traitors?"

"Owen, you're being . . ." Alysha trailed off, a thoughtful look on her face.

"Hard to accuse him of being too cautious now, isn't it, Miss Davis?" Miss Fanstrom said. "After all, do you know who supplied Sirabetta with her tattoos? Or whose help she seeks from the Order of Biology? In short, who can you trust?"

"Do you know who is good or bad and who we can trust?" Owen asked.

Miss Fanstrom frowned. "I face more limits than just rules,

Mr. Walters. There is much going on that is beyond even my knowledge."

Simon groaned. "Oh, that's just great! So anyone can be against us, right?"

Miss Fanstrom just looked at him.

Simon sighed; her silence was an answer. He rubbed his forehead. "If somebody's going to stop Sirabetta, it has to be us, then?"

Miss Fanstrom still said nothing.

"I'm only twelve," Simon said, his voice almost pleading. "I'm not ready."

"Weren't you eleven when you stopped her before?" Miss Fanstrom asked.

"Yeah, and she can't even use her tattoos anymore," Alysha said. "And Wanderby wasn't so tough. I'm sure we can handle this!"

Owen groaned. "You know, every time you say that, people get blown up."

"I'm afraid I must agree with Mr. Walters. If you choose to undertake this mission, you must be prepared for threats from anywhere and anyone."

"And if I don't accept the mission?" Simon asked.

Miss Fanstrom nodded her head. "A wise question, Mr. Bloom. Only a fool rushes headlong into certain danger without considering his options. Unfortunately, you risk much if you do nothing. If Sirabetta is restored to adulthood, her tattoos will probably function again. She'll likely come after you and the *Teacher's Edition of Physics* or another science-based *Teacher's Edition* and its Keeper. If she succeeds, she'll abuse that power, attack other Keepers, and steal their Books. I fear her efforts to remake the Union will damage or destroy life as we know it."

"Wait . . . what *exactly* is the mission you're suggesting?" Alysha demanded.

"Another wise question, Miss Davis. You can, of course, try to contact the entire Council and see what they want to do. You can try to rally the entire Order of Physics, or as many of them as you feel you can trust. Or . . ."

She trailed off, and Simon finished her sentence for her. ". . . or we can go to the Order of Biology ourselves to stop Sirabetta from turning herself back into an adult."

"That's a bad idea," Owen said. "She could have the whole Order against us!"

"Gilio wouldn't side with her," Simon said. "Neither would Flangelo." Indeed, Flangelo from the Order of Biology had been a great source of information to the kids when they'd first found the Book. His Bio power—the ability to turn into a sparrow—was of limited use in a fight, but he still risked his life to help them.

Simon sighed. "I guess we'll just have to wing it with the rest."

"Wing it?" Owen groaned. "How many times do we have to almost get killed before you give up on this whole 'wing it' thing?"

"I'm just wondering if he meant 'wing it' as a joke about Flangelo," Alysha said.

Upset as he was, Owen still managed a chuckle at that. "Fine, let's say we go to Bio. How do we get there? And where is there?"

The kids turned to Miss Fanstrom, who cleared her throat. "What do you think?"

"Obviously, you or the Narrator could tell us if you *wanted* to," Alysha said. "But if you're going to keep this hush-hush stuff going, Simon can probably ask Gilio."

The top of Miss Fanstrom's hair bent forward toward Alysha, as if nodding.

"This is the dumbest idea ever," Owen said. "What about school? It's Tuesday morning; are we supposed to go to the Order of Biology, save the universe, and be back in time for dinner?"

"Tut, tut, Mr. Walters. I am your principal, after all. I believe a special field trip aimed at furthering your science education can be arranged. You'd be amazed how much influence even a brand-new principal has with parents."

Simon nodded his head. "That's it, then. That's what I have to do."

"What do you mean 'I'?" Alysha asked.

"I can't ask you guys to go with me; we could get killed!"

Alysha snorted. "Yeah, 'cause last time was warm and fuzzy? It's risky, but it's like Miss Fanstrom said. Someone has to do it . . . and that's us. Of course I'm going."

Simon exhaled with relief; he was terrified at the thought of doing this alone. Then Alysha, Miss Fanstrom, and he looked at Owen.

Owen avoided their gazes. "What can you tell us about the Order of Biology?" he finally asked.

"Biology is the study of all living things," Miss Fanstrom said. "So their domain is filled with things that are alive."

"That tells me a lot, thanks." He grimaced but still didn't look up. "So we can expect huge, vicious creatures and weird, creepy plants? Oh, and Order members with powers over all sorts of life, too, right? And they'll probably all want to attack us!"

Miss Fanstrom cleared her throat. "Tut tut, Mr. Walters. You three are hardly helpless, are you?"

Owen was silent for moments. At last he kicked the ground and looked at Miss Fanstrom. "You know, I hate it when you say 'tut tut.' That's almost as bad as Alysha saying it'll be easy or Simon wanting to figure it out as he goes along."

The others said nothing.

"What does 'tut tut' even mean? Who says that?"

Still, they waited.

"Okay! You happy?" Owen shouted. "We'll go to Biology and get turned into newts or whatever. But I am *not* going to have fun while we do it!"

"I think we guessed that," Alysha said.

Simon and Miss Fanstrom's hair nodded in agreement.

CHAPTER 14

X MARKS THE SPOT

The kids had to wait until after school to ask their parents. Simon wasn't surprised by how Steven and Sylvia Bloom reacted to the idea. They were working in their home offices when he called them together and brought it up.

". . . so it's for school, and my principal says it's really important," he finished.

"Sure thing, pal," said his dad.

"No problem," said his mom.

Simon nodded. "Okay. You have to sign this—" They signed the form before he could finish his sentence. "Okay, thanks." He frowned as he took the paper back.

"Everything okay?" Steven Bloom asked.

"You're not coming down with something, are you?" Sylvia Bloom asked, placing her palm on Simon's forehead.

"No, just thinking about the field trip," Simon said.

"Great," his parents said at the same time. "Do you need a ride?"

Simon shook his head. His parents each gave him a quick hug and went back to their home offices, leaving Simon to go to his room and pack some things.

At the same time, Owen's mother was surprised to hear about the immediacy of the trip and her son's willingness to go on it. "Really? You *want* to leave town?"

"Yeah, Mom," Owen said, mustering a smile. "It'll be an adventure."

Owen's mother stared hard at him for a long moment and then signed the permission slip so quickly that she tore a hole in the paper. "Go. Have fun. Have"—her voice caught for a second—"an adventure."

Alysha's parents were the toughest to convince. "Missing school?" Max Davis asked. "Only three students going?" Jana Davis asked. "And on such short notice? What is this trip about?" they demanded to know.

Alysha did some fast and smooth talking, trying to stick as close to the truth as possible. "Guys, the principal hand-picked me for this. She says I could contribute so much to the trip." She paused a moment and unleashed her last-resort weapon: "And I'll bet it'll be great for my grades!"

Soon enough, Alysha was allowed to go, too. The permission slips said the trip was to upstate New York—Miss

Fanstrom didn't want the parents taking their kids to the airport. Instead, their parents dropped them and their bags at the school Tuesday evening (except for Simon, who used his friction control to skate over). The Davises and Ms. Walters met the principal and stared at her hair in shock. But after a few minutes of conversation, they were convinced their children were in safe hands.

As soon as the parents' cars pulled away, Miss Fanstrom's plastered-on smile faded away. "I am sorry we had to deceive your parents. I'm even sorrier that you have to face this alone. But I believe you will succeed. Be strong, be bold, and above all, be smart. Remember: you have formulas, but you also have your wits and your courage."

"Can we call the Order of Biology to tell them we're coming?" Simon asked.

"Not with a telephone. When you see the Order's domain, you'll understand."

The Book spoke into Simon's head. *Keepers can communicate via their Books.*

That's useful, Simon thought back. "Give me a second," Simon said aloud. He placed his hands on his Book and closed his eyes. After a few minutes, he opened them again. "We just need to take a Gateway to a certain place, and the Order of Biology's domain will do the rest."

"What, like the woods and the Breeze?" Alysha asked.

Miss Fanstrom chuckled. "Pardon me. But be ready for

something . . . different," she said. "Now, let's see about Gateways." She whipped out her notebook computer from her briefcase and opened it in a smooth and swift motion.

Simon felt a slight buzz from his Book, and it flashed a quick burst of blue at the computer. Miss Fanstrom's notebook computer gave off a quick gray flash, as if in response. But that meant—"Miss Fanstrom? Are you a Keeper, too?"

Miss Fanstrom smiled. "All that need concern you three right now is that I'm your principal. And I'm not shy about giving detentions, so be still." She tapped her computer screen a few times and nodded. "Regrettably, the Craftmen's Guild hasn't had a chance to install a teleporter device or Gateway access at this school, yet. The closest Gateway, in fact, is outside Dunkerhook Woods." Miss Fanstrom looked at the cloudy evening sky. "Might I recommend an aerial approach?"

The three friends left most of their bags in Miss Fanstrom's office. They didn't know how long they'd be gone, but they didn't want to be weighed down with too much luggage. Owen and Simon stuffed their backpacks with necessary items, and Alysha used a small duffel bag, taking more clothing than the boys.

Together the three put on their raincoats and flew to Van Silas Way. They landed on the street, where the trademark Union rainstorm was already in progress to keep their arrival hidden from Outsider eyes.

Simon gazed up at the majestic woods rising up in front of them. "Ready?"

"I felt pretty bad, lying to my mom like that," Owen said.

"It's not like we could tell them the truth," Simon said.

"It's better that they don't know," Alysha said. "When we come home, they'll be glad to see us and have no idea that we've saved the universe. For the second time."

"You mean *if* we come home," Owen said. "We might never see them again."

Alysha opened her mouth; I could tell she was ready to comment on Owen being a worrywart. But she stopped and closed it, suddenly struck by the very real danger.

The three friends stood there, the heavy rain blanketing the street everywhere but on them. Their raincoats once again kept them safe from the wet, but not from the gloomy feeling of the rain. Or, worse, the gloomy sense of what they were risking.

Finally, Alysha shook her head. "No way; no thinking like that." She put a hand each on Simon's and Owen's shoulders. "We'll be fine. We'll do what we have to do, and we'll come back, no problem." Then she gave both friends a gentle push. "Now snap out of it or I'm going to take charge of the mission."

That broke the tension for Simon and Owen. They smiled and relaxed a bit. The glowing Gateway sprang up, turning the water around them a beautiful blue.

"Here we go," Simon said. He started to walk toward the Gateway, then turned back. Alysha pushed Owen lightly ahead of her to get him moving, and seconds later, the three stepped through.

As they disappeared, a car screeched to a halt on the street. A hooded raincoat-clad woman dashed out and hurried into the rain. She paused as the Gateway disappeared into the ground, then she stepped into Dunkerhook Woods. She threw back her hood, revealing long red hair. Loisana Belane.

Loisana whipped out a cell phone and dialed. "It's me," she said. "I missed them. I'm not sure, but I think the Gateway was set for the Order of Biology. They should be taken care of there." She listened to a voice on the other end. "If I have to, I'll track them down sooner or later." She hung up and stared out to the street, her jaw set, her expression unreadable.

Simon, Owen, and Alysha emerged somewhere where it wasn't raining. They tossed back their raincoat hoods and looked around at a dark place lit only by the moon above them. It was a wide stretch of beach at the base of sheer cliffs that extended hundreds of feet above them. About thirty feet from the cliffs, ocean waves lapped gently at the sand. The Gateway sank into the ground, leaving more cliff face behind it.

Alysha laughed. "The way Miss Fanstrom was talking, I expected Biology to be in a volcano. But a beach? Does it come with umbrellas and fruity drinks?"

Owen looked around. "This can't be it, can it? I mean, where would they sit?"

"It's warm out," Simon said. "If this was the Jersey shore in October, wouldn't it be colder? Maybe we're not even on the East Coast anymore. Or the United States."

"And what do we do next?" Alysha asked. "Make sand castles while we wait?"

Owen stared at a spot about fifty feet away. "Look!" He pointed at a large X scraped into the sand.

The trio stood around the X. "Gilio said he'd leave a guide," Simon said. "I figured he meant a person. but this could count, right?"

"I bet it does." Alysha gestured toward the ocean. "Look, it's far enough from the ocean so no waves can wash it away."

"So what does it mean?" Owen asked.

"Let's find out." Alysha grabbed Simon's and Owen's arms and pulled them along as she stepped onto it.

Suddenly, a huge wave leaped out of the ocean and surged toward them. They had no time to move; Owen could barely scream the words "I knew it!" before the wave crashed onto them. When it receded into the water, the kids were gone from the beach.

CHAPTER 15

The Problem with Pebbles

The wave threw the kids into the ocean, but they didn't get wet; in fact, the wave wrapped around them and formed an air-filled bubble that left them dry and comfortable. All they suffered was a quiver in their stomachs as the bubble rocketed down . . . to somewhere. The bubble was completely opaque—all they saw was darkness.

Less than a minute later, the bubble disintegrated. Simon and his friends found themselves far from the beach. Far under it, that is. They seemed to be entirely underwater. The first big clue was the fact that the sand beneath their feet was now bordered by a nearby coral reef.

"Can you stop with all that drag-me-into-the-unknown stuff?" Owen shouted.

Simon and Alysha didn't answer. Owen followed their

gazes, and he, too, stared in wonder at the domain of the Order of Biology.

The off-white coral reef rose high above the sand, curving around behind the kids and standing like a wall to their left, stretching out as far as they could see. The reef was a huge living organism: a mini-ecosystem that was home to a variety of sea creatures. Colorful fish darted through and around the anemones and other reef animals, enjoying doing fishy things—nipping at one anothers' fins, snacking on vegetation, getting eaten by bigger fish. (Those getting eaten seemed to be having less fun than the others, though.)

But there was something strange about it. "I'm no expert," Alysha said, "but when you're underwater, shouldn't you be . . . wet?"

She was right: Simon and his friends were surrounded by—and thus breathing—air. Yet everywhere they looked was ocean. Around them, above them. Definitely not the best place to avoid drowning. Or at least extreme sogginess.

Simon walked to the nearest part of the coral border and reached out. His hand hit some sort of barrier several feet from the edge of the coral. "So we're underwater, but not *in* the water. But the coral is, with some sort of force field between us and the reef."

Alysha walked next to Simon and flicked the air with a finger; visible ripples spread outward, like when a pebble strikes the surface of a pond.

"Hey," Alysha said. "My hand's not getting wet!"

The ripples got smaller the farther they went; some arced high above them, revealing that the force field was in the shape of an enormous dome. By squinting, Simon could see the difference between the air-filled interior of the dome and the vast ocean on the other side. He took the Book out of his backpack and sent it a mental message. *Can you help me understand what I'm seeing? Even if it's not physics?*

Of course, Keeper, the Book thought back to him. *All the laws of the universe are connected, deep down. The divisions are for your sake, not ours.*

"Ours?" Simon asked aloud. "What do you mean?" The Book ignored that question, instead distracting him with information about the dome. "Ohhh, I get it. The barrier is made of water changed by physics, biology, and chemistry formulas set up and left in place, like those that hide Dunkerhook Woods. They mostly deal with surface tension to strengthen bonds between the water molecules and pressurization to balance the air inside and the water outside."

"I have no idea what you just said," Owen said.

Alysha gave a hard tap to the barrier and pointed to the tiny swells that flowed outward. "He means the formulas make the water act partly like a solid. Simon, you sound like a teacher. If you keep the Book, you'll ace every science class."

"Yeah. If," Simon said with a frown.

"Let's get going," Alysha said. "Hunting down Sirabetta should cheer you up. Think about how impressed the Board will be if we do well on this mission!"

"We should wait here," Owen said.

"Come on, Owen," Alysha said. "I know you're being careful, but we're on an urgent mission in maybe the most incredible place in the world. Why just wait here?"

Owen pointed a few feet to his right, in the opposite direction of the reef and dome wall. There, scrawled in the sand, was a message: WAIT HERE.

Simon saw a movement out of the corner of his eye; one of the reef fish came toward them. It was a foot long with red and white stripes all over. Simon stared at the fingerlike bristles at the tips of its fins and the numerous red and white spines along its back: it looked like a candy cane–colored sea porcupine. It swam right up to the edge of the barrier, stared at them with big black eyes, and then swam back to the reef.

Simon tore his eyes away from the reef and looked out at the interior of the enclosed world. "I'm with Alysha on this one. We don't know how long we'd have to wait before someone comes to meet us. What's the harm in scouting out the place?"

Alysha nodded. "Yeah—call it prep work. We'll get the lay of the land."

Owen shook his head. "What does that even mean? That's the kind of thing they say on TV shows before one of them gets killed. And I'll bet it'll be me!" He sighed. "Fine. But if we get eaten or killed, I'm not talking to either one of you ever again."

"Please, let us get eaten or killed," Alysha muttered.

They moved deeper into the domed space. The air was clear and fresh with no trace of humidity, so they breathed and walked comfortably. The reef fell into the distance, and all around them was just empty space over a sandy floor. Soon the sand gave way to finely ground gravel, then dirt, and finally a large plain with short grass as far as the kids could see. The dome arched higher and higher until it was impossible to distinguish between the air or the ocean beyond. At its highest point, it must have been many hundreds of feet off the ground.

"Kinda dull, isn't it?" Alysha asked.

"Dull?" Simon said. "This is the headquarters of Biology, the study of all life!"

Alysha twirled a finger in the air, the official "whoop-de-doo" motion. "Yeah, so you'd think there'd actually *be* some living things here. Besides all this lovely grass."

Simon frowned. "Wait . . . something's strange." His voice trailed off as he stared around him. It was something he'd felt before—a twisting sensation inside.

Alysha and Owen shared a look. "You okay?" Alysha asked. "You're not going to zone out and accidentally break the dome or anything like that, are you?"

"I'm fine. I feel like there's a sort of disturbance . . . but it's probably nothing."

Alysha nodded. "Good. So let's keep going."

In one direction, the short grass became waist high and

even taller farther along. In the other direction, the grass got shorter.

Owen frowned. "No way are we going through that high grass. There could be wolves or holes or sharks or anything."

Simon stared at the way the tall grass swayed gently despite the lack of any wind. "He's right—the last thing we want is trouble."

"Fine, let's stick to the golf course," Alysha said.

They kept going over the low grass but saw nothing special. There were several isolated patches of flowers and toadstools, but that was it. Occasionally they'd pass a pebbled path that led off into the distance. They followed the first path and found that it led to a small pool of water. They wandered along the other pebbled paths and saw each had a corresponding pool; the largest of them was the size of a modest swimming pool, while the smallest was like a big puddle— just big enough for someone to stand in.

Simon pointed to the nearest pool, which was about double the width and length of an average bathtub. "It's these things—they're what're bothering me."

Simon and Alysha approached and leaned over it, careful to keep their feet away from the edge. They saw only their faces reflected back.

Owen hung back and looked around. His gaze landed on another patch of toadstools near the pool. "You know, sane people usually avoid things that don't feel right. Let's go back and see if someone's come to show us around."

"Hold on," Simon said, unable to ignore the way that pool was messing with him inside. He picked up a pebble from the path and tossed it into the pool. It fell through the surface without a splash—only a sucking noise. Simon felt a twinge in his head. "Ohhh–kay. That's not right."

Owen grabbed at Simon's and Alysha's sleeves. "Fine, you've done your sightseeing, let's get out of here."

Without saying a word, Simon and Alysha turned away from the eerie pool and hurried to follow Owen down the path. Their footsteps made light crunching noises as they rushed across the pebbles. They had just stepped back onto the short grass when they heard a sucking noise much like the pebble made when it hit the water. Next they heard three loud crunches that sounded exactly like something—no, *three* somethings—hitting the pebble path.

The kids stopped short. "I didn't imagine that noise, did I?" Owen asked. A pebble clunked onto the grass in front of the three friends. "Or that?" he added.

"No," a gruff voice not belonging to Simon or Alysha answered.

The kids turned around and saw two men and a woman glaring at them. One man was tall and lean, with dark brown hair and a neatly trimmed beard. He also had a bloody cut, roughly the size of a pebble, above one eye.

"And I *know* I'm not imagining you three intruders in our domain," the other, shorter man said in a harsh voice.

"I am getting so tired of being right," Owen grumbled.

CHAPTER 16

BIG TROUBLE BY THE LITTLE PUDDLE

Simon and his friends stared silently at the three adults facing them. They looked like they were in their early- to mid-twenties. They also looked very upset.

"Well?" the angry man demanded. He was thin and pale with a shaved-bald head.

"Please, it's not what you think," Simon said, raising his hands in a calming gesture. "We're supposed to be here."

The woman swept her dyed black hair from where it covered her large blue eyes. "Outsiders? Supposed to be here? Don't think so. And what's with attacking Cassaro?"

"It-was-an-accident-we-swear!" Owen said.

"Yeah, and we're not Outsiders," Alysha added. "We're in the Order of Physics."

The thin, bald man glared. "We heard there was trouble

with your Order months ago." He concentrated, and the air around him shimmered. Within seconds, his whole body was covered by dark gray armor that made him several feet taller and much more massive. There were lighter, different-textured areas at his elbows, knees, shoulders, hips, and neck—all places that needed to be flexible. The armor over his face was almost featureless, like a huge gray helmet, but with black, bulbous eyes.

"Ewww," Alysha said with a shudder. "What's he supposed to be, a giant bug-man? I *hate* bugs!"

"Oh, Simon," Owen grumbled, "what did you get us into now?" He spoke his own formula and concentrated on the rocky trail. Six fist-size stones streaked up into the air, swooping and swirling in a steady, fluid formation between Owen and the three Biology members. He was ready to launch them at the adults if they got hostile.

"Hold on!" Simon shouted. "We're *not* here to fight! Gilio asked us to come!"

Cassaro shook his head. "Not buying it, fella. If you were here for a nice visit, what would shorty over there be doing with those rocks?"

Simon shook his head, but before he could say anything, the armored man nodded to the black-haired woman. "Targa, zap him!" he said, his voice booming out.

The woman scrunched her face up and gestured at Simon. He staggered, suddenly sluggish, and dropped to his knees. It was all he could do not to pass out.

"Whuuuut . . ." Simon slurred. "Whut . . . did . . . yuuu . . . do?"

Targa punched a fist into the air. "Totally messed you up, that's what! Try to fight us with your adrenaline levels all the way down. That's how *I* roll!"

"Leave him alone!" Owen yelled. He sent the rocks hurtling toward Targa, but the armored man leaped in front of her. The stones bounced harmlessly off his gray shell.

Cassaro laughed. "It'll take more than rocks to get through Kender's exoskeleton. Here, have some of these!" The tall man puffed out his cheeks and spat out a cloud of tiny, almost invisible, dots.

Owen launched more rocks at the center of the cloud, knocking away most of the gnat-size dots to land on the ground around him. A few got onto his clothes, though.

"Were those more bugs?" Alysha asked, scanning the ground in horror.

The dots, actually called spores, were a lot nastier than bugs. Or dots, for that matter. While I'm no expert on them, I know they're how fungi reproduce. Fungi, as in multiple of fungus, as in . . .

The spores in the grass started growing at an accelerated rate, each one becoming a different-colored mushroom. "Okay, that's gross." Alysha said. "But better than bugs."

The few that had landed on Owen started to grow, too. They weren't developing as quickly as the ones on the grass, probably because Owen's clothing was less nutritious

115

than soil, but they were still growing at an unnatural speed.

"Ahhh!" Owen screamed. "Get them off me!" The mushrooms kept expanding; the ones on the ground were already several feet high while the fungi on him—one on one sleeve, one on a pants leg, and one on the stomach area of his T-shirt—were already the size of small cats.

"First, the giant roach," Alysha said. She took a handful of coins from her pocket, filled them with electrical charge, and whipped them at Kender and his friends.

Targa and Cassaro dodged the attack but were flung to the ground when the coins blew up. Kender, confident in his shell's protection, didn't move. The coins exploded against his armor, gouging holes out of it and knocking him onto his back.

Alysha rushed to Owen's side. "Okay, this might hurt," she said.

Owen closed his eyes and braced himself as Alysha reached for the mushroom on Owen's sleeve. She discharged more stored-up electricity with a bluish spark and a loud *zzzap*; the mushroom turned black, shriveled, and fell to the ground.

"I think my arm's gone numb," Owen moaned.

"Stop whining and stand still," Alysha said; she didn't want to risk Owen moving and getting a shock. In seconds she'd burned the other mushrooms off. Owen smacked at his clothes to knock the charred remnants away.

Targa, Cassaro, and Kender rose to their feet. "That's a nice trick," Targa said. "But try pulling it after *I'm* through with you!" She pointed her finger at Alysha.

For long moments, Simon had been barely aware of what was happening . . . his vision was blurred and everything sounded as if he were underwater. But when Targa was knocked to the ground, Simon felt a bit more self–control creep back to him.

What do I do? he thought to himself. *How can I possibly fight this?* Squinting, he saw Targa taking aim at Alysha. That did it for him—he shoved his fear and exhaustion aside and let his anger surge forward. Anger, and the need to save his friends.

With great effort, Simon concentrated on the adults. Even with his mind sludging along at the speed of molasses, he was able to trigger his oldest, best power. The Biology members were suddenly hit by staggering weight as the gravitational pull on them was tripled. They collapsed to the ground with yelps and groans.

Simon felt better instantly, the exhaustion torn away like a blanket yanked off.

"You're okay!" Alysha said.

Simon nodded and got to his feet. "Getting there. How are you guys?"

Before they could respond, Kender slowly rose from the ground.

"How?" Simon gasped, taking a step back.

"That's the beauty of an exoskeleton," Kender said. "Augmented strength."

117

"You're going to need it, Beetle-face," Alysha said. "It's three against one now." She held up her fists, knuckles out, and let a jagged burst of electricity arc back and forth between them. Owen nodded, forming more stones into large, tightly balled clusters and raising them up in front of him.

A loud chirping cut through the air, and to everyone's surprise, a brown-and-white sparrow swooped between Kender and the kids.

The bird landed on the grass, flickered, trembled, and distorted until it morphed into a skinny, brown-haired man.

"Flangelo!" the kids shouted in unison.

"Stop fighting!" he cried out in his musical, almost singsongy way. "Kender, they're not enemies. And kids, stop beating people up! It's no way to greet strangers."

"They started it!" Owen shouted. "We were just protecting ourselves."

Kender stomped forward, each triple-weighted step making a three-inch-deep footprint in the ground. "They attacked Cassaro and were rude."

"And I'm sure you were an absolute angel to them," Flangelo said. "Trust me, Gilio invited them here for a reason, and he won't appreciate you hurting them."

Alysha snorted. "Hurting us? Look who's winning."

"Okay, I'm going to let those two up," Simon said. "But if any of you attack again," he said to the Biology members, "I'll make you weigh six times normal. More for you," he said to Kender. He gestured, restoring the gravity to normal.

Targa barely moved. "Trust me," she groaned, "I'm just going to lie here and ache for a while." She nodded weakly at Flangelo. "And who are you supposed to be?"

"He's in Animal Diversity with me," Kender said. He turned to Flangelo. "You'd better be right about these kids. You know how hard it is for me to molt and grow another shell."

"Yes," Flangelo said with a weary glance skyward, "we're all *so* concerned. Get it through your chitin skull, Kender. They're friends—back off."

Kender spoke a few words, and his human form stepped backward out of the massive exoskeleton. Then he spoke a few more words and poked the empty shell with a finger. It started to dissolve; within seconds, it was gone.

Cassaro struggled to rise to a sitting position. "Friends or not, they're sure tough. What was that you got us with?"

Simon shrugged self-consciously. "Gravity."

"Okay, okay, there'll be plenty of time to chitchat at the inter-Order picnic," Flangelo said, tugging on Simon's arm to drag him away. "Important business, now." Flangelo also grabbed Owen's arm and shouted, "Come on, spark plug, let's go."

"Wait!" Targa shouted. "Flatulo, or whatever your name is . . . what's the deal?"

"Love to stay," Flangelo chirped, "but these three have an appointment to keep and we're oh-so-late." He pulled the kids out of sight. "What's the matter with you?" he scolded them. "Do you know how long I've been looking for you?

Can't you read messages in the sand, or is WAIT HERE too complicated?"

"Yeah, it's nice to see you again, too," Owen said.

"Why are you yelling at us?" Alysha shouted. "If you were supposed to meet us, then *you* screwed up!"

Flangelo shook his head. "What, I'm not allowed to go to the bathroom?"

"We almost got killed because you couldn't hold it?" Owen asked.

Simon, Alysha, and Owen broke into laughter as they hurried along.

CHAPTER 17

Some Fish Do Need Bicycles

Flangelo led them back the way they came.

"Where are we going?" Alysha demanded as she was pulled along.

"To Gilio's," Flangelo warbled. "But I have to take you back to that entrance, because that's the fastest way I know to get to him. When he finds out what happened . . ." He shook his head.

Alysha pulled out of Flangelo's grasp. "Fine, but enough with the dragging!"

"Yeah," Owen said. "It's bad enough I had giant mushrooms on me!"

Flangelo dropped Owen's arm as if it were covered in dead fish or, more accurately, burned mushroom. "You could have told me." He stared at his hand. "Fungus . . . I'll be washing this hand for a week."

"Okay, Flangelo," Simon said, "you've got some explaining to do."

"Like how did we even get here?" Alysha asked.

"Yeah," Owen said. "One minute we're at the Jersey shore or something and the next there's a huge wave and sploosh!"

"Oh, that's Gilio's fancy entrance system. He's very cautious about who he lets into his home, you see." Flangelo let out a whistle-laugh. "He's got all sorts of ways to keep Outsiders from coming around here or noticing anything unusual."

Alysha shrugged. "Sure. That's what they said about Dunkerhook Woods, but look how that went with Simon."

Flangelo shook his head. "Well, there's no Breeze to invite people into our domain. And that's not New Jersey up there; I don't know where it is. The whole place moves—Gilio designed it to relocate regularly. Even Council members need Gilio's approval to have Gateways take them to the nearest beach, and then they still need the vesicle to bring them in."

"The what?" Alysha asked.

"That bubble that was your chariot," Flangelo said.

As they walked and talked, the grass beneath their feet gave way to sand again.

"So all the Biology members have to go through that each time they want to come to meet?" Owen asked. "Seems like an awful lot of work. And dangerous, too."

"It's at least as safe as the Gateway system." He paused.

"Which probably terrifies you, too, doesn't it, little lion-heart?"

Owen made a "sort-of" gesture with his hand.

"As for the coming and going," Flangelo said, "it doesn't happen as often as you'd think. Most of us live here."

"I thought Union members go around as teachers to help Outsiders discover stuff," Alysha said. "How does that work if you're all down here playing Atlantis and the rest of the world doesn't even know you exist?"

Owen gasped. "Is *this* Atlantis?"

Flangelo whistle-laughed. "No, but that's a funny story. Supposedly, a couple of guys in Physics were trying to impress a woman in another Order and . . . well . . . good-bye, continent, hello, annoying legend."

Simon pointed to a stretch of coral reef and the dome outline beside it. "That's where we came in. Do you think Sirabetta came through here, too?"

"Is *that* what this visit's about? That witch is back?" Flangelo warbled. "Wonderful. I'm pretty sure she didn't come through here, though."

"Why's that?" Alysha asked.

"Even if she managed to find this place and get past the protective formulas, she'd have been spotted by the guards. At the very least, they'd have told me about it."

"I hate to argue—" Alysha said.

Before she could finish, Flangelo fake-whispered, "Not likely."

Alysha rolled her eyes. "There were no guards when your vesicle-thingie brought us," she continued. "Maybe the same thing happened with Sirabetta?"

"No guard?" Flangelo chirped. "Oh, Phineas, care to meet our little guests?"

One of the fish from the reef came toward the dome wall. It was the red-and-white-spined fish that approached when Simon and his friends first arrived. As the kids stared, it swam straight for a spot on the dome a few feet above the ground.

Simon winced, expecting it to smack into the barrier. Instead, the fish plowed through without slowing down, bringing a beach ball–size globe of water into the dome with it. The aqueous ball separated from the dome and dropped to the sandy floor. The fish was entirely covered in this bizarre, reverse submarine.

Flangelo applauded lightly. "Good trick, isn't it? Every living organism is made of cells, and every cell uses something called *active transport* to take food or other objects in or out. Gilio designed the dome to work like a giant cell, complete with certain active transport sites. Ocean folk like Phineas get water-filled vesicles that let them move around in the dome's atmosphere. Air-dependent Order members get air-filled vesicles so they can go out among the fish. And you three get an express vesicle from the beach to this dome, with water jets propelling you at an extreme speed."

The water around Phineas shimmered. The bubble expanded around the fish's various spines and bristles, forming thin arms and legs. The fish lifted its water-sphere—its vesicle—off the sandy floor and walked over to them.

Flangelo gestured. "Simon Bloom, Owen Walters, Alysha Davis, meet Phineas. He's a lionfish and one of our best guards."

Simon reached out with one hand, anxious to see what the water-vesicle felt like.

Flangelo's hand whipped out and firmly grabbed Simon's arm. "Not a good idea, Captain Gravity." He gestured to the watery limbs. "The vesicle-formula lets him make those pseudopods: temporary, fake limbs so he doesn't have to roll around in here. But those spines? Poisonous. There's plenty of surface tension around each vesicle to keep the traveler pressurized and breathing properly, but if you pressed too hard on Phineas's . . . let's just say your mission would be over real quick."

Simon nodded and waved to Phineas. "Hi, there." Alysha and Owen took several steps back at the mention of poisonous spines and waved, too.

Phineas's wide mouth barely moved, but one of the bristle-pseudopods waved. "Likewise," he said in a gurgly voice.

"You can talk!" Owen gasped.

Phineas nodded—awkwardly, considering he had no neck; it was more like bowing his entire body. "Another of Keeper Gilio's great works." His voice was slightly muffled from going through water and air.

Flangelo shrugged. "The Craftsmen's Guild and your dear

125

Order of Physics probably helped Gilio with that, not that he'd admit it. Gilio likes to take all the credit."

"Back to the deal with Phineas, though . . ." Alysha said.

"He's one of many ocean recruits watching the active transport sites," Flangelo said.

Phineas performed another full-body nod. "No sign of anyone during my watch, nor any report from those before me. And if I do spot anyone, I will stop them." The lionfish gestured with a pseudopod to the kids. "I am quite agile on these. Though I'm waiting for Keeper Gilio and his wondrous Craftsmen to make a faster vehicle."

Flangelo whistle-laughed. "Like a bicycle!" There was no reaction from the others. "Never mind," he said with a warble. "We'd better get going, Phineas."

"Good-bye, friends of the Order," Phineas burbled, and then he strode back to the dome. His water-vesicle, legs and all, merged back into the barrier, and he swam away casually, if such a thing is possible, to resume his sentry position.

"See?" Flangelo said as he led the kids in a new direction. "Nobody saw anything, so you can breathe easier; I'll bet that bleach-blonde isn't even coming here."

Simon and his friends exchanged a look: they were not convinced. And if Flangelo was wrong, where in the dome was Sirabetta?

CHAPTER 18

BRING ON THE BAD GUYS . . .

In a distant region of the dome, there was a segment of coral that was bleached white: dead. Something—or someone—had killed off that region, so no fish swam by it. No anemones clung to it. No crabs or shrimp scuttled along it. As you might guess, there were no aquatic guards patrolling that area, either.

Oceans creatures are often on the move, however. That's why nothing seemed odd about the manta ray. If you've never seen a manta ray, I highly recommend it—they're beautiful and elegant. And big—that's important. They resemble undersea stealth bombers: black (mostly), almost flat, and wide with huge fins—like wings—for soaring through the water.

Unlike stealth bombers, they also have large mouths framed with hornlike limbs . . . and no bombs. Manta rays are also known to be gentle to people; this one even had two humans attached to its underside. The two people—one a thirteen-year-old blond girl, the other a middle-aged man—were wearing wet suits and diving gear. They were covered in puffy, hardened sheaths that protected them from the terrible pressure of the deep ocean; a special harness kept the protective suits attached to the manta.

The duo's expressions showed their fear. Though manta rays are graceful swimmers, they're also very, very fast. Being strapped to the underside of one wasn't too different from riding an underwater roller coaster (though without the long lines or the overpriced churros).

The manta approached the dome and picked up speed. Mere moments before hitting the solidified water, the manta curled its wings in toward its belly, tucking the two people safely against its body. A split second before impact, a woman's hand within the dome reached up and rested, palm out, beneath the target area.

A circle of dome dissolved there, just in time for the manta to plunge through. In the split second it took for the manta and its cargo to come through, tens of gallons of ocean water came with them. The woman's hand remained on the dome, and oddly enough, the water cascading over her dissipated as it touched her. The moment the manta and its passengers were through, the dome wall repaired as if the hole had never been.

No vesicle formed around the manta to keep it safe inside

the dome's atmosphere. Upon impact with the sandy floor, it tumbled forward and spread its wings. The two humans touched controls inside the protective suits, unhooking from the harness. They slammed to the ground, opened the sheaths from the inside, and rolled away from the manta as it writhed and gasped from lack of water and the sudden change in pressure.

The manta ray shimmered and vibrated before finally shifting into a tall, muscular man with spiky black hair. "Not pleasant," he groaned. The harness, which had fit tightly across his manta-body, slid to the feet of his human form.

The girl stood and brushed the sand off her face. It should come as no surprise that this was Sirabetta. "Don't worry, Preto. If all goes according to plan, you'll never have to sneak in again."

"Yes, Sir," the muscular man said as he helped the middle-aged man—Willoughby Wanderby—stand up.

A woman with tightly curled dark brown hair rose from where she'd been crouching by the dome. She stepped forward, staring at Sirabetta. "Sir? Is that really you? What did they do to you?"

"Get over it, Krissantha. I got enough of that from Wanderby when he first saw me," Sirabetta said. "Yes, I'm trapped at age thirteen. But not for long." She rubbed at her arms and legs, now covered by a long-sleeved wet suit. She paused and looked at Preto and Krissantha. "Thanks for opening the dome, though," Sirabetta said with hesitation, as if dealing with unfamiliar thoughts. She cleared her throat. "And Preto . . . good work bringing Wanderby and me down here. Pretty cool . . . I mean, well done, both of you." She blinked and set her jaw firmly. "Now, let's get out of here before we're spotted. I have my real age to reclaim."

Krissantha mouthed the words *"pretty cool?"* to Preto, who shrugged in response. They led the way along the sand while Sirabetta and Wanderby followed, hurrying to leave that area behind. They trekked through low grasslands and eventually passed into a region of jungle—that very jungle that Grawley the bear-man and his companion Kushwindro had been in earlier in this Chronicle. Krissantha escorted them through the thickly set trees and brush, seeming to follow no trail at all. Eventually, the dense vegetation gave way to a concealed cave.

"In here, Sir," Krissantha said, waving the youthful Sirabetta in. The three adults had to duck down under the cave entrance. A narrow tunnel sloped down gently, and the headroom increased as they walked along until the tunnel let out into a large cavern. Sirabetta glanced around as the others stretched. "Cool hideout. Weird, but . . ." She cleared her throat. "This will do." She folded her arms. "And Gilio won't find us here?"

Preto frowned. "Won't be looking," he said. Clearly he was a man of few words.

"I wish that was still true," Krissantha said. "Word's gotten around: three children with Physics powers got into a brawl with three Order of Biology members. A fellow who turned into a sparrow broke it up and dragged the children away."

Sirabetta narrowed her eyes. "Bloom and his friends! The brats followed me!"

"Does that mean we have to relocate?" Wanderby asked.

Krissantha shook her head. "No, I think we'll be okay here for a while. The jungle is vast and thick, and *she* carved out this cavern without Gilio's knowledge. Kushwindro's using his vegetation control to cover our tracks. But it'll help to have some guards out there."

Sirabetta nodded. "Set it up." She paused. "Where is she?"

Krissantha gestured to the far end of the cavern. Sirabetta walked over to a small chamber formed from the rear rock wall. An ageless, pale woman with long white hair was waiting at the entrance.

"My, my," the woman drawled. "How ever did you manage to do this to yourself?" she said, her tone making it clear she expected no answer. Though her face and hands were unlined, something about the way she spoke and moved made her seem as if she'd had many years of life. Experienced. Wise.

Sirabetta paused, staring at the woman for a long moment. "It's been a long time, old woman." Her tone was cold, but her voice quivered with emotion.

"Yes," the woman said. "But I'm here to make up for that." She showed no nervousness around Sirabetta, yet there was something unreadable in her tone.

"So, can you fix me?" Sirabetta asked with an edge of "you'd better" to her voice.

The woman gestured to a thin mattress in the chamber behind her. "Please, lay down."

Sirabetta did as she was told. The woman placed her hands on Sirabetta's head and closed her own eyes in concentration.

Long minutes passed like that until finally the old woman sighed. "This is hard work you have for me," she said. "Using biology to undo physics . . . and strong physics, too. Deep. Not just cells—molecules. No, deeper. At a level that I don't know—that only the Books know, perhaps."

"Aleadra, please," Sirabetta said, and for the first time since Wanderby had reminded her of herself, she showed vulnerability. Fear. "As long as I'm stuck like this, I'm powerless! Plus . . . I look like a child." She frowned. "Not a child—I mean, I'm a teenager, but . . ." She stopped and growled in frustration. "And that's another thing—even with my memory restored, I keep thinking like a thirteen-year-old!"

The woman known as Aleadra brushed some of the blond hairs from where they'd fallen in front of Sirabetta's eyes. "Not easy being young again, is it? Not easy living a different life at the same time as yours. Makes new weaknesses. Maybe makes new strengths, too, yes? Perhaps not all your changes have been bad."

Sirabetta half-rose from the mattress and gritted her teeth.

"Why is it that I can't understand what you're saying half the time?"

"Could be I've always been that way," Aleadra said. "Enigmatic. Or perhaps retirement has made me seem old and batty. But what matters is that I know what I'm saying."

"We don't have forever, you know," Sirabetta said. "Three children . . . powerful, interfering children . . . are hunting for me."

Aleadra nodded. "Yes, with the bird-man. I heard all about it, dear. Don't worry—I have plans for them. I still have plenty of tricks left from when I was the Keeper of Biology." She closed her eyes again. "Now lay back and let's see if we can get you back on track. Whatever track that is."

"Fine," Sirabetta said and did as she was told. She closed her eyes, too, prepared to pass the time with thoughts of power . . . and revenge. With the might of this former Keeper on her side, she would not fail again.

CHAPTER 19

The Long and Biting Road

"So this is the way to Gilio?" Alysha asked as they stomped along. "No shortcut?"

"This is the way he told me to use," Flangelo said.

"Maybe *he* should be guiding us," Alysha said. "You know, important mission?"

Simon swiped at his forehead with his sleeve. "Definitely," he said. The farther they walked, the hotter and drier it had become.

The sandy floor had long ago given way to rough, uneven stone with jagged points that the kids had to step around carefully. Large, twisted thorn-vines sprawled across the ground; a few twitched as the kids gingerly passed by. There was a bitter smell that stung the kids' nostrils and a heaviness to the air that made it harder to breathe.

Flangelo frowned. "I think we've strayed into one of the savannah regions in its summer phase."

"What's savannah?" Owen asked.

"It's a place in Georgia," Alysha said.

"No," Flangelo said. "Well, yes, but in this case I meant tropical grasslands. Gilio's got a duplicate of every ecosystem on Earth down here, and in every season, too. It can get a little confusing."

"I'm so glad Gilio made you our guide," Alysha muttered.

"Do you know where to go from here?" Simon asked.

Rather than respond, Flangelo stared off at something in the distance. Not far beyond them were sparse fields of dry brown grass, about knee-high on Flangelo. Past that, a herd of dozens of large, light brown animals with white and black faces grazed. They were vaguely deerlike but huge; the largest was four feet high at the shoulder, and each had a pair of three-foot-long black horns pointing up from atop their heads.

"Finally," Simon said. "Wildlife."

"Like the Nature Channel, but for real," Owen said.

Alysha noted Flangelo's expression and body language. "What's wrong, birdie?" she asked. "Got a problem with deer or something?"

"They're not deer; they're oryx—an almost extinct species of African antelope. But there's something . . ." Flangelo held up a hand. "Shhh!" he hissed. "Quiet, now!"

The kids followed his gaze to the gently swaying grass.

"What's—?" Owen started to say, but Flangelo clapped a hand over his mouth. A second later, the kids saw why. The grasses parted enough for them to catch a glimpse of gray, wrinkly skinned lizards. Though built very low to the ground, they were enormous—over twelve feet long. They'd have to be big to hunt those oryx.

"Those are Komodo dragons stalking the oryx." Flangelo said in a barely audible whisper. "They're an endangered species, too, but they're also predators. And if we don't leave them to their feast, you three might be on the menu, too."

"Why would they bother us?" Alysha whispered back. "Wait, you put dangerous animals in your headquarters and let them roam around?"

"They wouldn't attack *Biology* Order members," Flangelo hissed. "But I don't know how they'd react to you. Now let's—" He stopped talking in midsentence because one of the reptiles paused in its hunting. It turned its head sideways and flicked its tongue several times. Then it ran at full speed—about twelve miles per hour—toward him and the kids. It burst out of the grass, its short legs pounding at the dry dirt as its thick tail pumped from side to side.

Owen looked to Simon, who stood wide-eyed. Owen used velocity on the giant reptile, hurtling it back the way it had come. It hit the grassy ground hard and rolled to its feet; then it stood still, probably stunned or at least cautious, now. The other two Komodo dragons also turned from the oryx and swiftly flicked their tongues.

"That's their main sensory organ," Flangelo said. "They're literally tasting us."

All three Komodos ran at Simon and his friends. Simon shuddered. "We're not here to fight," he said quietly. He changed the pull of gravity on the Komodos so a spot in the distance acted like their ground. They started to slide backward on the dirt, scrabbling at it with their claws as they fell away from Simon and his friends. That ground was no longer regular dirt and grass to them—it was more like a vertical wall they were trying to cling to.

"Wait-anyone-notice-anything-weird?" Owen asked.

"You mean besides the attack of the killer iguanas?" Alysha asked.

"Yeah." Owen pointed to the herd of oryx. "Those guys aren't running off."

Simon looked at the huge antelope. "Maybe they're curious about us."

Owen shook his head. "That's not how it works on nature shows. Curiosity is bad for prey animals—they're supposed to scatter the second they know there's a predator, and then the predators take down the slowest one."

The oryx all cocked their heads in the same direction at the same time. They flicked their round ears in eerie synchronicity. Then, as a unit, they started to move.

"No," Flangelo said in a confused tone. "They're coming toward us!"

The antelope ran fast, their hooves pounding the dirt as

they moved. They burst through the grass with their horns aimed down, poised to spear the kids.

"What's going on here, Flangelo?" Simon demanded.

Flangelo shook his head. "I've never heard of such a thing," he said.

Owen used his velocity control on the oryx running in the front of the herd, knocking them sideways to trip the antelope alongside them. Those immediately behind the fallen stumbled over their herd mates, and many in the back came to a stop. Others, however, went around the traffic jam and kept coming, their lethal-looking horns ready for shish-kebabing. The fallen oryx, unhurt, slowly got to their feet, too. The herd spread itself out to cover more ground.

Simon went pale; this was getting worse and worse . . . and he was in charge, wasn't he? "I guess . . . I'll stop them." He reached out with gravity, straining to focus his attention on so many animals over such a wide area. In doing so, he let his grip on the Komodos slip. With the dirt floor suddenly acting as their ground again, the three monstrous reptiles resumed their attack. They ran alongside the oryx, passing right by them—even those that were still getting to their feet. Neither species reacted to the other, as if they'd forgotten all about that whole eat/be eaten thing.

"No," Simon moaned. "I made it worse! Everyone, grab your things—we're getting out of here!" Simon made his friends and himself weightless and they quickly linked hands.

"Don't bother changing, Flangelo. We can move faster through velocity."

Owen sent them soaring from the trees and far from the animals' reach.

"I don't understand," Flangelo squawked loudly to be heard over the roar of the wind. "They shouldn't have acted like that!"

"Worry about that later," Alysha said. "First figure out where we're going."

Flangelo shielded his eyes from the hot air blowing past and pointed. "There!"

Owen shifted his formula, sending them veering over increasingly stony ground. Soon they approached a lone, forbidding-looking tree with a thick gray trunk. It was over fifty feet high and twelve feet wide. The tree was barren of leaves or fruit; its rootlike branches were bent and curled, most extending outward like grasping fingers. It was easily the freakiest-looking tree I'd ever seen.

They landed at its base. Once they let go of one anothers' hands, Simon grasped at his head and stomach. That queasy, something-wrong feeling was hitting him again. "This tree . . . it's not normal," Simon said.

"I like it just fine," Gilio said, stepping out from the other side of the massive, gnarled thing. "Don't take it personally, Clive," he said, patting the trunk.

"Gilio!" Flangelo said with relief.

"What took you so long?" Gilio asked. "What were you doing, sightseeing?"

Four faces frowned back at him.

"Anyone else think we should feed him to the Komodos?" Alysha asked; the others raised their hands and chuckled.

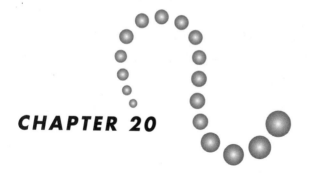

CHAPTER 20

No Jumping in the Pool

Flangelo and the kids filled Gilio in on what happened.

"This is very concerning," Gilio said. "I'm glad you're all safe. It's bad enough some of my Order members behaved so poorly, but the animals, too?"

"I saw a show on Komodos," Owen said. "They're not from Africa, are they?"

"No, Indonesia," Gilio said. "It's also a savannah climate. My dome has lots of animals and plants from different countries and time periods sharing ecosystems."

"That sounds unnatural," Simon said.

"Oh?" Flangelo said. "Says Mr. Gravity Keeper?"

"No, he's right," Owen said. "Wouldn't that mess with their lifestyles?"

"Maybe that's what screwed up the predator-prey relationship," Alysha said.

"It shouldn't have," Gilio said. "Trust me, the dome system has been working for decades; animals from different parts of the world and different time periods—sometimes even many thousands of year apart—have behaved normally until today." He shook his head. "Perhaps the Book has an insight into why they attacked."

He reached into his pants pocket and, in a move that defied all physical laws, pulled out his textbook-size, green-covered *Teacher's Edition of Biology*. Noting their stares, Gilio smiled. "The Books follow their own rules; you'll get the hang of it, Bloom." The Book pulled free of Gilio's grasp and hovered over his head.

Simon's blue-covered Book buzzed from within Simon's backpack, and Simon let it out. It floated above Simon's head and flashed a blue light at the *Teacher's Edition of Biology*, which flashed green in response.

The Book of Biology shifted to face Simon and flashed green again. Simon felt a tickle in his head, like the sensation from his own Book's mental contact. He sent a thought-message to the green Book. *Was that you? Can you talk to me like my Book can, too?* There was no reply, but the Books flashed subtle glows, as if talking.

Gilio arched an eyebrow, shifting his gaze from the *Teacher's Edition of Biology* to Simon and back. The two Books turned away from each other and hovered above their respective Keepers' heads.

Gilio sighed. "My Book either doesn't know or won't tell."

"Maybe someone who controls animals made them do it," Owen said.

"No Biology members can command antelope," Gilio said.

"Maybe there are new Biology members that you don't know about," Owen said.

Gilio arched an eyebrow. "That is impossible, my boy. A Keeper is the only one who can give people formulas."

"Except, like with Sirabetta, if they're somehow tattooed," Alysha said.

Gilio opened his mouth to reply but quickly closed it.

"One guy we fought said something," Simon said. "The one with the armor."

Gilio nodded absently. "Kender Mikarzan. He can form an exoskeleton, like arthropods have." He noted the blank stares from the kids. "Insects, arachnids, crustaceans; they have exoskeletons—their skeleteons on the outside. As opposed to mammals, birds, etc., which have endoskeletons—bones on the inside."

"Okay, well this Kender," Simon said, "he recognized Flangelo from some group—Animal Diversity, I think—but the other two didn't. How could they not know Flangelo if they're members of the Order?"

 143

"Biology has hundreds of members," Gilio said. "They're divided into groups relating to their area of focus. There are plenty of opportunities for them to get to know one another, but recent additions to the Order may not have met everyone else."

"Why so many members?" Alysha asked. "Physics has maybe forty."

"I *told* Ralfagon he needed to include this in his entrance exams," Gilio said with a frown. "You see, the Union changes as the Outsiders make strides in their learning. In the earliest days, there was only one science Order. Members splintered off into new groups as the Outsiders developed new areas of science. So Astronomy is mostly made up of members from Physics with some from Chemistry. Geology took many Physics members, too. Ecology took some Biology members, but also plenty from Chemistry and Physics."

"It sounds pretty confusing," Simon said.

Gilio waved a hand dismissively. "A little disorder is natural. But the Board hates it. They want everything done just so, with paperwork and planning and scheduling. They especially hate the overlap between the laws of Physics, Biology, and Chemistry. 'Too much redundancy,' they say. And the more the Union changes, the snippier the Board gets." He shook his head angrily. "It's that kind of narrow-minded attitude that lets all sorts of trouble slip in. The more rigid the system, the more problems will ensue. Mark my words," he said, "they're doing more harm than good to the universe."

Flangelo cleared his throat. "Gilio? I think you're scaring the kids."

Gilio coughed and smoothed out his sweater vest. "My apologies."

"If there are all these new Orders coming from older ones, where do their Books come from?" Owen asked.

"I don't know," Gilio said. He looked to his green Book hovering above him. It tilted away, as if trying to look innocent. "And no answer seems to be forthcoming."

How about you? Simon thought to his Book. *You must know where their Books come from.* After a long silence, Simon tried again. *Is it always going to be this way, even if the Board approves me? Will you always refuse to give me answers?*

The Book gave the mental equivalent of a sigh. *There are things you need to know and things you don't,* it responded at last. *At least not yet. Isn't it better to leave some information for when you're better able to handle it? To use it?*

"Hello, gravity-boy?" Flangelo said, snapping his fingers around Simon's head. "Anyone home, or has your brain gone off to space?"

"Give him a minute," Gilio said. "I think he's communicating with his Book."

Simon was considering what his Book said when another voice, similar but of a different timbre, sounded in his head. *We can't shelter him forever. Not with what's coming. Perhaps it is time now?*

Simon gasped and looked at Gilio's green Book. *Is that you? Book, is the* Teacher's Edition of Biology *talking to me?*

Simon's Book trembled for a moment; Simon got the impression it was upset. It sent a message into Simon's mind. *It shouldn't be. Not yet. Please, Simon. Trust me. Give it time. Give us time.*

Simon nodded. *Okay. But I'm still going to try to figure it out.*

Though the *Teacher's Editions* didn't have faces or any other means of showing expressions, Simon got the distinct feeling they were both smiling at him.

I'd expect nothing less from you, the Book of Physics thought to him. The floating blue Book sounded pleased.

Gilio looked from his green Book to Simon's blue, and then to Simon. "Were you somehow . . . ?" He shook his head. "No. I don't need to know. The affairs of the Books are the affairs of the Books."

Alysha groaned. "Yes, and they're all wondrous and powerful and made from cosmic trees or something. Can we chat about all this someplace nicer? We've only been in this fishbowl for a few hours and already we've had two battles."

Gilio frowned. "Indeed. There's no need to dally here when we're so close to my home." He gestured to the large tree. "If you'll all gather around Clive."

The tree trunk split down the middle. Inside its hollow center was a large pool of water like those they'd seen by the pebbled paths.

Simon winced; he felt an increase in that twisting sensation, just as he had by those other pools.

Gilio walked up to the water and gestured. "Come on in."

Owen stared. "Oh great, another puddle!"

Gilio cleaned his eyeglasses against his vest. "I'm surprised you haven't guessed what they are. These pools connect to one another. They use a principle similar to the Gateways, but these only work within the domain of Biology."

Simon's face brightened. "That's the weirdness I feel! They bend space, right?"

"You can sense that?" Gilio asked.

"Simon's on his way to knowing everything," Alysha said, crossing her arms.

"In my head and stomach," Simon said, ignoring her. "A tangle in normality."

"You're on the right track," Gilio said. "See, the dome has to be enormous to provide room for all these ecosystems. Such a setup requires ways of getting around quickly. Ralfagon and I designed these pools—they connect organically, somewhat like the intertwining root systems of a forest. Clive's pool is separate from the rest so I don't get unwanted visitors." He looked at Flangelo. "Care to show them how the system works?"

Flangelo nodded and hopped feetfirst into the pool. There was no splash, just a sucking noise, and he was gone.

"There's nothing to worry about," Gilio said. "Go on, you'll see."

Simon walked to the edge of the large puddle. "We've seen and done crazy things; what's one more?"

Owen frowned. "I think I've made my policy clear; all this teleporting can't be good for a person."

"Come on, Speedy, it'll be fun," Alysha said. "Last one in is fish food!" She ran at the pool and jumped, grabbing her legs in cannonball position.

"Wait!" Gilio shouted, but it was too late. She hit the surface and disappeared with a sucking sound.

Simon and Owen rushed to the edge and tried to see beneath the unrippled surface; all they saw was themselves reflected back. "What's wrong?" Simon asked.

"I'm sure she's fine," Gilio said. "But let's hurry after her, shall we?" The look on his face told Simon that Alysha might not be so fine after all.

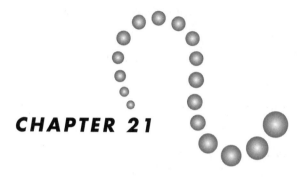

CHAPTER 21

GARDENING, BEATLES STYLE

Gilio nodded toward the puddle. "Please, just step in. Nice and gently."

Owen and Simon cautiously stepped into the pool and were sucked through. It was over in an instant; as with the Gateways, it seemed perfectly natural. Then they saw Alysha sitting on a cave floor holding her butt while scowling at Flangelo, who was whistle-laughing openly. Going into the pool hadn't gotten them wet; it had transported them to another part of the dome that, unfortunately for Alysha and her cannonball approach, had a hard rock floor.

"Are you all right, young lady?" Gilio asked, appearing next to Owen and Simon.

"You could have mentioned that it wasn't really water," she snarled. She stood up, rubbing her rear. "But yeah, I'm fine."

"Good thing you didn't dive," Flangelo said.

Simon looked around the small, barren cave. "What now?"

"Come this way." Gilio led them out onto a wide, flat mountaintop.

Simon stepped forward and gasped. "You have a whole mountain here?"

Gilio nodded proudly. "We have every ecosystem, all sorts of terrain. This is the highest point in the dome, located in the center. I have privacy from the rest of the Order when needed, yet I can keep an eye on everyone."

Simon and his friends walked to the edge of the mountain, thirteen hundred feet above the floor of the dome. The view was spectacular. The mountain rose up from a desert landscape; numerous landscapes stretched beyond that, one blending into the next. There were high grasslands, low grasslands, hills, lakes, and various wooded areas including snow-covered evergreens, temperate woodlands, tropical jungles, bamboo forests, and snowscapes. Someone had even made a few snowmen.

"The Order of Biology used to be based on land," Gilio continued. "Though near the ocean—after all, life started in the oceans. When I took over as Keeper, I decided we needed somewhere properly secluded from the Outsiders and the rest of the Union. Someplace with even more protection than Dunkerhook. So I got together with the other Council members and we shaped this."

Gilio pointed to smaller mountains in the distance. "I recreated an alpine ecosystem, complete with snow and wind, even though these mountain peaks are only a few hundred feet above the ocean floor. Each system mimics its surface version perfectly."

"Wow, look!" Owen said, pointing upward.

About fifty feet above the mountaintop, the kids could see the topmost curvature of the dome. I could tell how nervous the kids—even Alysha—were at the sight of thousands of tons of ocean above them, kept out by only a few formulas.

"Now," Gilio said, "to address your mission. Problem one: you have to find your nasty Sirabetta, who is someplace in the vastness of this dome. Problem two: there may be some non-Biology members who've been smuggled into this place. Problem three: there may be traitors within my Order. And if there are such enemies, they'd almost certainly wish you all ill."

"Yes, we've already met some of those," Alysha said.

"That might have been a misunderstanding," Gilio said. "Kender has a temper, Targa is a bit excitable, and Cassaro can be strange, but up until now they've shown no signs of disloyalty. I suppose I need to reexamine all my members more thoroughly, as well as check the borders and review guard reports. I can think of some who wouldn't stray no matter what. Flangelo, for example, is surely loyal."

"I'm glad to do whatever I can," Flangelo chirped.

"Excellent," Gilio said. "You'll be guiding these three around."

"Me?" Flangelo asked.

"Him?" Alysha blurted out. "Um, what if we get into another fight or something? I don't think being a smart-aleck really counts as a useful fighting style."

"Oh? It seems to be working for you," Flangelo warbled.

"I appreciate that, Gilio," Simon said, stepping between Flangelo and Alysha. "But Alysha's right, it might get dangerous."

Flangelo waved a hand. "I'm a changed bird now. Gilio gave me a second formula. One suitable for a fight."

"He'll be fine," Gilio said. "He'll also be able to fly around with you to seek out signs of Sirabetta as quickly and as quietly as possible. I'll flush out all the traitors in due time, but for now, speed and stealth are of the essence."

"Won't three kids flying around seem kind of suspicious?" Simon asked.

"Indeed," Gilio said. "That's why I want to give you a bit of Biology access."

Alysha grinned. "You mean we get new formulas?"

"Not formulas, exactly. As the study of all life, Biology has laws, yes, but so much more. Forms, aspects, communications, generators, processes." Seeing the kids' confused stares, he held up a hand. "Those vesicles are a variation on a cell's active transport *process*. Flangelo is able to take on the *form* of a bird and can *communicate* with other birds. Kender's exoskeleton is an *aspect* of arthropods. Cassaro can *generate* different fungi and accelerate their growth. Targa can affect adrenaline, also called epinephrine. It's a chemical that gives you energy; part of a *process* that's activated when you face danger, so you can run away or fight."

"Fight or flight!" Owen shouted. Gilio raised an eyebrow. "Nature shows can teach a lot," Owen said with a shrug.

"In any event," Gilio said, "I'll use my *Teacher's Edition* to give you the aspects of an animal that naturally uses camouflage. You'll be able to use that ability as easily as it can. And unlike your formulas, it won't tire you out. Not for a long while, at least."

"So, you're going to turn us into chameleons?" Alysha asked.

"No, you won't turn into anything, and no, not chameleons. Follow me." He led the kids and Flangelo along the mountaintop to his modest-size house. They walked around the house and stopped by a huge dirt plot containing countless beautiful, exotic plants of all different colors, shapes, and sizes. Some towered dozens of feet in the air while others were just a few inches high.

"This is my garden," Gilio said. "You'll never find a more diverse mix of species. There are plants from all over the world here, including several that are believed to be extinct. There are even some that haven't been discovered. Yet."

He guided them around the garden; a sunflower turned to follow them as they walked. They came to a blob of water about twenty feet wide and fifty feet high. It flowed and rippled but didn't spill; it was kept in place, presumably, by the same formulas as on the dome. In fact, the topmost part of it connected with the dome above them.

"This is my second-favorite garden," Gilio said, "and my little nod to the Beatles." As he gestured to it, a form became visible at the bottom of the water blob, near one of many piles of rocks set on the mountaintop.

Simon leaned forward and saw it was an octopus. This was an aquarium!

"Amazing creature, the octopus," Gilio said. "Wondrous natural abilities. They're very intelligent, too."

Simon touched the watery cage; as with the dome, it felt dry to his hand. A ripple spread out across the aquarium, and in response, the octopus approached. It placed the tip of one suction cup–covered limb on the same spot as Simon's hand. Simon could feel slight pressure as it pushed against the water; he pushed back and smiled.

"I can feel its tentacle," he said.

"Arm," Gilio said. "Squid and cuttlefish have two tentacles with their eight arms, but octopi just have arms."

"I'm still calling them tentacles," Alysha muttered.

Simon turned back to Gilio. "What else can they do besides camouflage?"

"They have many wondrous abilities. Why do you ask?"

Simon smiled. "I was just thinking . . ."

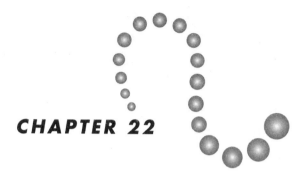

CHAPTER 22

THE WAY OF THE OCTOPUS

The first thing most people think of about octopi is that they have eight limbs. That's really no big deal: spiders have eight legs, and you don't hear them bragging about it.

The octopus also has gills for breathing underwater, but so do most sea creatures. Octopi can do so much more, though. There's that whole camouflage thing (you've got to admit, changing color *and* texture merits a round of applause). Plus they can detach limbs if a predator grabs one; they've got arms to spare, after all, and they grow back. Few octopi are known to limp.

They can also squirt a cloud of ink to help them escape: the ink, floating in the water, can look like a big, scary fish to confuse dumber attackers, or it can simply blind the attacker so the octopus can scoot away.

Certain octopi are also excellent mimics, using their flexible bodies and color–changing abilities to look like tougher or poisonous sea creatures. Gilio warned that combining two different aspects like that might be too difficult for the kids to handle.

Octopi can move quickly through the water by jet propulsion. Not that they actually hop into a small plane, but rather they shoot water out of a special organ so they can streak away from danger.

Alysha jumped at that one. "Do you know how hard it is to fight with electricity when the bad guys are standing far away?" she complained. "Throwing things I've electrified gets tiring. I have enough exercise in gym class, thank you!"

Of course, it wouldn't be practical for her to squirt water out (unless she was swimming at the time), so she'd have to use air. More problematically, she didn't have the organ to do so. It's called a mantle, with a muscular attachment called a siphon, and humans have neither.

"I'm going to have to assign another body part to act as your siphon," Gilio said. "Nose works best, I think."

Alysha grabbed her nose. "That's gross!"

Gilio frowned. "Can you think of a better body part?" Alysha shook her head. "Nose it is, then. Now at least one of you will need to take on camouflaging," Gilio said.

"Me," Owen said.

"Are you sure?" Gilio asked. "You'll have to focus on velocity while—"

"Me."

Gilio frowned. "It'll take intense concentration—"

"Trust me," Alysha interrupted. "If it'll keep us out of danger, he'll be a champ."

Gilio nodded. "And you, Bloom?"

"What's left?"

"How about flexibility?" Gilio offered. "I think it'll be invaluable, especially if you *do* run into problems."

"Sure," Simon said. "Why not?"

"Understand that once these are imprinted, they're biological changes," Gilio said. "You won't have to say any words to make them work, and Simon won't even have to activate his. It will always be on." He opened the *Teacher's Edition of Biology*. A pen rose out of the inside cover of the Book, much as with the *Teacher's Edition of Physics*, but this one was filled with bubbling green liquid. He pulled three blank pieces of paper from his pants pocket and unfolded them.

The Book, responding to a mental command from Gilio, started turning to the proper section. Simon, Alysha, and Owen watched the pages flip past. Of course, Alysha and Owen couldn't read the Biology symbols. As with the Book of Physics, most of the contents were nonsense squiggles and shapes except to the Keeper.

Simon squinted as he watched, unsure if he was seeing what he thought. "Hold on . . . can you stop the pages for a second?"

Gilio nodded, and the Book of Biology obeyed him.

"Can you go back to . . . there!" Simon pointed at the page. He leaned forward, marveling at how the shapes shifted, blurred, and then flickered into clarity. "That's the nausea formula that Sirabetta once used on me."

Gilio nodded. "You can tell? Incredible. There's always been a respect between Keepers and Books from other Orders, but that's unheard of. Can you read any others?"

The Book of Biology flipped through the pages more slowly, and Simon examined each. He shook his head until . . . "There!" He pointed to a series of green lines and splotches. "That's how to take on the form of a sparrow!"

Gilio blinked slowly. "Remarkable. You *can* read them. At least the ones you've come into contact with before."

Simon stared at the page and then turned to Flangelo. "I'd wondered how you could go from human to bird when they have such different masses. I get it now; when you become a sparrow, your extra mass is converted into another form like air molecules and dispersed around you. And when you change back to human, you convert other molecules from wherever you are to remake your old mass back."

Flangelo awkwardly whistle-chirped. "I just turn into a bird."

Gilio gaped. "You saw all that? On *that* page?"

Simon became self-conscious. "Sort of. There're all these comments and footnotes that imply it." He paused. "Can't you see them?"

Gilio took his glasses off, breathed on them, and rubbed

them. He put them back on and looked down at the page. "My boy, I can see the language of the concepts there and, from that, see how to turn a human into a sparrow and back. That's it. I know Biology, Chemistry, and Physics often rely on one another for their processes, but I only know that in an abstract way. I don't *understand* it on that level. But what you're seeing . . . what you're talking about . . ." He shrugged. "I'm not sure."

"That's so cool," Owen said. "You're like a super–Keeper!"

"Show off," Alysha said. "Told you he's going to know everything." But she said it with a warm smile.

Simon's cheeks reddened. "It's nothing, really. I just can read it." He wasn't used to so much praise, and he wasn't sure how to react to it.

Gilio glanced at the Book of Physics, which was hovering around Simon's shoulder. "Are *you* allowing this, somehow?" He looked at his own Book. "Or *you*?"

Both tomes did the Book equivalent of looking away and whistling innocently.

Gilio sighed. "I hate it when they do that."

"Especially since you *know* that they know," Simon said.

"Great, yeah, you should have a support group. Keeper's Anonymous or something," Alysha said. "Unlike Simon, some of us can't read that. So maybe you can give us those super powers now? Go Team Octopus and all that?"

Gilio cleared his throat. "Very well, let's proceed." The Book of Biology flapped to the right page, and Gilio started copying symbols onto the three pieces of paper. Each had a large blob in the middle and several smaller squiggles and shapes around it. Gilio scribbled each of the kids' names across the top of the proper pages and handed them out.

Simon saw nothing unusual while Gilio wrote out Alysha's jet propulsion or Owen's camouflage attributes, but he leaned forward with interest as his name was written atop a page with the flexibility information.

"What are *those*?" he asked. Simon was pointing to something in the Book that looked like nonsense to me, but it made Gilio turn pale.

"Why that symbol in particular?" Gilio asked.

"I don't know. I can *almost* see . . . something. Two lines coiling around each other." He reached out, and at Gilio's nod, touched the symbol on the Book's page.

"That's the core of this process," Gilio said. "The octopus DNA."

"I've heard of that," Alysha said. "It's this double–squiggle thing, right?"

"We call it a double helix," Gilio said. "A tiny double-stranded coil filled with things called genes. Every cell of every living being contains their DNA, and each gene in the DNA is a code that makes a living thing what it is. So octopus DNA has genes that decide what size an octopus will grow to, what color it will be: everything about it."

"And you're giving us octopus DNA?" Simon asked.

"I'm giving you each part of the DNA with one octopus

trait on it. You'll absorb it and make it your own. You'd need the entire DNA to take on a form, to *become* that animal, like Flangelo to a sparrow. Becoming an octopus wouldn't be practical for you."

"Good," Alysha said. "No offense, but they look kinda gross."

"Now, take a few minutes with your pages," Gilio said. "Here's a little secret that I don't usually tell Order members getting their first abilities: in Biology, we absorb the trait through touching the page rather than reading it. The DNA seeps through the paper into your skin and bonds with your own DNA."

"He didn't reveal it to me until he gave me my second form," Flangelo said. "He didn't want me to get nervous during the procedure."

"Really?" Owen asked. "Why would that make anyone nervous?"

"You absorb it?" Alysha asked with a shudder. "Yuck!"

Gilio smiled. "It will feel strange, but you should adapt quickly enough."

Simon held his page by the edges and held his palm over the shapes and squiggles on it. Before he touched them, they resolved into the image of an octopus surrounded by words explaining one facet of the octopus: its flexibility. *Weird,* he thought. *I haven't made contact yet.* Simon's mind bubbled with the memory of the full octopus DNA he'd seen in the Book. He remembered the different curves and the links between the two coils of the DNA double helix and the traits they represented.

This is going to be cool, he thought. But before he could place his palm on the image, he jerked his head around at the sound of Owen yelping. *Or*, Simon thought, *it could be another disaster!*

CHAPTER 23

The DNA Shuffle

"It itches," Owen shouted. He was jumping around and rubbing at his skin.

"Try to relax," Gilio said. "It's nothing you can scratch; it's your body adjusting. You're growing things called *chromatophores* under your skin; they're what let octopi alter their appearance for nearly perfect camouflage. Your muscles and nerves are changing to keep up with those chromatophores."

Owen groaned and dropped to the ground, rubbing his hands all over his body. "It hurts!" As he spoke, his body shimmered; different parts of him disappeared, blending in perfectly with the dirt around him. The camouflaging came and went, first in a few isolated patches and then in a wave that swept along his body from head to toe, then back up from toe to head. Then, suddenly, he was gone—all that remained was dirt.

"That's better," a voice said from the empty space.

Simon, Alysha, and Flangelo leaned forward, squinting to see better. "Is it just me," Alysha asked, "or is the camouflage working really, really well?"

"There's more to it," Owen said, reappearing right next to Alysha.

She jumped back with a shriek. "Don't *do* that!"

"Sorry, it's just so easy to turn on and off." As he spoke, he disappeared, reappeared, and then made different parts of his body do the same. "Look, it even works on my clothing!" He paused. "Good thing—I'd hate to have to go around naked."

"Yes, we'd all hate that," Flangelo said.

Alysha went back to her page, placing her palm firmly on the image there.

"Check this out," Owen said, reaching out to Flangelo. His touched Flangelo's arm, and it disappeared.

Flangelo gasped. "My arm!" He gasped even more loudly when his entire body vanished. "I can't see myself!"

Owen let go, and Flangelo returned. "I can share the chromatophores with anyone I touch!" Owen said. "But how come it didn't hurt him like it hurt me?"

"The Book lets you go far beyond what normal octopi can do," Gilio said. "When you're touching someone else, you're not changing them. You're actually spreading a thin coating of your own chromatophores over them. It's the same way you can camouflage your clothing."

"Ugh." Flangelo moaned. "You mean I had some sort of hyperboy slime covering me?" He smacked at his arms and clothing. "Please do not do that again."

Alysha, meanwhile, was clutching at her face. She wasn't screaming or complaining, but it was clear she was in pain from the way she cradled her nose.

"You okay?" Simon asked.

At last, Alysha pulled her hands away from her face. "No, I'm hideous!"

Simon, Owen, and Flangelo stared while Gilio chuckled quietly.

"What are you talking about?" Simon asked.

"My nose," Alysha moaned. "I can feel it. It's all . . . disfigured. And horrible."

"You look exactly the same," Owen said.

"Your changes are internal," Gilio said. "You don't look any different, but you can use your jet propulsion when you want. Think it; your body will do the rest."

"Really?" Alysha asked, gingerly feeling around her nostrils. She closed her eyes and scrunched her face in concentration. A burst of air surged out of her nose, shooting down and hitting the ground. It sent her zooming up into the air, screaming.

She stopped rising twenty feet up, and then started to fall

back to the ground. She quickly shot out another burst of air, but she'd since moved her head; the air jet now hurtled her backward. She tumbled in midair and probably wasn't sure which way was up; her next air burst sent her up at a sharp diagonal.

"Helllllllp!" she shrieked.

Owen used velocity to halt her flight and bring her down gently. When her feet touched the ground, she plopped to the dirt and sat there, gasping.

"Thanks," she said, finally. "That's trickier than you'd think. I think I'll need some practicing time." She rubbed her nose. "Ew. Sure cleans out the nostrils, too."

Simon and his friends all laughed at this. Before Simon could return to his own page and touch the image there, he felt a shooting pain throughout his body. He groaned and sank to the ground, dropping the paper as he did. Every part of him was burning up . . . not with fire but with internal motion. It felt as if his insides were shifting around.

Gilio, Alysha, Owen, and Flangelo rushed over to him. Gilio held up his hands to hold the others back. "Give him room," Gilio said. "His internal organs, bones—everything—are changing. He might go into spasms, but he needs to ride them out."

Instead, Simon rolled into a ball and lay there, unmoving. The squirming, shifting sensation made him feel as if he were riding a boat on heavy waves, only the rocking and swaying was all going on inside. Then, abruptly, it was over.

Simon uncurled and stood up; he felt the difference immediately. Just rising off the ground felt weird. His muscles, joints, and bones seemed to be made of gummi candy—they were soft and twisty, yet still tough and solid somehow. His shoulders, neck, elbows, hips, and legs had a rubbery feel to them. Experimentally, he grabbed his left arm in his right hand and pulled it around his neck. He was able to bend it at an impossible angle and wrap it around several times.

"That's . . . gross," Alysha said.

"Says the girl who shoots air through her nose," Owen said.

Simon let go of his arm, and it returned to its normal shape, but slowly. It didn't snap back like a rubber band but instead slid back like one of those squishy stress balls. He bent over backward completely, so the back of his head was touching the back of his legs. He placed his palms flat on the ground and stood that way for a moment.

"You know," he said, "this is probably the weirdest thing I've ever done."

"And that's saying something," Flangelo trilled. "Can you stop now, please? It's making me a little queasy."

Simon returned to his normal stance. He tried walking and felt his arms swinging too much. Worse, his body sagged slightly with every step. He walked around a bit more, and everything normalized, though there was a light bounce to each step, as if the ground was a bit springy. But it wasn't—*he* was. "Much better," he said.

"It's not something you need to activate," Gilio said. "When you need that flexibility, you'll have it."

"It's funny," Simon said. "I didn't even touch what you wrote on my page!"

"What?" Gilio asked. "Are you sure?"

"I was too busy watching Owen and Alysha deal with their changes."

"That can't be," Gilio said. "It's a physical transfer; that's how it works. Wait, you *did* touch the whole octopus DNA helix in my Book." He tapped a finger against the Book, deep in thought. "Hmm. Does your nose feel different? Or your skin? Like you can jet-propel or camouflage yourself, too?"

Simon shook his head. "Aside from this whole bendy thing, I feel fine."

"It should be impossible for you to absorb the entire octopus DNA from that touch. Only I, as Biology Keeper, can. Perhaps you did touch the images on the page but didn't realize it, distracted as you were by your friends. Yes, that must be it."

Simon tried not to stare as the Keeper fidgeted with his glasses, clearly bothered. Almost as if he were trying to convince himself of what he'd said to Simon. He didn't blame Gilio—all sorts of rules were breaking around him, some for better and some—like the oryx and Komodo attack—for worse. Was this what the Book had meant when it warned Simon about the end of things as he knew it? Why was it happening? Was there something—or someone—behind these changes? And if so, who?

Finally, Gilio glanced at his watch. "It's gotten late."

Simon checked his own watch. "What time zone are we in?"

"We're off the coast of Argentina. It's the same time zone you came from, but farther south. And *very* far down." He paused. "Perhaps you should get some rest now."

"The longer we wait, the more chance Sirabetta has to get away," Alysha said.

"Ralfagon and I examined Sirabetta shortly after you caught her," Gilio said. "Simon's space–time formula scrambled her in a way neither of us knew how to undo. If reversing it is possible for anyone but you, it won't be easy or quick."

Simon nodded. "Maybe we *should* have a meal, at least. With the day we've had and these new powers, we could use the recharge."

They followed Gilio to the front entrance. Simon glanced back and noted how huge the domed area was. How long would it take to search so many different environments? Was their search hopeless? Would they be too late? Was it already?

He absently bent his wrist back in the wrong direction, marveling at how easy and painless it was. *I hope we're in time,* he thought. *And that we're ready for what happens next.* But he feared they wouldn't be. That it would be him, now the big leader, who would let them all down.

CHAPTER 24

A Lot to Chew On

Gilio's house was basically like any other house. True, all houses have their differences—carpet color, type of furniture, whether they're made of straw or sticks or brick—but Gilio's didn't seem extraordinary.

Of course, it was atop a mountain located in a dome of hardened water under an ocean and was only reachable via a space-bending puddle hidden inside a huge hollow tree. But there's nothing like a kitchen with a space-saver microwave, an ice maker fridge, and a pedal-opening garbage pail to make you ignore the Octopus Garden just out the window and to the right.

Dinner was a rather mundane affair, too. Chicken, mashed potatoes with gravy, mixed vegetables, orange juice. It was very tasty, though.

Flangelo didn't have any chicken. When Owen asked him why, he huffed. "I'm a vegetarian, and I especially wouldn't eat other birds . . . flightless or not."

Owen looked down at the wing in his hands, shrugged, and resumed eating.

"Gilio, why aren't *you* a vegetarian or a vegan or something?" Alysha asked. "Aren't you friends with all the animals here?"

"I'm in charge of them all, but who said I was friends with them?" Gilio said. "There are a lot of rude chickens in the world. And what about vegetables? I assure you they're not thrilled about the variety of salad dressings."

Simon froze with his carrot-laden fork. "You mean vegetables can think?"

"A few plants in the garden asked the same thing about you," Gilio said with no hint of a smile. "Anything that's alive can think in a manner of speaking. They just might not do it in a way that makes sense to you. It's a shame that we need to eat to live, but the food chain is what it is, love it or not. Just be glad that humans are at the top."

"So is that what the Order of Biology does all day?" Alysha asked. "Change shapes, talk to animals, and think about the food chain?"

"We're similar to the Order of Physics, in a way," Gilio said. "We keep watch over life and make sure things are evolving smoothly. Plus we work with Outsider scientists, professors, and ordinary citizens to encourage them. New species, innovative theories, remarkable techniques—we're there to aid in their discovery."

Simon resumed eating, ignoring his vegetables. "Living down here seems like a pain, especially if you go to the surface to work with Outsiders. Why have the dome?"

Gilio slid his chair back from the table. "We've duplicated all of the planet's ecosystems to better understand how they work and so we can run private tests. After all, there's a lot about nature and life that even *we* don't understand. The same goes for everyone in the Union: there are deeper meanings, a larger scope." He glanced at Simon's plate. "Not eating your vegetables?"

"Nope," Simon said with a smile. "I don't want to be cruel to them."

"Sure, but you'll eat my cousins," Flangelo warbled quietly.

Gilio chuckled. "There are plenty of types of life worth preserving. That's the other purpose of the dome: as a sort of ark. We have certain species that have disappeared or are endangered up top, and we keep small numbers of other species around for our studies. There are a lot of problems with the world. It helps to stay separate while the Order of Ecology tries to do its work."

"How's that going?" Alysha asked.

Gilio sighed as he distributed bowls of ice cream to his guests. "They're a relatively new Order. Hopefully, they'll make progress. But we have this dome and others hidden throughout the oceans of the world in case the extinctions continue."

Simon looked across the table at a bottle of syrup, exactly what he needed to make his ice cream perfect. He realized it was too far to reach for and was about to ask someone to pass it when the syrup flew through the air and landed neatly in front of him.

Gilio looked sharply at Owen. "No powers at the table, please."

Owen shook his head. "It wasn't me, I swear!"

Simon stared at the syrup, not daring to pick it up. "I think it was me."

"You think?" Flangelo and Alysha said at the same time.

"I didn't use my gravity control; I thought about wanting it, and it came to me."

"I guess you're getting better at using your formula," Alysha said.

Gilio stared at Simon. "I thought I felt . . . no. It must be your gravity skill." He cleared his throat. Simon and his friends ate their ice cream while Gilio quietly watched Simon. From time to time, Gilio glanced over at his Book, which was lying on the table near him. Gilio squinted at it but said nothing, and it did nothing in response.

Soon, Gilio had Flangelo help him clear the plates and clean up in the kitchen. Simon, Owen, and Alysha used the time to talk quietly among themselves.

"Do you think it's going to be hard to find Sirabetta?" Owen asked.

"I don't know," Simon said, "but I'm starting to think I can *feel* her."

"How?" Alysha asked.

"Not sure. But I sense something, like with the pools, but different."

"I'll bet it's because of your space–time," Owen said. "Your gravity formula lets you sense gravity like mine does with velocity and Alysha's with electricity, right? Maybe your senses for space– and time–bending are sharper because of *that* formula? You can sense those pools that bend space. And since you made Sirabetta younger with it, maybe you can feel a disturbance in space–time or something."

"Wow," Alysha said. "That's pretty smart figuring, Owen."

Simon smiled. "And if you're right, we can probably track Sirabetta."

Nobody spoke for a few minutes.

"So does that scare either of you?" Owen asked quietly.

"This is going to be dangerous whether we find Sirabetta or not," Simon said.

"But I bet we'll find her," Alysha said.

"Okay," Simon said. "So it'll be *very* dangerous."

"Do–you–think–we're–ready–for–her?" Owen blurted. "I mean, she might not even be able to use her tattoos again, right?"

"Maybe," Simon agreed. "But maybe she will. And who

knows who she'll have on her side. We can handle Mr. Wanderby, but there might be others. More danger."

"We can handle it," Alysha said. She saw Owen staring at her. "What's with the look? Hey, I'm scared of what we'll find, too."

"You?" Owen asked. "Yeah, right!"

"We're in a strange place with new powers, a ton of pressure on us, and a lot of enemies," Alysha said. "I'd be stupid not to be worried."

"But you're always talking tough, going right up to bad guys and kicking butt!"

"So? Don't you get it, Speedy? Sometimes you have to talk and act tough even when you're afraid. Especially then. Otherwise your fear's going to beat you, and what good is that?" Alysha fidgeted with a saltshaker. "As much as I like my capacitance formula, I sometimes get freaked out about all that electricity flowing through me. Now I can fly, sort of, which is kind of crazy. And don't get me started on the plasma; I was terrified when those lights started coming out of me."

"And when you exploded?" Owen asked.

"Yes, Owen, that was not a comforting experience, either," she said.

"You were braver than us when we first got our formulas," Simon said to Alysha. "Even before you got yours. How do you keep it all from really getting to you? I mean, the whole Union could be in trouble if we screw this up. The whole universe!"

"Kind of like last time," Alysha said. "And does it matter how high the stakes are? Would you try any less if it was only *your* life on the line?" She cracked her knuckles. "Besides, I don't know if you guys noticed, but we're pretty good at fighting." She shrugged. "I don't like it, but I'd rather we be good at it than bad. Whatever nasty tricks, flunkies, and monsters Sirabetta throws at us, we'll handle it. All of us."

"What if we can't handle it?" Simon asked. "What if *I* can't?"

Alysha chuckled. "Are you kidding? You're doing things that even impress Ralfagon and Gilio! Simon, there's probably nothing you can't do." Simon blushed.

"That's right," Owen said. "If anyone can lead us through this, you can." Simon looked away, his face reddening more. Owen cleared his throat. "But just so you know, I'm kind of nervous about the mission, too."

"You don't say," Flangelo said, appearing in the doorway. "How shocking."

Alysha glanced at him. "Keep it up, maybe you *will* get shocked."

"Please, put me out of my misery," Flangelo said, walking out of the room. "Just wait until I've had some coffee first."

"Thanks," Owen said to Alysha. When he saw the puzzled look on her face, he smiled. "I mean for sticking up for me. Whenever Flangelo says something mean, you say something back."

"He's not really being mean," Alysha said. "It's just the

way *he* handles being nervous. Besides, I've said it before, I'll say it again: if anyone's gonna mock you, it'll be me."

They all laughed. "Come on," Simon said. "We've got a mission to get back to."

As they gathered their things together, Simon thought about what Alysha had said. He also thought back to what Ralfagon told him. Could it be that easy? To control your fears, you just have to keep them from controlling you? And the same with his Physics abilities?

He knew there was only one way to find out for sure, and that was the hard way. Because now that their meal was over, Simon and his friends were going to be looking for trouble, and like it or not, they'd almost certainly find it.

The only questions were exactly when and exactly what form that trouble would come in.

CHAPTER 25

THERE'S TROUBLE—
AND COFFEE—BREWING

My Viewing Screen shifted its perspective to Sirabetta's cavern.

It was spacious and well stocked with food and drink. A wide variety of plants grew within the cavern itself, without the benefit of sunlight. Of course, the entire dome—being well beneath the ocean—was without real sunlight. Yet all sorts of plants, including banana and apple trees, carrot patches, and even sunflowers flourished. (Though the sunflowers were a trifle annoyed at being deprived of the sun; it's in their name, after all.)

There were also modern touches like a watercooler and a coffeemaker, around which several of Sirabetta's allies gathered to chat while they waited for their leader.

Willoughby Wanderby stayed separate from the others. So

far as he knew, the others in the cavern were all from Biology; certainly none were fellow members of the Order of Physics. He wasn't interested in socializing with them anyway. He was more focused on making sense of what was going on.

Wanderby knew Sirabetta was tucked away in that back chamber, with that mysterious Aleadra trying to make her older. But that was only part of the story. Who, he wondered, was the one who had given him instructions and arrangements earlier? It wasn't Aleadra or any of those in the cavern . . . it was someone he'd never met or heard of. That silent organizer who had told him to make sure he was Sirabetta's caretaker while she was stuck as a hapless seventh grader.

How many other conspirators were there? And what was going to happen next? He wondered how he might find out. He strutted past the dozen men and women in the cavern. Surely they were even less informed than he; asking them about plans was pointless.

He walked up to Preto and Krissantha, who were chatting by the coffeemaker. "Anything to report?" Wanderby asked as he helped himself to a cup.

Preto shook his head, irking Wanderby; the man talked too little for his taste.

"For now, we'll just wait for *her* to get Sir back on track," Krissantha said.

Wanderby decided this was a perfect time to underline his authority. "Then this *Aleadra* should hurry up."

The collection of Biology members gasped quietly; they

were all clearly too impressed by that strange woman to refer to her by her Union name (or any name). They'd surely think him brave and important for having dared to do so.

Krissantha pursed her lips. "*She* is a former Keeper and a respected elder."

Wanderby's brow furrowed and his jaw tightened with anger at the implied scolding. "Listen, you mindless drone! If you think you can push me around"

"Think?" Krissantha asked. "I *know*. I know what you've done for Sir in the past. As long as she wants you here, I won't make a fuss. But if you had a brain in your head, you'd realize I could destroy it. Your brain, that is. How do you think I opened the dome for you?"

Wanderby sneered, "What . . . you control domes?!"

Krissantha smirked and walked over to him. Without saying a word, she stuck her index finger into Wanderby's coffee cup. There was a quick hiss. Wanderby looked down into the cup and saw only coffee grounds remaining.

"Fool, I control hydrogen bonds. Hydrogen, as in the element that's a major part of so much on this planet, including you. And bonds, those things that link atoms to other atoms. So I could destroy every cell in your body"—she snapped her fingers—"like that."

Wanderby paled. "I . . ."

"Yes, I know. You're sorry. You didn't know. You probably didn't even realize I'm from the Order of Chemistry, here to supervise Sir's forces. Or that I've witnessed *her* great works for many years, before Gilio came to power. Now you know. Now you can show me, and *her*, the respect we're both due."

Wanderby clicked his mouth shut, unsure of how to proceed. Fortunately, Preto chose that moment to approach. He glanced at Wanderby but addressed Krissantha.

"Someone's here. Says he wants to join us," Preto said.

"What?" Krissantha and Wanderby said at the same time. They followed him to the cavern's entrance and found themselves staring at a thin, bald man. Wanderby had never seen him before; by the look on her face, Krissantha hadn't either.

"Kender Mikarzan," Preto said. "Recent addition to the Order. In my group."

"Hmm. Animal Diversity." Krissantha turned to Preto. "He worthy?"

"Pretty tough. Fought the Physics kids," Preto added.

Krissantha looked at Kender. "How did you find us?"

"Word gets around among the discontent," he answered.

"Fine. Let's see what you can do." She turned to Preto and the three other Biology members standing nearby. "Preto, Kostaglos, Zillafer, Baharess . . . kill him."

Preto reacted instantly; his body shimmered and shook. Wanderby stepped back, curious; what could a manta ray do in the middle of the cavern?

The answer came quickly. Where a muscular man once stood, there was now a part man, part manta ray. A man–ta ray, if you will. Most of Preto's front and his entire back were black, much like a manta ray's body. He had legs, arms, and a muscular torso, just as Preto's human form did. His facial features were recognizable, but his head was much wider, with no clear division between it and his neck. His mouth was manta ray–size, though the manta ray horns were gone now.

He still had those winglike fins, now extending down from the base of his neck like a cape and attached to the back of his arms. He also had the tail, which he used to lash out at Kender as if it were a whip.

Kender leaped back, narrowly avoiding the tail strike. He activated his own formula and, within seconds, was encased in his slate gray exoskeleton. He launched himself at Preto with startling speed and threw a punch—just one—that sent Preto hurtling back toward the cavern wall.

Preto spread his wings and glided up and away, narrowly avoiding the hard rock.

The three nearby Biology members, two women and one man, snapped into action. One of the women, Zillafer, inflated like a human version of a porcupine fish: balloonlike and spiny. Her feet and arms protruded from her body just enough for her to aim her bounces toward Kender.

That's as far as she got, though; Kender spun and kicked, sending her boinging backward. One of her legs smacked into the other woman's head before she could attack. That woman, Baharess, sank to the ground, stunned.

The male Bio member, Kostaglos, opened his mouth wider than a human mouth should go; he lifted his tongue, revealing two hollow tubes like a cobra has in its mouth. He shot twin streams of a clear liquid from those glands, aimed right at Kender's head.

Kender raised his arm, blocking the spittle. A sizzling noise rose from where it hit his arm, but Kender didn't react; his exoskeleton didn't have nerve endings. He leaped forward, smacking Kostaglos aside before he could attack again. The thin man was sent crashing into the cavern wall and did not get up.

Preto descended, soaring downward with his fists pointed straight out in front of him to deliver a double punch. Kender was too fast—he sidestepped the fists and connected with a fierce uppercut to Preto's jaw. Preto's head snapped back and his body flipped backward; he hit the cavern floor and lay where he fell, unconscious.

Wanderby spoke his own formula, starting Kender spinning in place. Incredibly, the armored man kept coming, holding on to his bearings enough to move forward between rotations. Wanderby increased the speed, and the massively armored enemy was slowed down . . . but he still advanced. Wanderby spied a large watercooler bottle and, speaking his formula again, spun it toward Kender.

It shattered wetly on Kender's exoskeleton. Though the impact knocked him back, he recovered quickly and kept coming. Wanderby reached out with his formula to grab the coffeemaker, its pot filled with steaming coffee. He spun that, sending it smashing hotly against the armored man. That clearly wasn't enough either. Wanderby looked around for other possible weapons: rocks, furniture, the fallen Order members.

Before he could act, Krissantha shouted, "Enough."

Wanderby saw the look on Krissantha's face and obeyed, shutting down his formula. Kender stopped spinning and fell to the ground; he was back on his feet in a moment, ready for more action.

"I like your gusto," Krissantha said. "I like your determination. And I like your strength. But I have the power to destroy your shell and reduce you to a pile of ash."

Kender stood unmoving. "I didn't come to fight," he said, his voice echoing out from within his shell. "I came to join the cause."

"That," Krissantha said, "is a good response. Welcome to the revolution."

CHAPTER 26

Into the Big, Bad Haystack

Gilio led the kids and Flangelo outside; it was time to go.

Owen looked around. "Is it still nighttime? It's pretty well lit, especially for being under an ocean."

"I've arranged many bioluminescent life-forms inside and outside the dome," Gilio said. "Mostly mosses and kelp that give off a natural glow. Deeper into the biomes where the animals live, there's just enough bioluminescence to simulate moon and starlight; I didn't want to disturb the natural day–night cycle of the life-forms. By day, special devices provide artificial sunlight so it's much brighter where appropriate. It's a complex world down here."

"At least we'll always be able to see where we're going," Simon said.

"Now, you'll have to cover a lot of ground quickly without

being seen," Gilio said. "You're searching for a needle in a haystack, but a very sharp needle in a very dangerous haystack."

Simon explained his sense of space-time twisting, and Gilio nodded. "That'll be a big help. Can you tell where she is exactly?"

Simon turned around in a circle, feeling out the different twists in space-time across the expanse of the dome. The strongest tug came from the teleporting pool they'd used to get up to Gilio's mountain home, but he could feel much fainter pulling from the many other pools throughout the domain. He closed his eyes and concentrated, filtering out every other sense besides space-time.

There was so much to focus on, but he didn't let up until . . . "There!" Simon pointed. He felt a space-time distortion that was wildly different from all the others but familiar to him. "I think she's somewhere in that direction."

Gilio stared along the line of Simon's wavering finger. "Hmm. Lots of ground to cover that way," Gilio said. "First, desert. Then, depending on which way you veer, either there's dry, wintry savannah, or wetlands. After that, you've got more possibilities." He pointed to one direction. "If you angle that way, you get taiga, tundra, and mountain regions. Evergreens and snow leading to extreme cold and barren land with little life."

Simon pointed in a slightly different direction. "It's more like that way."

"Ah," Gilio said. "Wetlands, then a wide expanse of rain forest. Jungle."

"Wonderful," Flangelo said with a shake of his head.

"It's better than going back to Savannah," Owen said.

"*A* savannah," Flangelo said. "Not Georgia, remember?"

"Whatever, as long as we don't see any more Komodo dragons," Alysha said.

Gilio nodded. "You should be fine. While you're doing that, I'll send word to certain Order members and animals in the dome that I trust. I'll check in every direction in case your extra sense is wrong, Bloom. I have eyes and ears everywhere."

"That's gross!" Owen said.

"I mean spies," Gilio said. "If they've seen or heard anything unusual, I'll send a messenger-bird to you. Flangelo can understand and speak to them."

"Meanwhile, we follow Flangelo?" Alysha asked.

"I'm afraid so," Flangelo trilled.

Gilio looked Simon, Owen, and Alysha in the eyes. It wasn't hard—he wasn't very tall. "The camouflage works better when you're not in bright lights. Also, I wouldn't talk to anyone. Or get in anyone's—or any thing's—way." He frowned. "Flangelo, keep them in the air as much as possible, okay?"

Alysha chuckled. "Nice pep talk, thanks."

Gilio took off his glasses and cleaned them. "Bloom, a word, please?" Simon and he stepped away from the others.

"There are definitely strange things afoot, and I don't like it. Frankly, the Board must be having a fit—I'm surprised they haven't stepped in yet." He paused. "They must know *something*, and yet . . ." He shook his head. "In any event, your friends are going to need you to guide them. You're all very capable, but you are their leader. Keep your wits about you, be prepared for anything. And please," he said, looking away for a moment, "please be careful."

Simon nodded awkwardly—he was touched by Gilio's words, but he wasn't enjoying being reminded of how much responsibility he was carrying. He followed Gilio back to the others. "Ready?" Simon asked. They nodded. "Owen, do your thing."

Owen took Simon's and Alysha's hands, then triggered his octopus ability. With a mental command, he spread his chromatophores out to Simon and Alysha. A wave of color swept over them so they matched the appearance and texture of the dirt and air around them.

It was impressive and, I have to admit, a challenge to my narrating ability. I knew Simon and his friends were there and I knew they couldn't see one another. I could detect their feelings and surface thoughts, and I could sense a few things about them; for example, Owen's shoelaces were untied. As far as my eyes—watching them on my Viewing Screen—were concerned, though, the three kids had disappeared. As long as they kept physical contact with Owen, they, too, would be flawlessly camouflaged.

Simon eliminated their gravity to make them weightless, and Owen used velocity to raise them off the ground.

"Okay, Flangelo," Simon said. "You take the lead and we'll fly right behind you. I'll let you know if we need to change direction or if we start to get separated. Don't worry that you can't see us; you'll be able to hear us just fine."

"Lucky me," Flangelo warbled.

And with that, he turned into his sparrow form and took to the air followed by a perfectly camouflaged trio of youths. They soared off the mountaintop and swooped toward the ground. Flangelo flew as hard and as fast as he could, flapping his wings with all his might. Owen had no trouble keeping up; no matter how fast Flangelo went, Owen was moving at the speed of speed itself. He could go as fast as he wanted.

The first ecosystem they had to cross was the desert that surrounded Gilio's mountain. It's widely known that deserts are not fun to be in or, more to the point, to cross. They're dry and sandy with dunes, which are basically hills and valleys made of—you guessed it—sand. There are also long stretches of barren rock, which aren't much more fun than the dunes, but at least they're generally less sandy.

It was relatively dark for the first hour or so, and so the temperature was cool . . . even cold. As daybreak arrived, that changed. Whatever methods Gilio had used in designing the dome worked incredibly well—it really seemed as if the sun were rising. The air got steadily warmer until it became almost stifling. Flying became a lot less fun.

The heat and dryness made it, well, dry and hot, and the air that whipped past them (or, to be more accurate, that they whipped through) stung their faces. The sand occasionally blowing in their eyes, noses, and mouths didn't sweeten the experience either. At least Simon managed to lessen their friction with the air (called drag), so much of the stinging sand and air went around them.

Cruising over the desert, they saw a lot of spiny cacti in a variety of shapes, and the occasional desert animal. These weren't terribly exciting to look at, though. Scorpions scuttled, tarantulas crawled, snakes slithered, kangaroo rats hopped, lizards . . . crawled, too. (There are only so many verbs to describe that motion.) Hawks soared above; on occasion they circled, swooped down, and ate some unfortunate critter that wasn't scuttling, crawling, slithering, hopping, or crawling fast enough.

After seemingly endless hours, Simon could see the terrain starting to change. The way it felt to Simon's space-time sense, they'd be going across the wetlands and then the tropical rain forest. And that's where he hoped—and feared—they'd find the object of their quest.

CHAPTER 27

Out of the Drying Land and into the Mire

The sand and rock gave way to hard, dry dirt. They flew over a few teleporting pools and a handful of structures that looked like mud huts. I felt a swell of pity for whomever used them. If you had to live in the desert—and I think I've made my opinion about the place quite clear—you'd better live somewhere comfy. Preferably with air-conditioning and refreshing beverages.

Soon the land beneath them became increasingly lush, increasingly moist, and increasingly sticky. They were shifting from a dry and hot ecosystem to a wet and hot one, and that was not a nice change.

Things got worse when they found themselves being pelted by heavy raindrops. Flangelo angled sharply toward the ground, ignoring the complaints of the kids flying behind him. They followed him as he landed on the outskirts of a small lake. It was clearly real water, not another teleporting pool—the surface dented and rippled in the growing rain. All around the lake, a few hundred feet back from the waterline, stretched tall, thin trees.

The grass was thick and high, while the storm had turned the dirt into a muddy marsh. Each squishy, sticky misstep led to them having to yank their feet to get unstuck from the mud. It was a struggle, especially since their shoes often stayed in the mud and had to be pulled out separately.

"Why did you land?" Simon asked loudly. He didn't mean to yell, but having wind rush past his ears for so long had made it hard to tell what his volume was.

"Do you like flying through a downpour?" Flangelo chirped back. "I certainly don't." He held his hands out, letting the water smack against his upturned palms. "These hurt when you're a sparrow, you know! And what if there's lightning?"

"Okay," Owen said. "So why don't we fly above the storm?"

Simon shook his head. "I don't know how well I'll be able to follow the space-time trail from so high with a thunderstorm raging beneath me. It might interfere."

Alysha shrugged. "So Flangelo can fly with us in human form. I should be able to absorb any lightning that hits us."

"Should?" Owen asked, wide-eyed.

"Fine," Flangelo warbled. "But I'd like to rest a little." He waggled his arms. "Flying is tiring if you're using wings. Besides, I could really go for some water." He looked up at the clouds. "Not *this* water, but you know what I mean."

Simon nodded. "I guess we could all use a break." They reached into their packs, with Simon, Owen, and Alysha donning their raincoats to deal with the deluge. They were careful to maintain some contact with Owen so they'd remain camouflaged. "But not too long; we need to keep on Sirabetta's trail!"

"Yes, yes, whatever," Flangelo said. "Maybe we can discuss this under some trees, so we can get out of the rain? Or one of you can use your fancy Physics tricks to keep us dry? It's bad enough I'm talking to a bunch of invisible people."

"Hey, you're the one who decided to land here," Owen said. He started catching the rain above them with his velocity control.

With Owen reducing the rainfall around them, they could see the area around them better. "Ah," Flangelo said. "Possible trouble." He pointed in the distance.

Several shapes were moving. Some were on the opposite side of the lake, and most were keeping their distance from Simon et al. A few were passing right by them, but their slow pace and lack of interest made an attack seem unlikely.

As they stared, Simon and his friends were able to make out a herd of odd-looking horses. They had rounded ears, shorter-than-normal snouts, and very short manes. Others looked like variations of normal animals—such as armadillos, anteaters, and beavers—only giant-size. Across the lake, they saw huge creatures that looked similar to bears but with long, narrow faces and a slow, shuffling walk.

"Oboy," Flangelo said, then whistled. "Megafauna."

"What does that mean?" Owen asked. "Sounds like a type of giant robot."

"I'm surprised you haven't seen some show about them," Flangelo said. "They're unusually large animals, in this case, prehistoric ones." He pointed across the lake. "See those? Giant ground sloths. You can't tell from here, but they're about ten feet tall. And they're one of the shorter giant sloths. Sharp claws, too. That's our cue to leave."

"Wait," Alysha said. "They just want to drink from the lake!"

Indeed, the huge mammals paid no attention to the friends. Granted, Owen's camouflage was keeping them hidden, but the animals could surely smell them, too.

"I guess we don't smell threatening to them," Simon said.

"Well, let's hope they don't decide to go oryx on us," Owen said.

Once they were sure the megafauna were ignoring them, Simon and his friends tried to continue to the tree line. They struggled in the mire, breathing hard from the effort.

"This getting–stuck–thing is as much fun as getting soaked," Flangelo warbled.

"Who decided to land in the storm?" Alysha demanded, tugging at a stuck foot.

Owen lost his balance and fell to the ground, dumping

194

his collected water onto everyone with a splash in the process. "Sorry," Owen said. He couldn't get his hands and feet
unstuck. As his friends tried to help him up, they each stumbled in the muck. They became spread out from one another
and—it's important to note—far from Owen's camouflaging
touch.

They all noticed they could see one another, and they
suddenly stopped moving. Instead, they watched the various
megafauna carefully, looking for any sign of hostility.

"They don't care about you," Flangelo said. "I guess the
oryx attack was a fluke."

"Wait—does anyone else feel that?" Owen asked.

Everyone nodded; there was a light but steady shaking to
the ground.

"We should go," Owen said. "What if there's an earthquake? Or a dome-quake!"

"It's not a quake," Simon said, pointing to the tree line.
"It's *them*."

The group followed his extended arm and saw the source
of all that shaking. It was a herd of what looked like elephants
stomping out from the trees. Like elephants, these beasts had
thick gray skin with a few tufts of gray hair on their heads.
These were much bigger than modern elephants, though.

The largest in the monstrous herd was at least fourteen feet high at the shoulder, and fourteen feet long. That
one, stomping ahead of the rest, also had spiraled tusks
that stretched out at least fifteen feet in front of it; for a

moment, Simon wondered why the tusks weren't tipping them over.

There were seven in total, all huge and all headed toward the lake, a few hundred yards away. They were probably just looking for a drink like the other megafauna; it was unfortunate that Simon and his friends were standing between them and the water.

"Columbian mammoths," Flangelo said, his voice strained. "They were one of the largest animals to walk the Earth."

"You mean *are* one," Alysha said. "'Cause they're right there."

"We're fine," Flangelo said. "They're plant eaters like these others. Peaceful unless threatened."

"These other ones are leaving," Owen said.

It was true; the prehistoric horses, beavers, and other huge, extinct mammals were slinking away to the surrounding woods.

Flangelo shrugged. "I guess they want to give the mammoths room?"

The lead mammoth let out a deafening bellow and started to run at them. The rest of the herd trumpeted in response and joined in with a thunderous stampede.

Owen turned and glared at Flangelo. "Are any of you ever right about anything?"

CHAPTER 28

PLASMA MAKES PERFECT

"Should we feel insulted that the superbeavers didn't attack us, too?" Alysha asked.

"Maybe we can make jokes later?" Flangelo said. "After we fly away?"

Alysha tugged at her feet. "I can't—I'm stuck!"

Simon groaned. "Me, too!"

Owen, similarly bogged down, nodded as he frantically tried to get free.

Flangelo looked down; one of his feet was stuck in the swampy ground, too. "This is bad. And disgusting." He changed into his bird form. As Simon pointed out earlier, the extra mass of Flangelo's human body dispersed into the air and his sparrow form was small and light enough to avoid getting stuck.

Flangelo took to the air and flew at the lead mammoth. He chirped furiously as he winged his way around the creature's massive head, which was as big as a king-size bed. He hovered by one of its dinner plate–size ears, apparently trying to talk to it. Whether it understood or not, it swung its tusks and swatted its trunk at the sparrow. Flangelo easily dodged these attacks and returned to the kids.

He shifted back to human form. "Something's definitely wrong; they're not stopping. And it tried to attack *me*! I think something is controlling them!"

"You think?" Alysha said. "Simon, Owen, can you stop them?"

"They're huge!" Owen gulped. "I don't think I can move anything with that much mass and weight. Definitely not seven of them!"

"Simon?" Alysha yelled. "One of you at least try!"

Simon squinted through the rain at the uneven, muddy ground. Would friction work on that kind of surface? Would it work on something as big as the mammoths? These were like elephants from the planet Krypton. Massive in size and strength, terrifying in sheer power, with a stench—like a barnyard times twenty—worsened by the humid air and swampy ground.

It was his fault they were in this mess . . . he *had* to find a way out for them! He tried to redirect the gravitational pull on the mammoths as he did with the Komodos. The trees be–

hind them should have become their ground instead of the earth beneath them, and unlike the Komodo dragons, these beasts had no claws to grip the ground with. They should have been flung backward, literally falling to the forest. But it didn't work.

Alysha looked at Simon, slumping with defeat. "They're big—so what?" she yelled. "You control gravity! You sent Sirabetta's car flying once, and that was big!"

He nodded, but with no enthusiasm. Since he'd gotten his gravity formula, he'd done amazing things. But there were limits to everything, and he'd just found his.

"Those mammoths are a lot bigger and heavier than cars!" Owen said.

"Besides, I didn't consciously do that," Simon said. "I just changed gravity, and it eventually made the car fly." He shivered from the damp . . . and fear. What should he do? What could he do?

"Simon," Alysha yelled. "Try something! Anything!"

Simon grit his teeth. She was right—trying and failing was better than doing nothing. If he could make them weightless, maybe Owen would be able to use velocity on them. Simon tried to twist the weblike network of gravity away from them, but he couldn't budge it. It was as if gravity were a living thing that wouldn't let go of its grip on them. There might have been a way to do it, but he couldn't wrap his mind around how.

By now, the mammoths had gotten frighteningly close—maybe one hundred feet away and getting nearer with each earth-shaking moment. He couldn't redirect or take away the effect of gravity on them, but perhaps he could add to it. That wasn't fighting their enormous nature . . . it capitalized on it. He spoke the words and smiled as, with angry but weakened bellows, the Mammoths sank to their knees.

Simon had only managed to double their gravitational pull and thus double their weight. But these beasts naturally weighed ten to fifteen tons, which was not an easy amount for any land animal to go strolling around with. At twenty to thirty tons, their muscles strained and their bones creaked from their efforts to move.

"Great!" Owen shouted. "Now let's get out of the mud and go . . . anywhere!"

The kids pulled at their feet, but Alysha suddenly leaned back and shrieked. "There's something in the grass!"

"Oh, not again!" Owen yelped, staring wildly around him.

"Alysha, what's going on?" Simon yelled to her.

Alysha tugged harder at her leg and cheered when it pulled free. "Look, I saw that grass moving." She pointed toward the waist-high grass about twenty feet away.

"Great-just-what-we-need," Owen moaned.

"More of the megafauna?" Simon asked.

Flangelo pointed at the mammoths and uttered a warbling shriek. The kids turned to look and went pale; the tusked brutes were crawling forward on their knees, making slow but steady progress. They'd cut the distance between them and the kids in half . . . and less than fifty feet away was not very far when the animals in question were each the size of a garbage truck.

Alysha gasped. "Over there!" she shouted, pointing, causing the others to turn and stare. Something was slinking out of the higher grass: a shaggy, reddish brown giant cat. Not a cat of the scratch, lick, and meow type . . . but rather the tear, rend, and roar sort.

It stepped out from the grass, revealing it was huge. Lion huge. It raised his head a bit, sniffed with its massive, fist-size nose, and let out a roar that chilled Simon and his friends. Opening its mouth like that made something else clear . . . something more alarming than its size: it was no lion. It had seven-inch-long teeth, one on each side of its upper jaw jutting down.

"*Smilodon fatalis*," Flangelo said with a warbling whine. "Saber-toothed cat."

"This is the stupidest thing I've ever heard of," Alysha said. "I mean, who outside of the Flintstones keeps saber-toothed tigers around for kicks! Didn't anyone ever tell you that giant carnivores make bad pets?"

"It's Biology," Flangelo hissed. "Study of all life, not just what's cute and fluffy. Now get yourselves free so we can leave before—"

Once again, Flangelo stopped midsentence, this time because of the eight-foot-long, five-foot-tall bundle of death that came bounding out of the grass toward them.

Simon froze. *Again*, he thought. *I keep putting my friends in danger.*

Owen didn't hesistate; he grabbed it with velocity and hurled it at the nearest tree. *Smilodons* were agile, though—they were huge cats, after all. It twisted as it flew, landing feetfirst against the tree and springing forward again. Owen lashed out once more, this time using velocity to swing it around and fling it, with a loud splash, into the lake.

A series of powerful roars ripped out from the grass, and three more sabertooths came running out. They split up, each approaching the kids from a different direction. Simon got a grip on himself; this was something he could handle. Something he *had* to handle. One of the giant cats leaped, and Simon shifted gravity to pull at it from all directions. The beast was suspended in midair; it let out a whimper and flailed its baseball-mitt-size paws uselessly.

Another sabertooth ran at Owen, but Simon eliminated all friction on its paws. His worries about friction working on the uneven ground were unfounded—the beast slid helplessly past its prey. It kept going, unable to slow down as it skated over the dirt and through the grass. It smacked into and rebounded off a tree. The impact didn't hurt it much, but it was still unable to get any traction with its paws. It slipped in another direction, yowling furiously.

202

The fourth *Smilodon* moved toward Alysha with a snarl, legs tensed for an attack. Alysha snarled back, raising one hand above her head and lowering the other by her knees. She generated a huge arc of bluish white electricity that spat and sizzled in the wet air. It was enough to make the giant cat hesitate, but it didn't run away. It let out a low-pitched whine and tried to circle around her.

Alysha, her legs now free, shifted with it to keep her electrical arc between them.

"What now?" she yelled. "It's too fast for me to shock it!"

"Hold on," Simon said. He increased the gravity on her *Smilodon*, pinning it to the ground.

Alysha reached out and jolted it with an electrical charge that knocked it out.

Simon exhaled with relief; though he'd led his friends into terrible danger, he was able to lead them out of it, too. "We can do this!" Simon cheered.

A nearby trumpeting sound jolted him, perhaps the mammoth equivalent of saying, "Not so fast"; Simon whirled around in time to see a blur of white. A piece of ivory the size of a lamppost smacked him in his chest, lifting him up into the air and flinging him far, far back until he splashed into the lake.

The lead mammoth had reached them and hit Simon with a tusk.

"Simon!" Alysha, Owen, and Flangelo shouted together.

All the mammoths rose to their feet and bellowed, back to their normal weights. The floating sabertooth dropped to the ground, his regular gravitational pull restored, and the sliding sabertooth scraped to a halt, its friction back to normal.

Simon's formulas had stopped working: he was unconscious . . . or worse!

"I'll get him," Owen said, but he paused as the lead mammoth charged. Flangelo shifted to sparrow form and flapped away. Alysha dove to the side, ducked under the gigantic tusks, and rolled next to the mammoth's foot as it crashed into the muddy ground. She reached out and hit him with all the electrical charge she had left in her.

The mammoth shrieked in pain and shrank back from Alysha for a moment. But only a moment—the jolt hurt it, nothing more. It trumpeted in rage and reared up to strike. "Oh, no," Alysha moaned; she started to roll away as a manhole-size foot dropped down to crush her.

The foot never connected. Owen was standing, his arms outstretched, focusing his velocity formula on the creature. Beads of sweat slid down his forehead, joining the light rain, and with great effort, Owen knocked the immense Columbian mammoth backward. It fell on its hindquarters and toppled over with a wet thud.

Owen grabbed Alysha's hand and yanked her to her feet. "Are you stuck?" he asked, yelling over the angry trumpeting of the mammoth as it tried to right itself. She nodded and poured all her strength into tugging a mud-trapped foot.

Owen kept a hand on her and activated his chromatophores, camouflaging them both. They were frighteningly close to the mammoth, though; close enough that it could surely smell and hear them. "Hurry up," he hissed.

The mammoth got to its feet just as Alysha shouted, "Got it!"

Owen got a firm grip on Alysha and used his velocity to fly them up and away, narrowly avoiding the mammoth's tusk-strike.

Flangelo, back in sparrow form, chirped anxiously as he flapped over the lake—Simon was down there, probably drowning.

"Put me down, Owen," Alysha said. "I've got to make plasma, and I don't want to accidentally get you."

Owen returned Alysha to a relatively solid patch of ground, as far from the herd as he could. He noted the sparks around her as she began drawing in as much electrical charge as she could from the air around them. Without him touching her, she was no longer camouflaged: she would be trampled or smashed if he didn't do something.

A sabertooth reared up and lunged. Owen caught it in midair and flung it at the lead mammoth; the panicked *Smilodon* clawed and bit frantically at the behemoth as it tried to get a grip.

Owen let go of his camouflage, making himself fully visible, and then launched himself past the faces of the mammoths. He used his chromatophores to shift from one bright color to the next, making sure every prehistoric beasts' attention was on him, not Alysha.

Two mammoths veered toward her, so Owen used velocity to grab chunks of mud from the ground and fling them in their faces. The falling rain and a quick wipe from their trunks kept them from being blinded, but the attacks kept them angry and distracted.

Flangelo swooped wildly, zipping right up to the faces of the mammoths and pecking at them to keep their fury diverted from Alysha. Each attack brought him closer to being swatted by trunk or tusk, but he didn't dare stop.

Alysha was dimly aware of her friends' efforts, but it was taking increasingly more concentration for her to work at ionizing the air. She was focusing on invisible electrons, shuffling them from atom to atom, as if playing an imaginary game of checkers.

The air around her began to crackle as the ionization process grew ever more intense. Her hair began to frizz and, finally, stood on end as the electrical charge around her increased. There it was again—that scary feeling of power growing inside of her, building more and more, all the while becoming harder to hold back.

Hold on hold on hold on hold on, she thought desperately. She clenched her fists and squeezed her eyes closed as she strained to keep the gathering storm from breaking free too soon. *Simon's in the lake, those things are going to kill us, I've got to get this right, I have to own the power* . . . Then she hit that point, that level which she knew she couldn't go past. She only had seconds left.

"Guys!" she yelled. "Clear out!" She managed to open her eyes a sliver, narrowly seeing Owen zooming toward her with Flangelo in human form, clearly being dragged along by Owen's velocity. Then, through the glowing air in front of her, she saw massive shapes coming closer, closer, until they were almost on top of her.

She didn't know if Owen and Flangelo had made it behind her or not, but it didn't matter—there was no more waiting. She clamped her eyes shut again, feeling the hot breath of some gigantic animal on her, and then . . . Light.

The air in front of Alysha turned blue, then white, and then a bright pinkish hue. I whirled around and shielded my eyes just in time, because a split second later the colors burst outward in an eruption of ultraheated plasma.

The sound was deafening, tearing through my speakers and roaring across my entire apartment. The searing brightness of the light filled my living space through my Viewing Screen, leaking past the fingers over my face. It was less an explosion and more like someone bringing the sun down for a quick game of supernova.

A moment later, it was over, and I was able to look back at the Screen. All the grass for a hundred feet in front of Alysha was gone; the once-swampy ground was charred black and cracked, with steam rising from where puddles of water once sat. Alysha had wisps of purplish smoke curling gently off her hands and hair, but she was unhurt. She'd channeled the explosion but had been untouched by it. She looked back and smiled wearily when she saw Owen and Flangelo. Both looked well, though they'd been knocked to the ground from the explosion. They were staring at Alysha with eyes wide and mouths drooping open.

"You okay?" she asked. They nodded silently.

Alysha stumbled and started to fall, drained from her exertion. Though exhausted, too, Owen and Flangelo managed to grab her by the arms and keep her propped up.

"Thanks," she mumbled. She peered through the dissipating mist and saw the sabertooths and the mammoths sprawled across the ground, traces of plasma–smoke rising from their charred coats.

"Did I kill them?" she asked.

"Nah," Owen said, his voice hoarse from weariness. "I think you just stunned them." Indeed, though only patches of the shaggy sabertooth fur remained and there were pink burn streaks on the mammoths' skin, I could see that their chests rose and fell with ragged breaths.

Apparently, Alysha's spreading out the plasma attack to cover the whole battlefield had diffused the energy enough to knock the beasts out but no worse. Alysha sighed. "Good. That worked out nicely."

And that's when the last sabertooth burst out of the lake behind them and leaped at the trio.

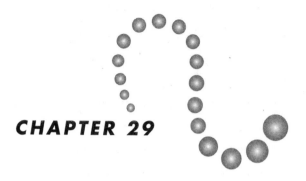

CHAPTER 29

The Unsinkable Simon Bloom

Let's not forget poor Simon. Getting hit with a mammoth's tusk and hurled into a lake was not the best approach to going for a swim. At the very least, it made it tricky for Simon to hold his breath, which he, being unconscious, was not doing anyway.

The lead mammoth's attack hit Simon hard; solid ivory was about as soft and cuddly as a baseball bat. That, combined with the impact of hitting the water at race car speed, should have left him with countless broken bones or, more likely, dead. Add the whole sinking-to-the-bottom-of-the-lake thing, and Simon's remaining part in this Chronicle should have been from beneath a tombstone.

Which was what made his opening his eyes so surprising. Unfortunately, he also opened his mouth wide in an expression of surprise and panic. It's worth noting that opening his mouth underwater wasn't the smartest thing for Simon to do; it should have been just the latest on his laundry list of deadly problems. But let's address the being-crushed-or-killed problem before the drowning-quickly one.

Thanks to the octopus trait he'd taken on, Simon was much more flexible and resilient. He was still a human being with muscles, bones, organs, tissues, and all that, but they were now much harder to damage with the impact of, say, an enormous mammoth's tusk smacking him like he was a flesh-colored golf ball.

There was no breakage, no puncturing, no internal bleeding; Simon just got a nasty bruise all across his left side and chest. On the other hand, the one-two punch of the tusk-strike and smacking into the pond's surface did knock Simon out, and that was a bad thing to be when at the bottom of a lake. No amount of flexibility would save him from drowning.

That was the funny thing about Simon waking up underwater: he was breathing. When you've spent twelve years of your life breathing air in one way, you catch on swiftly when you start breathing in a totally different way. Simon felt at his throat and gasped from surprise at what he found there.

Stunned at his ability to gasp underwater, he gasped again, though he felt terribly foolish afterward. He continued to touch the area around his throat, sure that humans weren't supposed to have multiple slits in their throats where he did.

Especially not slits that rose and fell so rhythmically. It didn't take Simon long to realize what they were.

True, Gilio had only given Simon one octopus attribute—the flexibility. But Simon had touched the symbols for octopus DNA in the *Teacher's Edition of Biology*, and, as noted, Biology abilities are transferrable by touch. Simon's connection to the Books of Physics and Biology was apparently enough to allow him access without Gilio intending it. So Simon had absorbed many—perhaps all—octopus attributes, and as mentioned earlier, they most certainly had gills. And now, so did he.

Simon didn't realize the *why* of this, yet. For now he was content to focus on being alive. That and *staying* alive. More importantly, he thought about his friends. While he was at the bottom of a lake, his friends were on the surface, fighting for their lives. That would not do. He used his gravity to reverse the normal pull into a push, launching himself up through the water at three times a normal falling rate. He burst through the surface of the pond and flew high into the air.

Simon opened his mouth and gasped, sucking in air and reveling in its fresh taste. It was a delight to breathe normally again, to taste the air as it moved through his nose and mouth. He noted the peculiar sensation of his gills closing up, presumably disappearing until needed again.

Simon hovered in midair for a moment, squinting to make sense of the scene before him. Down by the lakeshore, Owen and Flangelo were facing Alysha, who was turning and stumbling toward them. Beyond them were mammoths and sabertooths lying on the charred and smoldering ground.

Simon smiled: his friends had done it! He couldn't wait to celebrate their victory and tell them about his remarkable new discovery. He shifted gravity so he was falling toward them, zooming through the raindrops that smacked against his already soaked face and body. He was so intent on reaching them that he didn't notice the *Smilodon* until it was too late; the beast was already out of the lake and pouncing on his friends.

What happened next was almost too quick for me to follow. Owen and Alysha, sluggish after all their formula use, moved too slowly, but Flangelo was a hair faster. He shoved Owen toward Alysha, placing himself between the *Smilodon* and the kids.

At the same time, Simon instinctively stretched his arms out toward the huge cat, as anyone might do when they saw something disastrous happening far away. Normally such automatic reactions were futile, but Simon Bloom was far from normal.

He felt the result instantly; the gravitational pull around the sabertooth changed, yanking it back from his friends. Even so, Simon wasn't in time; the beast's claws raked Flangelo's shoulder and side, tearing through his clothes and his skin. Simon followed through with gravity, hammering the *Smilodon* into one of the fallen mammoths; it connected with a thump and lay still.

It would only be much later that Simon would realize he

hadn't actively triggered his gravity control; he'd reached out with his arms and the formula had somehow responded. An important detail . . . but for later.

That moment, however, Simon focused on getting to Flangelo as soon as possible. He tore through the air and landed by the bleeding man's side just as the startled Alysha and Owen caught him midfall.

Simon stared at the bright red of the wound, almost hypnotized in his horror. True, the injury would have been much worse had Simon not stopped the *Smilodon*, but the damage was done. He had to do something! But what?

Simon felt a mental flash from his backpack, still on the ground where he'd dropped it when the mammoth had knocked him into the lake. The flash was a message from the Book, tucked cozily inside during the entire battle.

The apple, was all it said, but that triggered memory flashes for Simon. The apple with a bite missing. Ralfagon chewing. The apple whole, as if never bitten. Simon whispered the words of his space-time formula, focusing on an image of Flangelo as he was before the attack.

Flangelo was sagging in Owen's and Alysha's arms when the four gushing claw marks began to ripple like the surface of the storm-smacked lake behind Simon. Before his startled friends' eyes, the slashes shrank and the blood flowed in reverse. The red stains on Flangelo's and Owen's clothes and the spatter on the ground rose up into the air and returned to Flangelo's body.

After a moment, the blood and wounds were gone: not healed so much as never happened. Simon had moved time backward around Flangelo's wound, making it so it never happened. Even the rips in his shirt were gone. If someone were to look at the sabertooth who'd attacked Flangelo, they'd find the blood gone from its claws . . . though it would still be unconscious from Simon's gravity-attack. As with the apple at Ralfagon's office (and with Sirabetta at the end of the last Chronicle), the time-reverse was highly localized to its target.

Simon exhaled in relief, and Flangelo stared at him with an amazed expression. "What . . . what happened?" he chirped weakly.

"Simon!" Owen shouted with relief. "You saved him!"

"And you're okay!" Alysha added.

Simon might have looked okay, if rather soggy, but in truth he was far from it. His mind was reeling. The last few days' events had already been fairly stressful physically, mentally, and emotionally. But the last five minutes took things a bit too far.

"I think that's enough for today," Simon said. And then he passed out, dropping to the muddy ground with a plop.

CHAPTER 30

Great Mileage in City or Desert

Owen, Alysha, and Flangelo rushed to Simon's side.

Owen was closest; when he reached Simon, he knelt into the mud and did his best imitation of a TV-drama paramedic. He checked Simon's pulse, listened to his breathing, and pried open his eyelids to check his pupils.

"Well?" Flangelo asked. "What's wrong with him?"

"How should I know? I'm not a doctor," Owen said. "But he's alive."

Alysha knelt beside Simon, too. "Look, if you got smacked around by a giant mammoth, drowned in a lake, and then miraculously healed a sabertooth wound, you'd need a nap, too."

"Not healed—undid," Flangelo said, pointing at his undamaged clothes. "Maybe that was too much for him, though."

"He's got two Books on his side and a ton of power," Alysha said. "There's probably nothing that can stop him. He'll wake up when he's ready."

Flangelo frowned. "I hope you're right. But if being in the Union has taught me anything, it's that even the weakest can hurt you and the strongest can get hurt."

Owen looked around at the mammoths and sabertooths scattered across the smoldering ground. He noticed several pairs of eyes staring out from the tree line and remembered the many other types of megafauna they'd seen before. "Maybe we should go someplace safer to talk about this?"

"Is there a place we can hide out?" Alysha asked Flangelo.

"Normally I'd say there were plenty, but I don't know what might attack us."

"What about those huts we passed over in the desert?" Owen asked.

Flangelo nodded. "It's worth a try. Shame to backtrack, though."

"More of a shame to get eaten," Alysha said. "Dealing with Sirabetta will have to wait until Simon recovers."

"You're right. Follow me," Flangelo said. He looked around. "And hurry."

"If we want speed, let's just fly with Owen's velocity," Alysha said. "No offense, but he can move us much faster than you can go."

"Wow, lightning rod," Flangelo warbled. "Did you just say 'no offense'?"

"What happened to 'hurry'?" Owen asked.

Owen and Alysha put on their backpacks and gave Simon's to Flangelo to wear. The kids grabbed Simon's arms and Flangelo put his hands on Owen's shoulders; Owen used velocity to lift them, and his octopus camouflage kept them hidden. They soared into the air, keeping high above the ground to avoid any further danger or bad weather. They soon reached the border of the desert and landed outside one of the huts.

"What's the deal with these?" Alysha asked. "Can't you make nicer homes?"

"You'll see," Flangelo said, "so long as we can find one that's empty."

Owen closed his eyes and concentrated on sensing velocity. He pointed to a hut. "That one. I can't sense any movement inside; it's either empty or everyone's asleep."

"Wait here," Flangelo chirped. He shifted to sparrow form and flew around the hut. He changed back to human form and entered. A few moments later he came out and waved to the kids.

Moments later Alysha led the way while Owen used velocity to float Simon into the hut. It was, to put it mildly, quite nice. It was considerably larger on the inside; they'd walked into something the size of a small trailer made of mud and found they were in something the size of a spacious, well-decorated one-floor house.

The temperature was perfect, but it took my link to my

Chronicle subjects to fully appreciate this. To Flangelo, it was like the climate in a shady, slightly moist forest. To Alysha, a big fan of tennis, the air resembled the fading warmth of late afternoon on a sunny day. For Owen, happiest parked in front of his television, there was a slight chill to the air and a flat, still quality to the room that basically screamed naptime.

In other words, rather than adjusting the room to the inhabitants' needs, the hut was adjusting each inhabitant's body to make them feel comfortable. Quite a neat trick.

Flangelo walked up to a large window on the wall opposite the door. He tapped the side of a large black box beneath the window; the box unfolded like a flower's petals. Something vaguely like a steering wheel formed, and Flangelo tapped the center. He touched his foot to a raised rectangle on the floor, and the entire hut jerked forward.

After that initial sense of movement, there was no indication that they were going anywhere. Only the window–view of barren ground and windswept dunes whipping by made it clear that they were crossing the desert.

Flangelo talked to the kids over his shoulder as he drove the hut. "There are things like these in a few other biomes, too; they're all very cozy inside. Some Order members live in the midst of nature, some have real houses like Gilio's. Almost nobody lives in these cruisers; they're mainly for comfortable travel."

"And Biology formulas make them possible?" Alysha asked.

"I'm sure Gilio got Ralfagon and some folks from the Craftsmen's Guild to change the space inside of them and make them move around."

"Why do you need these when you have the water-teleport things?" Owen asked.

Flangelo looked away from the window, and for a moment, the hut veered wildly to the side. He quickly turned his gaze back to the window and spoke over his shoulder. "The pools go between biomes, not within them. Places like the forests or mountains don't have these cruisers; they can't exactly fit between trees or boulders. But for the tundra, the polar region, the grasslands, and especially the desert, they're essential."

A few minutes later, Flangelo parked the cruiser-hut behind a large sand dune; he tapped the center of the steering wheel-thing and turned away from the window.

"We should be safe here. There aren't many animals that would or could look for us here. I'd like to see a mammoth try to cross the desert."

"I wouldn't," Owen said.

"We'll keep an eye on the view-port, just to be sure," Flangelo said.

They helped Simon drink some water, and he opened his eyes. "What happened?"

"You passed out," Alysha said. "Right after you did something incredible."

Simon smiled. "That space-time formula's not bad, huh?"

"Very not bad," Flangelo said. "Thanks for saving my life."

"And thanks for saving ours," Alysha said to Flangelo. "If you hadn't stepped in front of that sabertooth . . ."

"Okay, okay," Flangelo said. "Let's not get gushy."

"Looks like you got the plasma working," Simon said to Alysha.

She smiled and nodded. "I'm not in a hurry to try it again, but yeah. I guess we all kinda kicked butt."

"How did you do that whole not-drowning thing?" Owen asked.

"That sort of happened underwater," Simon said. "I might have a few more tricks," he said, thinking of how he threw that last sabertooth. "If I can figure them out."

Simon looked away for a moment, his mind abuzz. He did have a lot to figure out about the changes he was going through, but he knew one thing: he was doing okay. Better than okay—he was getting stronger and more capable. Was that enough?

"Hey, Flangelo, we still haven't seen this tough new formula you were bragging about," Alysha said. "But you did nice work distracting those things, at least."

"You'll see me in action the next time we're in trouble, I swear," Flangelo said.

Simon turned his attention to the part of his mind that could sense space-time. By concentrating he felt that distinctive Sirabetta signal; he was almost positive she hadn't been restored to her normal age. Yet. "I think you'll have a chance to prove that," he said to Flangelo. "We all should eat and rest up; our formulas won't be much use if we're exhausted." He thought about Sirabetta and whatever other surprises were waiting for them. "And we're going to need our strength to-morrow."

CHAPTER 31

A CALL TO ARMS

Once they'd eaten, Alysha, Owen, and Flangelo went to the hut's sleeping quarters. But Simon lingered in the kitchen and pondered how different throwing that sabertooth had felt compared to his normal use of gravity. He squinted in the dim light and noticed a half-eaten snack bar twenty feet away. He thought about reaching for it but was careful not to activate his gravity formula.

"Whoa!" he whispered to himself. The snack rose up in the air and floated toward him, exactly as if he were using an invisible arm to pick it up. A very long invisible arm.

Simon looked around the room at other items, like his sneakers, his backpack, some discarded napkins. He closed his eyes, folded his arms, and thought about picking up the items. His arms never moved, but he had the sensation of grabbing four of them. When he opened his eyes, he saw those items move through the air to him.

The strangest thing was that Simon *felt* as if he'd picked them up, even though his arms were still folded. When he closed his eyes again, he could imagine—almost sense—four more arms. Simon opened his eyes and, with a thought, made the items he'd grabbed float to wherever he willed them. He could feel disruptions in normal gravitation; the objects' movements were connected to his gravity formula. But how?

Book, he thought, using his mental connection to the *Teacher's Edition of Physics*. *Do you know what's going on?*

The Book took its time. Simon imagined it stroking its chin or rubbing its forehead while debating what to do; the image was limited by the Book's lack of chin, forehead, or fingers to stroke or rub.

Finally, the Book responded. *Why didn't you drown?*

Because I grew gills, Simon thought back.

And how did you do that?

Simon was much too tired to deal with puzzles. *I don't know.* When the Book didn't respond, Simon gave it some real consideration. *Because of the octopus DNA? Maybe when I touched it, I somehow absorbed it all?*

The Book didn't move, but Simon felt the mental equivalent of a nod. *And what else do octopi have besides gills?*

They can do what Alysha and Owen can, they're flexible, they can

spew ink. Eww, can I do that? There was no answer. *Fine, what else? They can lose a limb and grow it back, they* . . . He paused and whispered aloud, "They have eight arms."

If there was a way for the Book of Physics to think a smile at him, it surely was.

But I don't have eight arms. He waved his two arms around. *Just these. Trust me, I'd notice more.* And he really, really hoped he wouldn't grow them. That would be not only gross, but he'd also have to get custom-made shirts!

After a pause, the Book sent a quiet thought. *Must all arms be flesh and bone?*

Simon stared blankly for a moment, then closed his eyes again. There they were again—four arms he couldn't see or even feel. But he knew they were there.

See, the octopus DNA had changed parts of Simon's body, but it had also changed the way his mind worked. He could now think like an octopus. That didn't mean he'd start daydreaming about seafood and avoiding fisherman's nets but, rather, that he could apply his attention the same way octopi could.

Simon, being human, only had two arms and two legs, but he also had control of great forces. Without even realizing it, he used one of those forces to fill in for the four arms that were missing from his octopus-self. So while his flesh and blood arms and legs were just flesh and blood, his extra four arms were extensions of pure gravity.

Simon opened his eyes again and, at last, saw the new

limbs. He held them in front of his face and twisted them around, examining them from every angle. They were nothing like his human arms: they looked just like octopus arms, except they were entirely made up of distortions in the gravitational field around him. He found he could use them as solid arms to pick things up or wrap around things to squeeze. This led to a big mess with a juice box. He also found he could use them as hollow tubes of gravitational pull that sucked things in through the walls of the tube (which worked well to clean up the spilled juice).

I don't know if I should be thrilled or freaked out, Simon thought to the Book. They moved like octopus arms, coiling and uncoiling restlessly unless he focused on them. That was another thing about octopi—each arm has its own mini-brain that lets it act independently. So Simon only had to think about moving an item in the room, and one of the gravity arms would launch into action. With effort Simon could make them stay still, but he preferred letting them coil and uncoil. It was an amazing sensation, like discovering a color he'd never noticed or a great new part of a book hidden between two familiar chapters.

Definitely thrilled, he decided. This was it! These arms could give his friends and him the edge they'd need if they ran into more danger. And he was quite sure they would. Once again, he thought of the Book's warning: the end of things as he knew it.

Book, Simon thought to it. *Can you tell me anything more about*

that? There was no response. That was okay—Simon would just practice more with his new power.

"Whoever's moving stuff around—knock it off," a grumpy voice warbled.

Simon sighed. Or he could get some sleep now.

CHAPTER 32

GROWING UP IS HARD TO DO

Miles away in the cavern beneath the jungle, Aleadra and Sirabetta had not budged from that small chamber in the back. Aleadra sat cross-legged facing Sirabetta, who was stretched out on the mattress. Their eyes were closed, their jaws were tight, and their faces were beaded with sweat. The air was stale and the mood was tense, as if they were in the middle of a big exam and had forgotten to study. Or bring pencils.

Aleadra's eyes snapped open, and she stared off into the distance. "They've won another victory," she said with a grunt.

Sirabetta kept her eyes closed. "Who?"

"Your enemies. Those children. They defeated some beasts I sent after them."

"Are you sure about that? You're not Keeper anymore," Sirabetta said. "You might be mistaken."

"I'm positive. You're not the only one who has powers she shouldn't have."

"Well, then good," Sirabetta said, opening her eyes at last. "I want to take care of Simon Bloom myself. I want to see the look in his eyes when he falls!"

"My, my, aren't you the bloodthirsty one," Aleadra said. I couldn't tell whether she was saying this with concern or pride. "Don't worry, you'll have your chance soon—they're headed this way."

"Perfect," Sirabetta said. "As long as we're ready for them." She hesitated; when she next spoke, it was as a nervous teen. "We'll be ready, right? This'll fix me?"

"I've been preparing for this ever since you were changed," Aleadra said. "Of all the Biology abilities I've regained, my best are those dealing with the physical form." Her voice softened. "I'm here to make you better. And I'm almost done."

"I don't feel any different," Sirabetta said.

"It's as if I've spent this whole time finding the right key and learning how to fit it in the lock," Aleadra said, her voice wavering with fatigue. "Now I need only turn it."

She closed her eyes and held her hands, palms down, over Sirabetta's head and heart. She spoke a long chain of words, presumably several Biology commands. Sirabetta's body glowed bright green, shimmered, and then shook.

Sirabetta let out a whimper as her entire body changed. "It hurts," she cried. "Why does it hurt so much?"

"Let me describe what I'm doing to you," Aleadra said,

keeping her tone soothing. "I'm aging you twenty years, which means shedding your dead cells and adding new ones as your body matures. I'm making your muscles, your organs, your internal systems, everything—even those tear ducts you're using right now—develop, and I'm making sure they work properly. At the same time"—Aleadra paused, breathing heavily—"my formulas are giving you the nourishment you need." She exhaled slowly. "It's not as easy to do as it sounds, so try not to disrupt the process."

"Okay," whispered Sirabetta. "But please, do a good job."

"I always do," Aleadra whispered back. Sweat was pouring from her forehead. Minutes passed until, finally, she sank down, collapsing onto the edge of Sirabetta's mattress. "Finished," she murmured.

Sirabetta unclenched her eyes. "Yes," she said. "Yes, you have!" She stood up and looked at her hands, her arms, her legs, her torso: all were as they should be for a thirty-three-year-old woman. The blotches of color on her skin had been replaced, too, with dozens of tattoos properly spaced along her arms and legs. "Beautiful!" Sirabetta shouted, triumphant. "You've done it!"

Aleadra looked up and smiled. "Welcome back."

"Thank you so much," Sirabetta whispered. "You didn't let me down this time."

She rubbed at the tattoos, each one tingling at her passing touch. She winced; with their return came the pain they brought. Because they were not imprinted as formulas should be for Union members, they constantly struggled against her control.

Sirabetta activated a painkiller tattoo, one of her many Biology powers, and sighed at the relief it brought. "Now," she said, "I'm ready to crush my enemies."

Suddenly, Sirabetta lurched forward. She clutched her stomach, and her face twisted into a grimace, but the only sound she could make was a pained moan.

Aleadra stared, and her mouth dropped open at the sight of Sirabetta's entire body rippling like a lake in a storm. "No!" Aleadra shouted. She leaned forward and held her hands out, speaking formula after formula. "Stop!" she gasped as the rippling continued.

It was no use; with a burst of white light and a puff of dusty-smelling air, Sirabetta's body snapped back to her thirteen-year-old self. She dropped down to her knees and wept into her palms, one of which was once again covered with a useless splotch of multicolored ink.

Aleadra placed a hand on the crying girl's shoulder. "I'm so sorry."

"What happened? Why am I like this again?"

Aleadra exhaled wearily. "I'm not sure."

"So what do we do now?" Sirabetta whined.

Aleadra sipped some water. "Now we rest a bit. Then we try again and we keep trying until we get it right."

"Again? How much longer is this going to take?"

"Teenagers today—no patience," Aleadra said with a cluck of her tongue.

"Don't patronize me," Sirabetta said acidly. "After all those years focused on your own life! And then you refused to help me get justice, leaving me to face one punishment after another from the Union—you're in no position to act superior!"

Aleadra nodded. "You have every right to be angry with me for the past, Sara Beth. But I'm here for you now, and I will do everything I can to help you."

"My name is Sirabetta!" she shouted. Then her expression and tone softened. "I know you're trying your best. It's so hard to be patient; we have to finish before those children get here." Her features twisted again. "I want Bloom to pay!"

Aleadra took more water and smiled coldly. "Don't worry, my dear. If they arrive before we're ready, we have our foot soldiers to greet them. This is my vow: I *will* make you better, and you *will* have your justice."

CHAPTER 33

THE ROAD TO YUCK

The next morning, my Viewing Screen showed me the interior of that mud hut where Simon and his friends were asleep. Minutes ticked by, and they continued to sleep. I checked my wristwatch (official, custom-made for Historical Society Narrators) and considered nipping back to my bedroom for a nap.

Then a squat, rectangular alarm clock went off in the hut, delivering a mild buzzing sensation directly into the bodies of the four sleepers. Each of them sat up, jolted by the unpleasant but very effective alert.

Simon, a bit cranky from having stayed up too late, thought of reaching out for the alarm clock. In response, a gravity arm reached out, coiled around the clock, and smashed it against the far wall.

"Oops," he said.

"They do shut off automatically once you're fully awake," Flangelo said.

They got up, ate, and prepared for what they hoped was the end of the quest.

"Too bad we can't travel by those pools," Owen said.

"We'd have to know where we were going," Flangelo said.

"I do," Simon said. "I know exactly where."

"Like I said," Flangelo chirped, "let's take the pools."

"Wait, how do you know?" Alysha asked.

"Yeah, did your powers change in that lake so now you can see the future, or did an octopus come to you while you slept and tell you or what?"

Everyone turned to stare at Owen with mouths agape.

Owen blushed. "What? Is it really so impossible?"

Flangelo and Alysha shrugged in unison; he had a point.

"No. I felt a strange twitch in space–time; something made Sirabetta really stand out. I'm almost positive she's in the rain forest. Beneath it, maybe."

"Okay," Flangelo chirped. "We'll take a pool to the out-skirts of the jungle and explore until we find her." He pulled a piece of paper from his pocket and unfolded it. It was a map of the pools: a maddening tangle of different colored lines that showed no sense of organization as the routes criss-crossed one another.

"You can make sense of that?" Owen asked.

Flangelo looked skyward. "Please. You just have to know how to read it."

Alysha leaned forward. "I think it's upside down."

Flangelo's cheeks grew red. "I was getting a different perspective."

"Here," Simon said. Without looking, he pointed to a spot on the map.

"That's right!" Flangelo said. "But how . . . ?"

Simon chuckled. "An octopus came to me while I slept."

"Ha–ha," Flangelo muttered as he walked to the steering control.

Simon looked away. He didn't know how he knew. Maybe his contact with the Order of Biology's Book had forged some sort of connection to the domain.

Flangelo guided the cruiser, gliding across the desert to the transporting pool they needed. It was an isolated spot, far from the border they'd originally crossed and the other mud huts they'd passed.

Flangelo drove the cruiser in a circle around the pool's unmoving surface, staring out of the large window as he went. He scanned the patches of shallow grass and brittle bushes, checking for any sign of surprise enemies lying in wait.

Finally he parked the cruiser, closed the black box around the steering column, and followed the kids outside. They all flinched from the change in temperature; the dry heat felt almost physical, like standing near a pizza oven. Compared to the climate control in the mud hut, it was awful.

"Okay, you know the drill," Flangelo said. "One at a time, feetfirst," he said, directing his stare at Alysha.

She bared her teeth at him and stepped into the pool. Owen carefully followed her, and Simon hopped in after. Flangelo went last and, in an instant, was beside the kids at the outskirts of the jungle region. They were suddenly up to their ankles in thick, moist grass and, worse, sticky humidity.

"Ugh," Alysha said. "After this, let's go to one of the cold ecosystems, okay?"

"Focus on the present, squidlings," Flangelo said, "I suggest you let mini-motormouth do his camouflage trick on you. There are plenty of animals that could attack you in there, and it's a lot harder to see them coming when you're in the thick of it."

"You, too," Simon said. "If they're out to get us, they might be after you, too."

"I suppose I'd rather have chromato-gunk on me than get eaten," Flangelo said.

They all joined hands and Owen activated his camouflage. Within seconds, his chromatophores spread across them, making them blend in with the air and grass around them. They turned to face the rain forest one hundred yards away.

The trees were very different from those in Dunkerhook Woods. Many had thin, almost white bark, while others had a rough, dark coating on them. Most were tall and some were thick, but they weren't nearly as massive as Dunkerhook's. They compensated for their lack of size with attitude, though. Most had their upper branches intertwined in a way that made them look like they were huddling together. Like they were ganging up on someone. It was not a welcoming effect.

Simon made them weightless, and Owen flew them onward; as they got closer, Simon noticed a variety of leaves, including several broad, prehistoric-looking ones poking out in various directions. The vegetation was thick and lush along the border, but that was nothing compared to the top.

"What is that?" Alysha asked. "Nature's way of saying 'go away'?"

The dense leaf-coated branches above formed a canopy: an impenetrable-looking roof. "I don't think we should try to fly through that," Simon said with a frown. Their camouflage did nothing to hide their scent or the sound they made, and crashing through that canopy would not be quiet.

"Even if we could," Alysha said, "anything could be waiting in those branches!"

"I've seen TV shows about jungles," Owen said. "There could be apes, monkeys, snakes, leopards. Gigantic spiders. Tiny poisonous frogs."

"Or bugs," Alysha said with a shudder.

"And that's in modern jungles," Flangelo said. "This one could have beasts and bugs from any time period, all only too happy to try to munch on us. Trust me, you don't want to meet a prehistoric insect."

"I can feel Sirabetta in there," Simon said. "So we have to get in somehow."

Simon and his friends landed at the edge of the jungle;

holding hands to maintain the camouflage, they followed Simon's lead one by one. Owen came next, then Alysha and Flangelo in the back. With a gentle tugging, Simon guided them toward the least wall–like part of the heavy vegetation at the border.

As he stepped into the biome, Simon was struck by how dark it was. Though the dome's artificial light source made the morning bright and sunny outside the jungle, the ceiling of branches and layers of leaves allowed only for a dim, gloomy view inside it. Vines and creepers of different thicknesses wrapped around many of the trees. Others hung down from branches, some reaching all the way to the jungle floor.

It was hard to walk without brushing against some type of plant, especially since the group had to keep their hands linked. They moved in a straight line and tried to be as stealthy and alert as possible.

That level of caution was stressful enough, but the atmosphere made things really unpleasant. It was less hot than the desert or the savannah, but the humidity was terrible. The air had a thick, clinging feel that made breathing a labor. Each moment was sweatier than the one before, especially for their clasped palms. Every step was like trying to walk through a wet, stinky sponge.

The stench was ripe and always present: the odor of decay mixed with vibrant life stung the group's nostrils and tongues. The closest comparison would be to take a few thousand rotten eggs and sprinkle them with a ton of cedar chips.

Add in a lot of dead plants, some fresh flowers, and a dash of paprika, and there it was—not quite *eau de rain forest*, but close enough.

Then there was the noise. Unlike the barren desert they'd just left, the jungle was a thriving ecosystem. Every second provided another sound: a buzzing insect, a croaking frog (often trying to eat a buzzing insect), a squawking bird (sometimes going after a frog), or some sort of mammal. Whether swinging among the trees, ambling along the ground, or dozing on a branch, the mammals didn't seem interested in trying to eat the birds. They were still pretty loud, though.

The rain forest floor wasn't sweetening the deal; it was covered in several inches of moist leaves, rotting branches, loose soil, and an assortment of colored molds, mosses, and fungi. Within minutes, the group's feet and shins were coated in muck.

"Simon, you'd better be right about this," Alysha whispered. "This is probably the most disgusting thing I've had to do."

"It is for all of us," Flangelo warbled in a low voice.

"Shhh!" Simon whispered. "We're supposed to be sneaking!" He used the sleeve of his free arm to mop at the sweat on his forehead, and then he stared past a copse of dark green, ivylike plants. "We're not too far."

They went in silence after that, all aware that they were walking toward a deadly enemy and whatever surprises she'd gathered for them. It made them appreciate the muck they walked through; though unpleasant, at least it wasn't trying to kill them.

For now, they were putting a lot of faith in Owen's camouflage to give them the element of surprise. Fortunately, the noises their footsteps made were covered by the sounds of the jungle. Unfortunately, they didn't notice the tracks they were leaving in the rain forest floor as they went.

But anything—or anyone—familiar with the sights and sounds of the jungle would be able to pick them out easily.

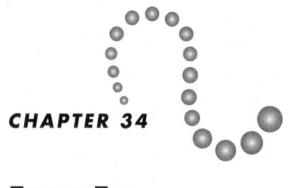

CHAPTER 34

ON THE RUN . . .

"That's it. We're done here." Aleadra stood up from her position by the mattress and leaned against the wall of the small chamber.

"Done?" Sirabetta asked, sitting up. She held out her hands. "These are not mine." She felt her face. "*This* is not mine." She smacked a hand against the mattress. "This is the face of a thirteen-year-old girl." She gingerly touched her nose. "Great—now I'm getting a zit!"

Aleadra wiped her sweaty brow. "Sara Be—, Sirabetta, I've turned you back to thirty-three years old again and again. And each time you've snapped back to this age. Whatever that boy did to you goes deeper than I can reach. Maybe deeper than anyone can without using the same formula he did. I've reached my limits; I can't restore you."

"You've failed me again, Aleadra. What about my power? My revenge?"

"Perhaps you should focus on your loftier goals. When you started this, you were dead set on fixing the Union. "

"I can *also* want revenge, can't I?" Sirabetta hissed. "But I can't do anything if I'm stuck like this!" Her raging turned to sobs.

Aleadra knelt stiffly and awkwardly hugged her; Sirabetta flinched at first but soon accepted the embrace. "Step-by-step, you can do what's necessary to fix this foolish system. And perhaps, along the way, you'll find the satisfaction you seek, too."

Sirabetta rose to her feet. She wiped the tears from her cheeks. "Maybe you're right." She frowned at Aleadra. "What other choice do I have?"

Aleadra shrugged. "Keep your sights on the Book. "

"Well, then," Sirabetta said, "there's only one thing to do. I'll need to get some new tattoos. Ones that work. Ones that will let me topple those jerks—" She caught herself and frowned. "Those *wretches* in power."

She helped the exhausted Aleadra stand. "Someone's coming," Sirabetta said.

Krissantha appeared at the entrance to the cramped chamber. Her eyes widened at the sight of Sirabetta's still-youthful form. "Forgive my interruption, Sir." She turned to Aleadra. "Madam." At a nod from Sirabetta, she continued. "I have important news."

Sirabetta spoke with the commanding tone of her old self; gone was any sense of sorrow or insecurity. "The children are in the jungle and closing in on our position."

Krissantha's mouth dropped open. "How—?" She caught herself. "Yes, Sir."

"We've done all we can here," Sirabetta said. "Krissantha, you and Preto will accompany Aleadra and me on a new mission. I want a force to stay behind to take care of these nuisances. Include that new guy, the one with the exoskeleton."

Krissantha's mouth again gaped; nobody had told Sirabetta about the new recruit yet. "Yes, Sir. What are your orders?"

Sirabetta absently rubbed her exposed arms as she considered what she wanted. She'd tried showing them mercy before, and she'd suffered for it. She glanced down at her arms, then her palms. Those children did *this* to her! They were as guilty as the Council of Sciences and the other Union members who'd imprisoned her and left her to rot. Who'd made the Union intolerable for those who didn't conform to their rules. These *children* had caused her plenty of pain and suffering; they deserved the same.

"My orders are to defeat the children and any with them. Do whatever it takes to keep them from coming after us. Except—make sure Simon Bloom is brought to me alive. Bloom and all his possessions. *All* of them, untouched. Understood?"

Krissantha nodded.

"Good. Wanderby will stay behind and command those

242

who remain. He knows who Bloom is, and he can inform the others."

"Yes, Sir," Krissantha said, and she left to pass on the word.

"Are you sure that's the best plan?" Aleadra asked. "You're willing to risk them taking the Book for themselves?"

Sirabetta shook her head. "The Book won't open for them without this." She held up her palm with the multicolored tattoo on it. "And they don't know how to get it. But until I get this fixed, the Book won't open for me either." She stared at her palm and rubbed at the colors there. "Without my tattoos, I'm useless in this type of fight. Our troops would notice, and that would lessen my hold on them." She clenched her fists. "No, better to get my powers restored first. That way, I'll be ready for anything and everything."

Even being thirteen and powerless, Sirabetta brimmed with confidence and menace. "Now let's go. Soon enough, it will be a different universe. Mine."

AND NOW A WORD FROM MY KEEPER

As Sirabetta and her closest allies began their preparations for leaving and Simon and his group labored through the jungle, my Viewing Screen changed.

An image of the front of Julius Henry Marx Junior High—Simon's school—appeared. Classes were in session, and aside from the duck–shaped weather vane atop the school making a squeaky revolution from time to time, things were quiet. The front door opened and Miss Fanstrom emerged, briefcase in hand. She leaned against one side of the large concrete archway of the school's main entrance, took out her notebook computer, and opened it. To my frustration, I could neither see the screen nor tell what she was thinking.

The top of her hair swiveled so that the tip was pointed

at the angle from which I watched, miles away. The top of her hair was somehow aimed right between my eyes.

Miss Fanstrom glanced up and met my gaze through my Screen. "Of course you can't tell what I'm thinking, Mr. Geryson. Who's the Keeper of whom, after all?"

I gasped. She'd read my mind!

"Mr. Geryson, you read your Chronicle–subjects' minds all the time. You'd be a rather poor sport to whinge about having it done to you, especially by your Keeper."

I was too flustered to respond. I found myself wondering how much she knew about me and my Chronicle.

"Quite a bit," she said. "Now, if you'd like to keep your private thoughts private, perhaps you should speak aloud rather than think to yourself all the time."

That *did* seem to make sense. "I mean, that makes sense," I said aloud. "But Miss Fanstrom . . . what are you doing?"

"Monitoring your Chronicle along with you." She tapped the computer.

I was flabbergasted. Surely there were numerous Narrators at work across the world, yet she was focused on me?

"Tut tut, Mr. Geryson." She sighed. "I can follow many Chronicles at the same time. But with the exception of some shenanigans the Math League is up to again, no subjects of other Chronicles are holding the safety of the universe in their hands."

"Pardon? You're saying that Simon and his friends . . . ?"

"Yes. Their mission will decide the fate of all things. Are you surprised? You've made references to that several times; were you just being colorful?"

"Er, no," I stammered. "I'm just not used to this sort of conversation. Talking with someone who knows more than I do."

Miss Fanstrom chuckled. "Ah, that's part of being in the Knowledge Union. No matter how much you know, there's always someone who knows more."

I shuddered. "What happens now?"

Miss Fanstrom checked her watch. "Now—ah! Here they are." She was looking at the street in front of the school, where an ordinary unmarked white van pulled up to the curb. A man and a woman, both wearing denim overalls and baseball caps with GUILD stitched across the front, got out.

I recognized them from my last Chronicle—they'd installed a teleportation device in Miss Fanstrom's office when she became principal of Simon's elementary school.

"Thank you for coming," Miss Fanstrom said to the Guild members. "I have much work for you, more than the standard setup package."

The woman took a large toolbox out of the van while the man took out a red and white cooler, the kind often used to hold beverages. The various gauges and switches on the cooler and the unusual tools in the toolbox made it clear these were not ordinary items.

"Excuse me," I said, "what exactly are they going to do?"

Miss Fanstrom crooked a finger to the Guild members, who followed her into the school. "Mr. Geryson, they are going to do what the Craftsmen's Guild does best: prepare me for whatever may come. You keep your eyes on your Screen, I'll keep mine on mine, and hopefully that's all we'll need to do."

"What else might we have to do?"

Miss Fanstrom showed a mysterious half-smile and a shrug. "I can tell you this: I fear we may be earning hazard pay in the near future."

Hazard pay? But I don't get *any* pay!

"A minor quibble, Mr. Geryson," Miss Fanstrom said. "We'll worry about that later, if there is a later." A beep from her notebook computer distracted her. "For now, we both have work to do. And friends to worry about."

And with that, my Viewing Screen changed its focus: the Chronicle was to go on.

CHAPTER 35

When Rain Forests Attack

"Are you sure this is the right way?" Flangelo quietly asked for the third time.

"He's sure!" Owen and Alysha hissed at the same time.

"Just getting tired of stomping through all this mush," Flangelo chirped.

"It's not far now," Simon whispered. "Wait, something's changing. She's moving." He concentrated. "She's slowly headed that way now," he said.

"Slowly?" Alysha said. "If she's not flying, maybe her tattoos aren't working."

"But *we* can fly after her," Flangelo said. "I'll go as a bird; I'm tired of Owen's sweaty hand." He yanked his hand away from Owen's and wiped it on his pants. "It's like holding an eel!"

Flangelo paused and stared down at his hands and body, which were rapidly becoming visible. "Wait, how come I'm starting to see myself? Oh, I'm going to regret that, aren't I?"

And that's when the jungle sprang at him.

A vine lashed out from the nearest tree and wrapped around Flangelo. It yanked him off the ground, wound him up like a yo-yo, and flung him back to the floor.

It happened so fast that the kids barely had time to avoid his hurtling body. He squished to a landing in the muck beyond them, while the act of dodging forced the kids to let go of one anothers' hands. Alysha and Simon's chromatophores disintegrated, leaving them fully visible, too.

"Surrender!" a familiar voice bellowed.

Simon, Alysha, and Owen turned at the sound of a voice that used to holler at them through seemingly endless gym classes. "Mr. Wanderby!" they shouted.

"Stay camouflaged, Owen!" Alysha shouted. She looked down at the moist rain forest floor. "And watch out for your footprints!"

Owen used velocity to launch into the air and slowly circle above his friends.

"Forget him," Wanderby yelled. "You, lad," he said, pointing at Simon. "You have something I want, and I want it now!"

Alysha burst out laughing. "Do you ever get tired of sounding like such a jerk?"

"You watch how you talk to me, lass!"

"You're not our teacher anymore!" Owen shouted, his

voice floating down from the seemingly empty air. "And we never liked you then, either!"

"Spread out and prepare for battle," Wanderby said over his shoulder, in the commanding tone of a military leader.

Simon gulped; stepping out from the foliage were eight Biology members he didn't recognize plus Kender, already encased in his exoskeletal armor.

Grawley, still dressed in all brown, cracked his knuckles. His body shimmered, shook, and grew until he'd shifted to his massive, eight-foot-tall grizzly bear form. Then he let out a roar that shook the branches around him.

Simon felt that roar deep inside his stomach, and his face went pale. *Oh, no, here we go again!* He looked from Grawley to the other enemy Bio members. *What did I get us into?*

"Simon?" Alysha said, her face scrunched up with worry. "Come on, focus. We need you if we're going to get through this."

Wanderby laughed. "That's the point, lass—you won't." He turned to the Bio member who'd been with Grawley earlier. "Kushwindro, bind them!"

Kushwindro nodded and gestured with his hands. Dozens of green, ropy vines dropped from the canopy above, lashing out through the area where the kids stood. He then spoke an unintelligible string of words, causing the dirt, leaves, and moss on the rain forest floor to reach up and encase Simon's and Alysha's legs. Before they could try to free their feet, their bodies were snared by the animate vines.

"Watch–out–he–can–control–the–jungle!" Owen shouted.

"No kidding," Alysha groaned. "Don't give away your position!"

"He doesn't have to, little lady," Kushwindro said with a chuckle. "This is *my* rain forest; I'm all–powerful here." He gestured, causing more vines to swing through the air between the canopy and the jungle floor.

One of them grazed Owen's unseen arm and suddenly several more flailed around that area. Within moments, Owen was entwined. He was still camouflaged, though—the vines appeared to be holding onto part of the jungle itself.

"That was even easier than I'd expected," Wanderby said. "Sir will be pleased."

"Don't worry, kids, I'm coming!" Flangelo shouted as he rose from where he'd been thrown. Another vine wrapped around him, but Flangelo turned into a sparrow, leaving it holding empty air. He flapped hard, dodging other grasping vines.

"Okay, now I'm getting angry," Alysha snarled. She generated a current of electricity through her body, killing the vines and burning away the rain forest muck that held her. "Simon, snap out of it!"

For a moment, Simon was lost in his head. Feeling stupid, feeling useless, feeling like the worst thing to ever happen to his friends. To the universe. *Wait a second,* he thought. *If I give up now, that's even worse.* He glared at Wanderby, fumed at the other Bio members who were moving forward around him, and raged at Sirabetta for putting his friends and him through this. *No. No more!*

Simon used gravity to fling away the mud and decaying vegetation that held his legs, and then he used friction to slide out of the vines' grasp. Kushwindro sent more vines swinging and whipping after him, but Simon formed arms out of gravity and tore them apart. He did the same to the vines wrapped around Owen, freeing him, too.

"You never learn, Wanderby," Alysha shouted. "Don't underestimate kids—especially us!"

"Do I look worried, lass?" Wanderby yelled back. He raised his hand and opened his mouth, but he paused when two more Bio members burst through the foliage, breathing hard as they slammed to a halt at the battle site: it was Targa and Cassaro.

Kender nodded his bug-eyed head at them and turned to Wanderby. "Those are my friends. They're here to help." He chuckled, the sound echoing deep inside his exoskeleton as he cupped one fist in the other. He suddenly spun around and swung his fists at Grawley the Grizzly Bear, knocking him back into the trees with a shocked whine.

"Don't worry, kids," Kender shouted. "We're on your side."

Wanderby turned to look at Kender. "You traitor!"

"Traitor?" Kender laughed. "By betraying betrayers?" He shrugged his massive, gray-armored shoulders. "My friends and I only picked a fight with those kids so I could join your

252

group and wreck your plans. We joined this Order to improve things, not to pull some conquer-the-world scheme!"

Flangelo shifted from sparrow to human form. "All right, Kender!" He turned to Alysha. "Okay, spark plug, as promised, I'm going into warrior mode. Prepare to be impressed." With that, his body shimmered and once again changed shape into a bird. This time, however, he didn't become a sparrow.

Where slender, pale Flangelo once stood was now a huge bird. He had a two-foot-long, black-feathered neck; a head the size of a softball with a triangular black beak; and a light gray, fluffily feathered body. His legs were three feet long, each ending in a three-toed, sharp-clawed foot. He wiggled his head, rose to his full height—over six feet tall—and let out a few grunts from deep within his throat.

Wanderby grimaced. "You think we're scared of a few kids, three punks barely out of college, and an ostrich?"

The large bird shifted back to Flangelo's human form. "For your information, I'm an emu, not an ostrich."

"This is a battle, not chatter time!" Alysha hissed. Flangelo blushed and returned to emu-form.

"Whatever type of bird he is, you should be scared, loud-mouth," Kender said to Wanderby. "It's almost even numbers—seven versus eight—and we're gonna flatten you!"

A ferocious roar split the jungle, and Grawley burst back into the region. He tackled Kender, slamming him to the ground with a wet thud. Grawley swung softball-size paws tipped with three-inch-long claws and bit with a tooth-filled snout the size of a loaf of bread. Kender punched at the bear-man, and the two began rolling back and forth along the jungle floor, fighting fists against paws, teeth against head butt.

"I guess it's seven against nine again," Alysha grumbled.

"Guess again," Wanderby yelled. "Najolo, Demara, call your armies."

Najolo, a tall, thin man with messy hair, shimmered and shook and turned into a gibbon—a three-foot-tall, black-haired ape. He inflated a grapefruit-shaped air sac on his throat and let out a piercingly loud gibbon hoot.

It wasn't a monkeylike "ooh-ooh-ahh-ahh" or the usual deeper, apelike "ooh ooh." It was a high-pitched "wooooh, wooooh," like a cowboy having fun. Answering hoots came from throughout the jungle, and distant trees shook with what must have been hundreds of gibbons approaching.

Demara, a blond, curly-haired woman, spoke some unintelligible words, and in response, the jungle began to vibrate with a buzzing sound.

"What's that?" Alysha asked, her voice quivering.

Demara grinned. "My army of insects: flying beetles, mosquitoes, cicadas, bees, and flies. Many thousands of them. And they'll be here in a few minutes."

"Bugs?" Alysha shrieked. "You're fighting with bugs? I *hate* bugs!"

Zillafer the porcupine fish–woman stepped forward and

triggered her Bio-power, inflating her body into a huge, spike-covered sphere. Kostaglos, the venom spitter, moved to her side, hissing as he opened his mouth wide to reveal his poison-shooting tubes. Two more female Biology members joined them with faces set in grim expressions, ready to unleash their own Biology abilities, too.

"Now do you see what you're up against?" Wanderby said.

"Simon," Alysha hissed, "if you've got a plan, this would be a really good time to mention it."

Simon looked from her to the assembled enemies, with the hoots and buzzing of more on the way ringing in his ears. "Yeah," he said with a gulp. "I'm working on it."

CHAPTER 36

Rain Forest Crunch Time

"Okay, team—get them!" Wanderby snarled. "Failure is not an option!"

"I didn't think anyone really talked like that," Owen said as he used velocity to yank handful-size globs of mossy jungle-gunk, loose branches, and torn vines from the rain forest floor. He bombarded Wanderby with them, forcing his former gym teacher to back away while covering up as much as he could with his hands and arms.

Flangelo let loose with a booming sound—the emu equivalent of a roar—and rushed at the nearest enemy: Zillafer the porcupine fish-woman. Before she could react, Flangelo spun and kicked her hard, sending her bouncing off into the forest.

Cassaro stepped forward. "Nice shot! Let's see how they like this." He spat a cloud of mushroom spores toward Wanderby and a cluster of enemy Order members; several attached themselves and began growing at an accelerated rate.

"This is going to be easy!" Targa cheered, throwing her fists into the air.

But she spoke far too soon. Kostaglos rushed forward and shot streams of well-aimed poison at most of the mushrooms growing on his friends. The fungi dissolved quickly, melting to the ground in bubbling puddles.

Kushwindro gestured, shifting the thick, long leaves of nearby bushes and trees to smack at the group. He also launched more vines from the canopy, sending them snaking down toward the heroes. Several wet leaves clung to Owen, revealing his location.

While Owen was busy tearing the leaves off, Wanderby used the break to turn his rotational formula on Flangelo. The fierce but goofy-looking bird crashed hard into Cassaro, knocking him unconscious; the remaining giant mushrooms stopped growing. Wanderby whirled Flangelo faster and faster, causing the emu to let out tormented honks.

Zillafer bounded back into the battle area, squashing some leftover mushrooms as she arrived. Chunks of torn fungus clung to some of her spikes. "I hate getting bounced around," she bellowed. "I'm going to enjoy squashing these guys."

"Here," Kushwindro said. "Let me help you with that." He gestured, and more vines grasped at his enemies. Zillafer aimed herself at Simon, Alysha, and Targa, who were standing near one another in a relatively clear part of the jungle.

Wanderby grinned cruelly as he spun Flangelo faster and faster. "Trurya, make sure they're defenseless for the attack."

Trurya, a short, slender woman with extremely thick glasses, gestured at Simon, Alysha, and Targa.

Alysha reached into her pocket and brought out a handful of coins; she was about to fill them with electricity and throw them, but Trurya's attack had an instant effect. "I can't see the bad guys anymore!" Alysha gasped. "I've gone blind!"

"Me, too!" Targa yelled. She waved her hands in front of her own face. "No, wait—I can still see things close by, but not far away." She slapped at some grabby nearby creepers, but once they got more than a foot away, she flailed helplessly at the air.

Simon knew what it was. "Myopia," he whispered. "She made us nearsighted." He strained to see past a foot, but everything was blurry. "Owen, can you still see?"

"Yes–but–I–can–only–see–jungle–attacking–me," Owen yelled. He was flying back and forth, using velocity to tear away the vines, branches, and leaves that were coming at him from all directions. "Camouflage doesn't help when there's jungle everywhere!"

"This will be like bowling," Zillafer said, aiming at Simon, Alysha, and Targa.

"We're sitting ducks like this," Targa shouted. "Kender, we could use a hand!"

As they battled, Kender and Grawley went crashing

through the foliage, rebounding off large trees and snapping smaller trees they smashed into. "Little busy right now!"

Not two minutes had passed since Alysha had called for Simon to think of something, and in that short time, everything had gone from bad to worse. Simon squinted but, try as he might, he couldn't see beyond a foot or so.

"I don't need to see like that," he muttered. He closed his eyes tightly and extended his sense of gravity, letting him feel everything happening around him. Everything, moving or stationary, was being affected by the gravity around them. It may have been Kushwindro's rain forest, but it was all part of Simon's world.

There were so many enemies, though, and beyond them he could sense an enormous swarm of insects flying in from one direction and an army of gibbons swinging over from the other. It was too much for him to focus on.

"No," he whispered. "I'm tired of worrying and I'm sick of being pushed around." He might well be a terrible leader, he decided, but the others were looking to him for guidance. He'd gotten them into this mess—he'd get them out.

"Hey . . . adrenaline woman!" he shouted, sensing her nearby.

"Name's Targa," she said.

"Can you reverse that sleepy trick? Make someone hyperalert and energetic?"

"Yeah, sure. Who?"

"Me."

"When?"

"Now!" Simon shouted.

The effect was immediate: Simon's eyes immediately jolted wide open as Targa's epinephrine surged through his bloodstream. He felt as if he'd just chugged twelve cans of soda, but without having to pee after.

Every heartbeat was a gong-strike, every intake of breath was a cyclone in reverse, and every muscle was a contender for the be-like-Superman club. Most importantly, this triggered another chemical (called norepinephrine) in his body; it turned his mind into an Indy 500 of racing thoughts and sharp, precision calculations. His gravity-sensitivity was amplified, giving him hyperawareness of everything around him.

"Wow!" Simon said. "*That's* going to come in handy."

Sensing Zillafer bounding toward them, Simon reached out with his gravity arms, using all four to grab at her. Rather than try to stop her, Simon took advantage of her mass and momentum. He swept her up off the ground and swung her in an arc, whipping her back the way she came. Back at his enemies.

Simon could tell which one was Trurya the same way he knew she'd caused shortsightedness . . . though he didn't yet understand what that way was. All that mattered, though, was he knew where to strike and he had a good weapon handy.

"What's happening?" Zillafer shouted as she streaked through the air.

"Kushwindro!" Wanderby shouted, taking his attention away from Flangelo. The dizzy, weakened emu stumbled and collapsed to his knees.

Kushwindro diverted all the vines in the area to grab at Zillafer, but she'd built up quite a bit of speed propelling her mass. She tore through the foliage, slowed but not stopped, and smacked into Trurya and Kostaglos.

They were flung far back, plowing through numerous large plants before landing with a splash into a lichen-covered puddle. They didn't get back up. As for Zillafer, she slammed into a particularly large tree. All the air she'd used to inflate herself burst out of her mouth, and she sank, unconscious, to the jungle floor.

"I can see!" Alysha shouted. "And I've had enough of *The Jungle Whisperer* over there." She activated her jet propulsion, aiming her nose so she launched through the air and streaked toward him. Kushwindro sent branches and creepers at her, but that didn't stop her from flinging a handful of electrically charged metal pieces at him. They exploded around him, sending him senseless to the ground.

The grasping leaves, vines, and rain forest muck dropped harmlessly, freeing Owen. Alysha smiled. "Three down." She glared at Wanderby. "Next!" She launched herself through the air toward him with another rocketlike nose-whoosh.

A short, chubby Biology woman stepped forward and let out a massive belch aimed at Alysha. The result was a deafening boom of sound and, worse, a stench so bad it was almost visible. Caught head-on by this, Alysha rolled on the ground and covered her face . . . more her nose than her ears.

"Well done, Baharess," Wanderby said. "Makes up for your failure in the cave. Now let's get rid of the rest of these troublemakers."

"No way," Simon said. He used an old trick on Baharess, robbing her of friction to make her feet slide out from under her. When she crashed flat onto her back on the forest floor, Simon shifted friction so her arms, legs, and torso were stuck to the ground.

He saw Baharess taking a deep breath and guessed she was getting ready to let out another burp. "Owen, block her!"

Owen used velocity to yank a cluster of broad leaves from the nearest bush, covering her head and chest. The pile of platter-size leaves arrived just in time to make the woman's gaseous attack rebound back into her own face.

Baharess gagged and choked; still stuck to the ground, she couldn't even fan her face with her hands. "Is *that* what my burps smell like?" she moaned, then passed out.

"Alysha, you okay?" Simon called out.

Alysha sucked in clean air. "This might be the grossest day of my life."

Simon, sharply attuned to every change in gravity, looked into the distance. "It's about to get worse." The tree canopy shook and the leaves parted. Suddenly, a gigantic cloud of insects burst through from one side. And from the other direction, hooting loudly, a horde of gibbons swung in.

CHAPTER 37

Apes and Bugs and B Teams, Oh My!

Owen suddenly became visible just a few feet above the ground. "There's no way I'm staying in the air with them!"

Alysha grit her teeth. "Any new ideas?"

"Can you do that plasma trick again?" Simon asked her.

"No way—I might burn down the whole jungle or blow us up!"

Simon nodded, having guessed as much. "Listen, if I keep your feet anchored, can you use your, um, nose as a weapon?"

Alysha frowned. "Ugh. Seriously, yuck. But yeah, I think I get what you mean."

"Good." He pointed at the insects. "Aim for the middle."

"Now you'll pay the price for resisting," Willoughby Wanderby shouted.

"Is he still here?" Owen asked.

"I have an idea that'll take care of him, too," Simon said to Owen. "But first you need to stay close to the ground and follow my lead."

"What can I do?" Targa asked.

"Just keep that epinephrine stuff coming," Simon said. "I'm going to need it."

Flangelo rose unsteadily to his feet, pivoting his emu head back and forth between the two approaching masses of creatures. He let out a loud emu grunt, as if to make sure Simon and the others were paying attention to the danger.

The attacking insects, in a thundercloud–size formation, zoomed down at the friends. "Alysha, now!" Simon said, shouting to be heard.

Alysha activated her jet–propulsion ability, aiming her nostrils at the center of the swarm. She was rocked backward by the powerful burst of air, but her feet were firmly planted and stayed that way thanks to Simon's friction formula.

Her air attack struck the middle of the collective, punching a beach ball–size hole into the front of the cluster. Those insects hit ones next to and behind them, leaving a gap in the back end the size of a small car. The impact wasn't fatal, though; the displaced bugs regrouped while the rest of the swarm, though slowed, didn't stop coming. But they were spreading out more and more.

At the same time, Simon reached out with his gravity arms, using them to grab at and scoop up as many gibbons as he could. There were hoots of dismay and surprise as the apes were suddenly snagged midswing or midjump and flung over their targets—the small gathering of people and emu—and to the insects beyond them.

Owen did the same with velocity, snaring gibbons in groups of six and seven and yanking them over to the insects. The two boys had to act quickly, so they just tossed the apes the few dozen feet to the target area. Soon the hundreds of hairy enemies were displaced to the far side of the battle site.

Alysha shot burst after burst of air through her nose, tilting her head slightly to scatter section after section of bugs. "Simon, I can't keep this up," she yelled. "My nose is going to fall off, and I think I've pulled every muscle in my legs and butt!"

"You can stop," Simon said with a smile. "It worked perfectly." He pointed as the gibbon army desperately grasped at branches and vines around them, only to find themselves in the midst of the huge collection of flying bugs. Flying bugs which, it just so happened, gibbons liked to eat.

Gibbon and insect forces met in midair, and the result was mayhem. Gibbons used their hands and prehensile feet to snatch at the tasty, crunchy treats while the bugs stung and bit at their attackers. Simon, Alysha, Owen, Targa, and Flangelo—still in emu form—crouched beneath them, watching the strange, noisy war.

Demara put her hands to her head in dismay. "Najolo," she screamed, "make your apes stop eating my insects!"

Najolo, in gibbon form, let out a loud hooting: clearly a scolding in gibbon-speak. The gibbons halted their feeding frenzy and leaped down after Simon and his friends.

Demara closed her eyes and sent a mental command to the bugs, making sure they backed off the gibbons and attacked the people below.

"Now comes the tricky part," Simon muttered. He closed his eyes to focus his Targa-boosted thoughts, and then he shifted the gravitational pull of the area above his friends and him. Suddenly, the descending gibbons found themselves zooming in the reverse direction. The insects did, too, but they had wings and had no trouble resisting.

"Alysha," Simon shouted, "bug zapper!"

Alysha glared at him for a moment. "This is going to be completely disgusting," she muttered. Then she closed her eyes, held her arms outstretched to her sides, and surrounded herself with a field of bluish white electricity. She kept sucking electrons away from nearby atoms and channeled them into a steady flow of electrical charge.

The insects were drawn to her, much as they would be to someone's backyard bug zapper. And when they flew to that irresistible light, they met the same end. There were still many hundreds of the flying attackers, and the air was filled with the loud snap, crackle, and pop of their shocking deaths.

Unfortunately, this meant that Alysha was completely surrounded by the very creatures that she found so vile, their corpses piling up around her. And she did not sound happy about it.

"Siiiimmmmoooon!" she shrieked, loud enough to be heard over the buzzing and frying. "I'm going to get you for this!"

"Stop!" Demara shouted. She closed her eyes and concentrated, commanding the surviving insects to ignore that alluring blue-white light. The bugs obeyed and, finally, turned on their intended targets.

The cicadas weren't dangerous (they don't even have mouths), but they were loud and distracting. The bees had their nasty stings, while the flies, beetles, and mosquitoes could—and would—bite. Though Alysha was safe, the others were vulnerable.

But Simon wasn't done. He had a final stage to his plan that seemed crazy to him but, if it worked, might finish the job. And he was determined not to let doubt get in his way anymore. He twisted his gravity arms into a funnel, sucking the insects in and sending them speeding down a narrow path. He made the gravitational pull fierce along the borders of that route, so the insects were hard-pressed to fly anywhere but where he wanted them.

They streaked through that tunnel as Simon shifted it, forcing them away from his friends and him. Instead, it directed them right at his former gym teacher.

"Hey, Mr. Wanderby," Simon shouted. "Catch!"

At that moment, Wanderby was staring open-mouthed as his battle plans fell apart. Suddenly, hundreds of insects came winging their way in a tight stream at him. He activated his rotational formula, spinning bugs away by the dozen, but more kept coming. Finally, the flow broke through Wanderby's defenses and slammed into him. He was thrown backward, his entire body coated in squashed bees, flies, beetles, mosquitoes, and cicadas. He was also knocked out, but that was almost beside the point.

The gibbons, unfortunately, were finding their way around the reverse-gravity zone. They used the branches of the trees to head down toward the enemy their leader ordered them after. Once past the gravity-twisting layer, they had no problem attacking.

Gibbons swung around Alysha, but after the first few were singed and stunned by her electrical field, they kept their distance. Owen and Simon were able to use velocity and gravity to keep most of the gibbons off Targa, Flangelo, and them, but there were too many apes for them to fully defeat.

Everyone—even the gibbons—turned in the direction of a tree-shaking roar. Grawley, in bear form, soared through the air in a wide arc, crashing through dozens of branches before smacking to the floor, hard. He half-rose to his feet but plopped back down with a whine. He changed from grizzly to human and lay there, unconscious.

Kender, his exoskeleton torn with many deep, claw- and tooth-shaped gouges, stomped out of a thicket and let out a triumphant yell that echoed across the suddenly quiet patch of jungle. "Okay, who's next?" he bellowed.

Dozens of gibbons piled onto Kender, slapping and biting at his shell. "Stupid question," he said as he sagged to the ground under their assault.

Flangelo let out an angry honk—emu-speak for "enough is enough!"—as he ducked under a pair of leaping gibbons. He scanned the rampaging apes and found the one he was looking for: the only one hanging back and watching, occasionally giving a hoot of encouragement or command.

Flangelo-emu let out a booming cry and dashed forward, leaping and kicking his way through the gibbons that grasped at him. He delivered a spinning kick that sent the lead gibbon flying through the air and smacking into the ground, hard. It shifted back into human-Najolo form and did not rise.

The army of gibbons paused in their attack, hooting quietly and staring at their fallen leader. Kender grunted and spun around, flinging the distracted animals off him while Simon and Owen continued to toss the hairy primates around.

Flangelo turned back to human form. "It's okay, everyone; stop fighting them."

There were many pained hoots and angry grunts from the gibbons, but they weren't violent by nature. With Najolo in human form, the gibbons' leader had suddenly vanished; they had no reason to attack the other humans (especially since attacking kept getting them hurt).

The next-largest gibbon, taking over in Najolo's absence,

gave a command. As one, the gibbons went after the remaining insects and fed with even more eagerness than before. Then they dispersed, swinging and leaping back to their homes in the trees.

"My insects!" Demara shrieked. "But there's more where *they* came from."

"No. More. Bugs," Alysha snarled. She tackled Demara and discharged a jolt of electricity that left the insect-controlling woman out of commission.

For a long moment, nobody moved or spoke. Cassaro woozily got to his feet and looked around at the ruined stretch of jungle around him. "Did I just see a bunch of monkeys running away?" he asked.

"Apes," Owen said. "They're gibbons; it's a type of ape, not monkey."

"This is not the time or the place for a science lesson!" Alysha said. She paused and considered what she'd said. "Fine, it *is* the place, but not the time."

"We won!" Targa crowed, raising her arms in the air in triumph.

"Not yet you haven't!" a man shouted. Two more adults burst out from behind some trees. One, a man with a mustache, hurled a rock at Simon's head.

Owen grabbed it with velocity and sent it flying back at the man, conking him on the head and knocking him out.

A pale woman standing next to the fallen man stuck her hands up. "I surrender!"

A lean, dark-haired man stepped out next to her with his fists poised, ready to fight. He frowned at the woman. "Jaynu, you quitter!"

"What do you want me to do, Branto?" the woman said. "I'm bioluminescent: I can glow in the dark. I'm not cut out for this kind of fighting."

"So? Cubec's ability only deals with tracking, but he's willing to fight!"

The woman pointed to where the mustachioed man, presumably Cubec, now lay unconscious. Branto followed her finger, sighed, and raised his own hands in surrender.

"Wait," Owen said to the lean man. "What's your formula?"

The man sighed. "I study hibernation; I could make one of you fall asleep, but it tends to make me nod off, too."

Alysha chuckled. "Glowing, tracking, and putting yourself to sleep? What kind of powers are those?"

"Powers?" the woman asked. "We're not here to be superheroes, you know. We have jobs. We advance knowledge. Some of us have formulas that can be used aggressively, sure, but we're here for the science."

"Yeah? No wonder you're the B team," Alysha said.

"Tell me where Sirabetta's headed!" Simon said.

Branto frowned. "Why should we tell you?"

Alysha held out her palm, threatening him with a large electrical spark. "Because it's going to hurt if you don't. A lot."

"Oh, knock it off, Branto," the pale woman said. "I'll tell you whatever you want to know."

"No!" Branto said. He gestured to Jaynu, who yawned deeply and slid to the rain forest floor, sound asleep. Branto folded his arms with a smug smile but frowned a split second later. "Oh, no," he said before he, too, slid to the ground, snoring loudly.

Alysha rolled her eyes. "You know, I'm starting to get really tired of this Biology place. Let's catch Sirabetta so we can go somewhere that isn't so annoying."

CHAPTER 38

THE FAILURE OF THE FISH

"Okay, now what?" Targa asked.

"Can you sense which way Sirabetta's gone?" Alysha asked Simon.

Simon closed his eyes for a moment and concentrated. "That way," he said, pointing through the jungle.

"Good, can we please go after her?" Alysha asked.

"But what about these guys?" Owen asked. "If we leave them here they might wake up and escape."

"Or attack other Bio members," Flangelo said.

"We could always trap them in their cavern headquarters," Kender said. "At least as a temporary measure." He pointed in the direction Simon had. "It's on the way."

"It still feels like Sirabetta's moving fairly slowly," Simon said, "but we should hurry." Owen and Simon used their formulas to move the traitor Biology members into a pile; soon Simon had all eleven floating weightlessly.

"Wait," Alysha said. "Where's Wanderby?"

Simon pointed to a pile of squashed insects. "That's where I got him." They saw the footsteps left behind in the muck; he'd woken up and run off in a different direction.

"Should some of us go after him?" Targa asked Simon.

Simon only hesitated for a second. "No, we stick together. There might be more enemies around. Plus we don't know how tough the Bio members with Sirabetta are."

"At least one—Krissantha—seemed dangerous," Kender said.

"Tell us about them as we go," Simon said. "At least now we don't have to worry about trying to be quiet—we can fly the whole way. Owen, can you manage all of us?"

The way Owen rolled up his sleeves would have been comical if not for the fierce look of determination on his face. "I guess I'll have to."

"Then let's go," Simon said. "We can finish this right now!"

Simon used gravity to make his friends and allies weightless. Then Owen flew them through the jungle to the cavern, following Kender's gestured directions. They went fast, with Kender in the front so every tree branch or thick leaf that they had to plow through was torn aside harmlessly against his shell.

They arrived in minutes. Kender cleared away the vegetation at the entrance to the cavern, and they hurried to the sloping passage. Simon used friction to make the tunnel ultraslippery so they could move quickly. Kender and Cassaro fell a few times, but Targa was a natural.

They left the villains in the cavern and hurried back out to the jungle. Simon used his gravity-arms to yank on the rocky entrance. He strained for a few moments until, with a thunderous, dust-raising crash, the entrance collapsed. "I'll clear that away when we get back," he said.

"Hopefully my lungs will start working again by then," Flangelo said, coughing.

"Okay, everyone form a circle and join hands," Simon said. "Flangelo, stay human; it'll be easier and faster."

"I don't like the sound of that," Cassaro said.

"Sorry," Simon said, "but they have a huge head start. From what Kender told us it doesn't sound like they have any strong fliers, so maybe we can catch up . . . but only with speed."

The seven of them linked hands, and Simon made them all weightless. "Ready, Owen?" he asked. Owen nodded, and Simon took a deep breath. "Brace yourselves."

Simon used his gravity-arms to force the trees apart and tear through the leaves, branches, and vines of the jungle canopy. "Owen, now!"

Owen lifted them as a group, launching them straight up through the gaping hole in the rain forest Simon had made. In less than a minute they'd soared past the enormous trees and were above the entire jungle ecosystem.

 275

"That way," Simon said, pointing with one leg to direct Owen.

They streaked through the air, moving as quickly as they could while still being able to breathe. Their hair blew back, their clothes ruffled from the wind, and their cheeks started to push back from the pressure, but Owen didn't let up.

The jungle whizzed by beneath them and the dome zoomed past above them. Targa, Kender, and Cassaro gazed up in awe; I could tell they'd never been so close to the top. An entire ocean held a few feet beyond their heads was an impressive sight.

The landscape below changed from jungle to low grasslands and, very quickly, to sand. "There!" Simon shouted, and Owen sent them soaring down to where the dome touched the beach.

It was a dizzying landing for Kender, Targa, and Cassaro, who weren't used to this type of flight; Targa and Cassaro bumped into each other and almost fell over, while Kender leaned forward with his hands on his knees for a moment until he adjusted.

"Can you still feel her?" Alysha yelled.

"Yes," Simon said. Then, "Oh no!" He ran to the edge of the dome and planted his hands against its curvature. "There they are!"

In the distance the black shape of a manta ray moved swiftly through the water. It was already far away, though;

within seconds it was beyond the bioluminescent kelp around the dome. Past that boundary there was only the impenetrable blackness of the deep, dark ocean. The fleeing enemy was quickly gone from sight.

Simon could feel the space-time tug from Sirabetta dwindling, too. He turned to the Biology members. "How can we go after them? How can we go outside?"

"Kid," Targa said, "that's the ocean out there! Can you spell *drown?*"

Simon waved his hands. "I'll be fine—I can breathe underwater!"

"Doesn't matter; there's nothing we can do," Flangelo said with a low, sad whistle. "There isn't an active transport point nearby; there's no way in or out of the dome here. Besides, what about them?"

Flangelo pointed at the coral reef ringing the dome. As if injured, a small variety of marine life was drifting along at odd angles above the reef. There was a moray eel, a large stingray, a small shark, and a few other fish. Simon recognized one as Phineas.

"Oh no," Owen said. "Are they okay?"

Targa squinted. "They're breathing; I can see their sides moving."

Phineas wiggled in the water and started to swim, though with a slight tilt—the aquatic version of a limp. He came next to the dome.

Simon put his ear to the wall of water and heard Phineas talking: the same formulas that let him talk through a vesicle clearly worked through the dome.

"I am sorry, friends. I was on my way to guard duty when they made their illegal breach. I gathered as many helpers as I could from the area"—he gestured with his spines to the sea life around him—"but we weren't enough."

"You tried your best, Phineas," Simon said. "We'll tell Gilio."

"Many thanks," the lionfish said. "And if you should cross fins with these villains, I only ask that you thrash them for me."

Simon nodded. "Gladly." The other fish and sea creatures started to stir as Simon turned away from Phineas; the brave guards were recovering. Still, Simon's face fell—their enemies had gotten away and he had no idea where they were going. What could they do now?

WHAT THEY DID THEN

I watched as Simon used the Book to contact Gilio and ask him to meet the group back at the cavern. I could sense everyone's tension as Simon and Owen cleared the cavern entrance; they figured the rogue Biology members might be looking for more trouble. They needn't have worried. Most were still unconscious (or, as with Jaynu and Branto, sound asleep), and the others were eager to surrender.

When Simon collapsed the tunnel, he'd disrupted the cavern's artifical lighting and climate control. Without that climate control, the place was as cold as you'd expect something to be at the bottom of the ocean—that is to say, quite. The few traitors that were awake and alert enough to be a possible danger were too busy huddling around the semiconscious Grawley—in battered and exhausted bear form—for warmth.

Alysha lit the place with an arc of electricity, and Simon had no trouble wrapping the collected villains in the firm grip of a gravitational field. It was almost ridiculously easy to transfer them to a special holding cell Gilio had arranged to keep them asleep until the Board of Administration was ready to deal with them.

Gilio had Simon, Alysha, and Owen over for a hearty meal and good night's sleep; their traveling, battling, and chasing had made for an exhausting day. He told Flangelo, Kender, Targa, and Cassaro to join him the next morning for breakfast. Flangelo quietly chirped something about hoping there were no eggs there, but Gilio ignored him.

This left me with some downtime, and I wondered what to do. What could I do? How many times would I have to ask myself that? My job, I was realizing, was an exercise in admitting my own helplessness.

This never bothered me before when chronicling Simon Bloom's life; in fact, there was a certain amount of satisfaction in knowing I had no responsibilities besides watching.

But now . . . now I wanted to be a part of it all. To do something useful. Or, at the very least, to understand more about what was going on. Frankly, it was embarrassing to be almost as clueless as those I watched.

As if in response to my wishes, my Viewing Screen changed

scenes. Something was happening. Something important. To celebrate the occasion, I popped two pieces of different flavored gum in my mouth. I took a moment to appreciate why no company had ever marketed peppermint-banana gum, paused to spit out the poorly chosen combo, and watched the new scene take form.

CHAPTER 39

ᗩᑎOTᕼEᖇ ᛁᑎK ᑕOᗰᛁᑎG

The image shifted to a place I could barely see, which was odd; the Screen had gizmos to counter lighting problems. It should even let me see infrared, ultraviolet, and other wavelengths of light not in the visible spectrum.

Now, though, I could make out a large room with heavy shadows. Several people walked into the room, but the darkness persisted; I could only see shapes.

"Let's get this over with, LaCurru," said a familiar, gruff thirteen-year-old girl.

The lights went on, revealing many devices with dials and wires; rubber tubes; glass vials and beakers with colorful liquids; and metal: tables, stools . . . even chains. It was a place decorated with style in mind, assuming that style was "Mad Scientist's Lab."

Sirabetta, Aleadra, and two men entered. One man was average height and average weight with no hair on his head. Not only was he bald . . . but he also had no eyebrows or eyelashes. His skin was so white that most Narrators would call it alabaster or porcelain.

That wasn't enough for my descriptive tastes; I'd say he was a full moon made flesh. Polished ivory crossbred with an albino rat fed a strict diet of white paint. Just to underline my point, I'll add some adverbs: the man was luminously, gleamingly, blindingly pale. His eyes, by the way, were chestnut brown.

There was a gleam in those brown eyes that made the man seem a bit off. Unstable, in an active volcano sort of way. That barely maintained sanity, coupled with the assorted lab devices around the room, led me to believe he really was a mad scientist.

That, and the white lab coat he wore. Always a dead giveaway.

The other man stayed by the doorway, cloaked in shadow. Usually not the sign of a warm and sunny personality. I could tell he was tall, thin, and not afraid of the dark.

The mad scientist—LaCurru—gestured to a cushioned table, like in a doctor's examination room. He used a sheet of tissue paper from a thick roll to cover it.

Sirabetta climbed up, dressed in a sleeveless shirt and a pair of shorts. It took me a moment to realize what was strange about that sight. Then it hit me—I was seeing bare skin. Her tattoos were gone!

"Removing the old tattoos was simple for someone of my talent and knowledge," LaCurru said. "My esteemed Keeper Lombaro couldn't have done it," he muttered, "yet *my* special solvent made short work of them." He frowned. "Putting new ones on will be challenging, even for *me*. It'll be a long night, Sir; brace yourself for more pain."

"We've done this before," Sirabetta said. "It's a pain I know well. Just make sure you do it right. Aleadra, be ready to do your part: make sure they adhere to my skin and attach to my nervous system properly. And make the changes we talked about."

The ageless woman nodded. "I've done it before, too. Remember, we both have special gifts from him." She gestured to the figure still standing in shadow. "But can your thirteen-year-old form handle the strain? With the changes you want, these are going to hurt a lot more than before. Especially when you use them."

Sirabetta clenched her teeth. "Oh, I'll handle it. I have even more reason to bear the suffering than I did before. And remember," Sirabetta said to LaCurru, "arrange them the way I said."

"Maybe we don't have to do this. Are you sure our forces failed?" Aleadra asked.

"I've gotten word from Willoughby Wanderby," the thin, tall man said from the shadows in a cold and emotionless voice. "The others were captured, but he escaped."

"I knew before Wanderby called in," Sirabetta said. She

noted LaCurru's puzzled look. "An ability left over from my days in the Order of Psychology."

"That sounds useful," LaCurru said. "How does it work?"

"I can displace my consciousness," Sirabetta answered. "Send part of my awareness somewhere else. It came in handy both times the Union wiped my memories, though I needed help bringing them back. It also lets me sense what's happening beyond where my physical form is. That's really hard to do, though, and it doesn't always work. But it was enough to let me watch part of the brats' battle with our forces."

"You always were a marvel," the hidden man said. Once again his voice was flat, but there might have been a hint of something . . . pride, perhaps? "But surely Bloom and his friends will guess you'd go to Chemistry? It's the rational next step."

"Not everyone is as rigidly logical as you," Sirabetta said. "And the captured Biology members didn't know the plan. Now, have you brought what I need?"

The thin man nodded and handed several sheets of paper to LaCurru. The mad scientist took them gingerly . . . even fearfully . . . though it wasn't clear if he was afraid of the papers or the man handing them over. Or both.

"Is that all you need from me?" the shadowy man asked.

LaCurru nodded. "Yes, thank you. I wouldn't have needed to bother you at all, but the old papers disintegrated after I tattooed her last time."

"As it must be," the other man responded emotionlessly.

"These are only meant to be used as backups for the Books. There are many in my organization who wouldn't approve of our using these papers for this purpose. If they were even to discover I'd taken them, it would be a disaster. At least before we're ready."

LaCurru nodded. "I was wondering about the other Board—"

"Never refer to them aloud," the shadowy man said, his voice extra cold.

"Of course not!" LaCurru said quickly. "My apologies."

"It is unwise to mention them—it might draw their attention." While the man's voice had been emotionless before, it somehow became even more so, like something lifeless managing to die twice over. "It is bad enough that I had to return here. See to it that I never have to again."

"Enough chatting, gentleman," Sirabetta said, irritation plain in her voice. "I have some suffering to do . . . before I can share it with others."

LaCurru gulped and held up one of the pages he'd gotten from the hidden man. "We'll start with this one," he said. With his other hand he picked up what resembled a yellow, thick-handled pen with a sharp, yellow, glowing point. He touched the point of the pen onto the surface of the paper, and the tip became multicolored.

"Sir, please give me your palm," LaCurru said.

Sirabetta closed her eyes, and Aleadra put her hands on

her shoulders, ready to aid the process. The pen was about to touch Sirabetta's palm when she clenched it into a fist.

"Wait—I'm sensing something!" Sirabetta said. She opened her eyes. "It's Bloom's Narrator—he's watching us!"

"Are you certain?" the thin man asked from the shadows.

Sirabetta nodded. "I started to detach my awareness to help deal with the pain the tattooing would bring. I felt his presence; he's narrating all this."

"I don't have a shielding device, has he seen me?" the shadowy man asked.

"I don't know," Sirabetta said. "LaCurru designed this lab to be able to block out spies; it should at least limit the Historical Society. But you'd better go, to be safe."

The man backed into the doorway and pulled out what looked like an ordinary clipboard. He tapped it a few times with a thin, black stick. "Very well. You have all the tools you need for your mission, Sirabetta. Do not fail again." He tapped the clipboard again and disappeared in a flash of multicolored light.

"I don't trust him," Aleadra said.

"You should've thought of that thirty-three years ago," Sirabetta said.

"Nobody likes a smart aleck," Aleadra said.

"I don't trust him either, but he's serving our purpose. When we're done, will it matter?" Sirabetta angled her head so she was looking right at me, and then she glared. "But first, our observer has gotten too much information as it is; I'll have him taken care of soon. For now, block him out, LaCurru, and then get back to work on my tattoos."

LaCurru reached for a switch on the wall. "Yes, Sir," he said. Then he flipped the switch, and I was left staring at the blank Viewing Screen.

Sirabetta had two more allies, and she was about to get her tattoos back! Plus she could sense me, and one of her allies had a way to block my narrating abilities!

I was shaking. From confusion? From worry? From fear? All of them, I realized. And, of course, the usual helplessness.

"Not this time," I whispered to myself. I had an idea—a way that might save Simon and his friends. And, as so often was the case, salvation rested with pizza.

CHAPTER 40

DEFINITELY NOT THIRTY MINUTES OR LESS

It was Friday morning; Simon and his friends were at Gilio's, chatting over the remains of breakfast.

Kender, no longer in his exoskeleton, looked sheepishly at his Keeper. "Sorry to say, Gilio, but there were plenty of rumors of dissent in the Order."

"I've been a fool," Gilio said with a shake of his head. "I've long suspected this but did nothing. Clearly I've isolated my-self too much from my people."

"Most of the traitors were new members," Targa said. "Maybe because they hadn't fully established loyalties to you yet?"

"Makes sense," Flangelo said. "New members usually only have one Biology ability and could be greedy for more."

"Doesn't explain Preto, though," Gilio grumbled. "He's

been a member since before I was Keeper. I even taught him that silly half-man, half-manta form."

"How did you infiltrate the traitors?" Flangelo asked Kender, Targa, and Cassaro.

"It was easy once we found out kids were in the dome," Targa said.

"There are lots of toadstools in the grasslands they walked through," Cassaro said. He noticed the kids' perplexed looks. "Oh, I'm able to sense things through fungi."

"Right, so we knew you were here and exactly where you were," Targa said.

"And none of the Order members has their kids living in the domain," Kender added. He nodded to Simon, Alysha, and Owen. "Union rules: no parents can tell their children about their secret until they're of age and have passed certain Union tests."

"That's a stupid rule," Alysha said.

"Yeah," Owen said. "Just because we're not allowed to drive or do fancy grown-up stuff doesn't mean kids can't do a lot of other things!"

"Indeed," Gilio said. "A pity your talents don't include grammar or syntax."

"So we still don't know who controlled the mammoths and oryx?" Simon asked.

"As I said before, nobody in my Order should be able to," Gilio said.

"A lady sent different insects after us, and there was that gibbon guy," Owen said.

"Demara's *communication* ability only lets her control insects," Gilio said. "And Najolo can command gibbons because he can transform into an alpha of their species. A leader. It's the same with Flangelo; when you last fought Sirabetta, he was able to command sparrows in Dunkerhook Woods because he took the role as alpha of their flock. If he found a flock of emu, he'd be able to do the same."

"Maybe it's this *her* that Kender heard the traitors talking about," Simon said.

"Can't you make the prisoners tell you?" Alysha asked.

"You can't go around shoving a handful of electricity into everyone's face demanding information," Gilio said. "Besides, a Board member took the traitors away last night, soon after I contacted them. Which is odd—the Board is usually slow, with maddening procedures and paperwork. I thought it would be days before they came."

"The BOA will tell you if they find out anything, right?" Owen asked.

"One would hope," Gilio said.

A tapping sound came from a window at the far end of the dining room. Gilio walked over and spoke quietly with the source: a large sunflower leaning over from the garden. A moment later, Gilio returned to the table.

"That's . . . interesting," he said. "I have animals patrolling the beaches near the dome. They keep an eye out for nosy Outsiders or suspicious-acting Union members that haven't been invited."

"Except Sirabetta," Alysha said.

Gilio ignored her. "A seagull sent word through the chain of command: an item was left on the beach at the exact spot the X was left for you three."

"What was it?" Simon asked.

"A pizza box, prepaid and delivered from a pizzeria in the nearest town." He frowned. "That's going to raise suspicions; I'll move the dome by midday."

"So someone left a pizza on the beach, big deal," Alysha said.

"Ah, but this pizza had black olives carefully placed to spell out: 'Simon, hurry: visit Narrator'," Gilio said. "Take note, Owen Walters—they even had anchovies for punctuation."

Simon coughed on the juice he was drinking. "It's Greygor!" He ignored Gilio's puzzled expression and turned to the people at the table. "Anyone up for a trip to New Jersey?"

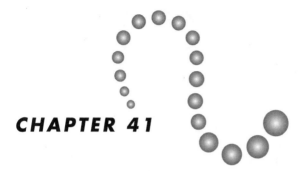

CHAPTER 41

Iꜰ Tʜɪꜱ Kᴇᴇᴩꜱ Uᴩ, I'ʟʟ Nᴇᴇᴅ ᴀ Bɪɢɢᴇʀ Aᴩᴀʀᴛᴍᴇɴᴛ

"I'm glad you've already eaten," I said as I opened the door. "There's not enough pizza in the world to feed you lot. Now come in quickly before my neighbors complain that I'm having a party."

I shut my door behind the group as they shuffled in. I sensed the newcomers' disapproval of my garb. "This bathrobe is standard issue for all Narrators."

Flangelo raised his eyebrows. "If you say so," he trilled. "Is that also your excuse for this layout?' he asked, gesturing to the interior of my apartment.

"If you have a problem with my decor, you may perch outside on the windowsill."

Flangelo frowned but said nothing. Score one for Greygor!

There were a few awkward moments as the four Biology

members gaped in astonishment at the sight of themselves and the rest of us on my Viewing Screen. Then Kender broke the tension. "Can you get basketball on this?"

"Not really what it's for," Alysha said. "But I'll let you in on a little secret: when he's not doing a Chronicle, the answer is yes!"

I sighed. It was true; when the kids weren't making me re-play their exploits, they were getting me to show their favor-ite movies or the latest sporting events. Alysha was definitely a scream–at–the–television sort of sports watcher, too.

Simon made the necessary introductions between the Bi-ology members and me, but, of course, they weren't necessary for *me*. I was, as ever, the perfect host, welcoming them into my home with refreshments and access to my knowledge. Of course, some people have a one–track mind.

"Hey, Greygor, can we watch some highlights?" Owen asked. "I want to see the fights!" He turned to Kender, who'd won the recliner debate. "We fought these giant elephants. What were they again, Flangelo?"

Flangelo warbled with exasperation. "Columbian mamm-moths. Big, mean, smelly. Ho–hum. Can we discuss something besides the dumbos beating up the Dumbos? Such as why we've been summoned here?"

Flangelo's snarky way was even more difficult when it was aimed at me, but he was right: I had much to tell them.

"I have much to tell you," I said.

Kender, seated in my recliner, leaned forward to look at

the Recording Monitor. "There it is, just like you said, Owen," he said, touching the screen.

"Do you mind?" I asked as I stomped over to him and turned the Monitor away from him. "If our speed-talker has told you of the Monitor, he's surely told you I don't like people reading as I narrate."

Kender, for lack of a better word, sulked as he settled back into my chair.

I told them what they needed to hear (leaving out my conversation with Miss Fanstrom, of course). I revealed Loisana's suspicious behavior, I shared the identity of the mysterious *her* who was allied with Sirabetta and how she had failed to restore Sirabetta's age, and I told them where I last saw Sirabetta and Aleadra: the Order of Chemistry.

"A former Biology Keeper?" Alysha asked.

"How can we fight a Keeper?" Owen asked. "Isn't she all-powerful?"

"Doesn't sound like she's a Keeper anymore," Simon said.

"Right," Alysha said. "Don't they lose their powers or something?"

"Officially, when they give up their Book they do give up most—if not all—of their formulas," I said. "Their names are crossed off the Book's Keeper list, and they shouldn't be able to communicate with the Book at all."

"When I met the *Teacher's Edition of Biology*," Simon said, "I felt Gilio's mind linked to it. But I didn't feel anyone else's. Unless she's got a way of hiding that."

"To do what she did with Sirabetta, she must have had substantial Biology abilities," I said. "More than any retired Keeper should. Aleadra said the man in the shadows was connected to Sirabetta getting her tattoos and her abilities, too."

"Great," Owen said. "We have at least two enemies who can break the rules of the Union and do whatever they want, and *another* mystery guy who hates us."

"I did research Aleadra, though," I added, walking over to my bookshelf. I took down the proper volume dealing with the Council of Sciences. "She was Keeper right before Gilio and retired about thirty years ago." I rubbed my chin. "She stepped down willingly like Ralfagon; the official record states that she claimed she had personal matters to tend to. Sorry to be so vague, but that's all it says."

"That could mean anything," Simon said.

"There is a footnote," I said. "It's just a rumor, though. Supposedly, she became involved with someone in a position of great power and responsibility."

"Maybe our mystery guy?" Owen said.

I shrugged. "I couldn't say. That's all I was able to find out."

"Okay, now what?" Alysha asked.

"We can go to the Order of Chemistry to get her," Simon said.

"Keeper Olvero Lombaro's a good guy; he'll help us," Targa said. "I know him from my Chemistry orientation—my formula's technically Bio-chemistry, you know."

"There's a problem," I said. "I don't know where at Chemistry they were; the Order is spread throughout a big city with many places to hide and plenty of ways to flee quickly. It would be harder to search than Biology's dome."

Targa nodded, confirming this.

"Then what do we do to stop these guys?" Targa asked.

"*We?*" Alysha asked. "Are you guys volunteering?"

"You kidding? That fight was ka–razy; I can't wait for the next one!"

Kender chuckled. "Ironic, isn't it? Targa's an adrenaline junkie. As for me, I can muster up a fresh shell. I'm sure I can be of some help."

"Don't know what good a bunch of mushrooms will be," Cassaro said. "But I'll do what I can."

"And you'd be helpless without me," Flangelo chirped.

"Now we just need to find someone to point your beak at," Alysha said.

"I've been thinking about that," Simon said. "I can still sense Sirabetta with my space–time connection. Not well enough to pinpoint her exact location, but maybe there's a way to pull on that link and bring her here."

"You're kidding!" Alysha said. "Couldn't you have thought of that before we traveled through Biology and fought every-one and everything inside?"

"It's tricky," Simon said. "I'm thinking about something called a wormhole: it's like a tube between two spots in space and time that can take you long distances very quickly. It's not as neat as the Gateways or the Biology pools, but hey, teleportation's teleportation, right? Problem is, I still don't know much about the formula."

"Besides," Owen asked, "would it even work so far away from her?"

Simon's mind raced with ideas about the space–time continuum: the complex network of space and time that enveloped the entire universe.

What do you say, Book? he asked mentally. *Is there a way to reach her?*

Simon tuned out the noise in my apartment while he waited long moments for a response. Finally, the Book answered. *With the level of control you have, it will be difficult. Given your power over gravity and space-time, there are ways, but they must be for you to think of, Keeper. For you to figure out. And they will be dangerous.*

Simon thought about it. He knew Einstein's theory that gravity was caused by curves in the space–time continuum. He also knew gravity could reach anywhere in the galaxy— maybe beyond. It wasn't as strong at large distances, but it should be enough to locate and grab Sirabetta.

Then he thought of the place where he'd first forged that space–time connection to Sirabetta. It would be the best place to do what he had in mind: poke a hole in the space– time continuum, then send a gravitational pull along space– time, dragging Sirabetta through the hole to where he was waiting.

Simon nodded to himself; it was as good a place for a

fight as any. "This might not work, but it's worth a try. And if it does work, we won't have to worry about Aleadra or any other of Sirabetta's buddies. We'll have her—alone—against all of us."

One by one the members of the group nodded or spoke their agreement. Simon, Alysha, Flangelo, and I all stared at Owen when he said yes.

"What?" Owen asked. "It sounds like a good plan to me. It's not like *I'm* the one being teleported!"

"Good luck to you all," I said. "I wish I could go with you and help."

"It's been nice meeting you," Targa said, clapping me on the shoulder.

"This has been . . . interesting," Kender said. "We never even knew Biology had a Narrator, much less had a chance to meet him."

"Your Narrator is a *she*, I believe," I said. "I've never met her, but she's surely observing us right now." They all looked around in a rather useless attempt to spot her. "I suppose you Biology folk are welcome to visit again. I've given up on try-ing to stop Simon, Owen, and Alysha . . . I might as well not even bother with you lot."

Simon turned to Owen, Alysha, and Flangelo. "Okay then—we'll just make a quick stop at the junkyard, and then I think it's time to introduce our new friends to Dunkerhook Woods."

CHAPTER 42

SOMETIMES NOTHING IS BETTER THAN SOMETHING

The group stopped just inside the entrance to Dunkerhook Woods, basking in the soothing Breeze and the energizing air that filled the place. Targa, Kender, and Cassaro stood in awe at their first entrance into the woods.

"It's like nothing I've ever seen before," Kender said.

"And that air! It's like super-epinephrine that you can inhale!" Targa said.

"And look at all the incredible mushrooms!" Cassaro said, pointing off the path. The others gave him a strange look. "Fungi are my thing," he said with a shrug.

Alysha and Flangelo shared a look of disgust.

"Come on, let's get moving," Simon said. "We've got to prepare for this if we're going to get it right." They hurried along, with Alysha and Owen carrying duffel bags that clanked as they moved.

They hadn't gotten far before finding they weren't alone in the woods; a woman was waiting for them.

"Loisana!" Simon, Owen, and Alysha shouted at the same time. They spread out, ready for a fight. The Biology members reacted more slowly but did the same. I was pleased to see they were heeding my warnings about Loisana's possible nasty intentions.

"Hey, guys," Loisana said. "What's wrong with you?"

"Wrong with us?" Alysha asked, generating a threatening electrical arc between her outstretched hands. "What about you?"

"What?" Loisana asked, taking a step back. "What do you mean?"

Simon stared. "Kind of convenient that you happened to be here."

"Yeah," Owen growled. "Who are you working for and what do you want?"

Loisana leveled an uncomfortable glance at the Biology members. "What are you talking about? And who are these guys? They're not Outsiders, are they?"

"We're asking the questions here," Alysha said. "Why are you stalking us?"

Loisana put her hands in front of her in a "take it easy" gesture. "I have been waiting for you, but I swear I'm not up to anything sinister."

"I don't trust her," Targa said.

"You don't have to believe me," Loisana said. "You can ask the person who asked me to watch out for you." She carefully reached into her pocket and pulled out her cell phone. "Call the last number dialed," she said.

Simon snagged the phone with a gravity arm, whipping it through the air to his hand. He did as she requested and was surprised to hear a familiar voice.

"Er, hello?"

"Ralfagon?" Simon said. "You sent Loisana after us?"

"After you what?" Ralfagon said through the phone. "Oh, you mean to follow you? Yes, my boy. I needed to observe you, and my skills at surveillance aren't what they used to be."

"It's one thing to go all private when you're chatting with the *Teacher's Editions*," Alysha said. "But maybe you can share this with us?"

"Sorry," Simon said. He pressed the speakerphone button on Loisana's cell phone. "What were you saying, Ralfagon?"

"What *was* I saying?" he replied.

"Needed to observe me," Simon prompted.

"Ah, yes. How else was I to know if you were ready to take over as Keeper? I asked Loisana to practice with you to see your leadership skills in as natural a setting as possible: with your friends. You did beautifully."

"Wait a second," Targa said. "How do we know someone's not pretending to be this Ralfagon guy?"

"I assume you're from the Order of Biology," Ralfagon said. "Would you like me to discuss some of your Keeper's habits? Such as how Gilio always wants to watch *It Came from Beneath the Sea* each time there's an Order movie night?"

"Anybody could have told you that!" Kender said.

"Told me what?" Ralfagon asked.

"It's Ralfagon," Simon, Owen, and Alysha said at the same time.

"Told you," Loisana said.

"That's great," Alysha said. "So why is she here now?"

"After you took over as Keeper, I asked Loisana to offer her help to you," Ralfagon said. "She missed the Gateway to Biology, though, and I figured it was better for her to wait here than to try finding you in *that* place. I get lost almost every time I go there. I'd have joined her in person, but I'm supposed to keep a low profile until the meeting with the Board this Sunday. I could risk it if you feel you'd need my aid."

"No, but thanks, Ralfagon," Simon said. He thought of how much faith Ralfagon had shown in his leadership and his control. "For everything."

"My boy, it's my pleasure. Be careful, though I know you'll do well. I look forward to hearing the whole story later."

Simon hung up the phone and floated it back to Loisana. "Sorry I doubted you."

"You can't be too careful these days," she said. "So what's going on?"

Simon introduced her to the visiting Bio members and shared their plan.

"You're bringing Sirabetta here to fight?" Loisana asked. "Is that wise?"

"Even if she has her powers back, we outnumber her," Simon said.

"We have the element of surprise," Alysha said.

"But her allies? A former Keeper?" Loisana asked.

"They won't even know what happened; she'll disappear and reappear here, leaving them behind," Simon said.

"I'll stick around, if you don't mind. An extra formula pitching in couldn't hurt."

"Sure, why not." Simon said. He wasn't too worried about Loisana's lack of battle experience; after all, he figured this would be a quick and easy fight.

They continued along the path until they reached the spot where Simon had turned Sirabetta into a thirteen-year-old. "Here we go," he said.

Kender generated his exoskeleton and stood between the target spot and the path to the entrance, ready to nab Sirabetta if she tried to run.

Cassaro spat out a cloud of spores on either side of the path and speed-grew them into huge mushrooms that would block Sirabetta from dashing into the forest.

Targa used her adrenaline powers to boost Simon, who'd

need a lot of focus if he was going to make this space–time twist work.

Flangelo changed to emu form, ready to kick or head–butt as needed.

Alysha continued to draw in electrical energy from the air around her, storing up as much as she could muster. She wouldn't mess with plasma; she didn't want to risk any damage to the woods. Instead, she took two handfuls of assorted metal pieces out of the duffel bag she was carrying. There was plenty more to grab, if needed; she'd filled the bag at the town junkyard.

Owen stood between the path and the clearing. He took some metal rods and several small but heavy appliances from his and Alysha's duffel bags, also gathered from the junkyard near his house. He could use them to batter or at least distract Sirabetta if she tried to flee through the other end of the woods.

Loisana positioned herself alongside the trees. She turned some of the moisture in the air into water, letting it flood across the ground. Zeroing in on the area where they expected Sirabetta to appear, she froze the water into a thin sheet of ice. When Sirabetta materialized there, she'd lose her footing on the slippery ground.

Simon surged with intensity from Targa's influence. He stood a few feet apart from everyone else so he could better concentrate on his space–time control. "In case we can't knock her out quickly, make sure she can't see those tattoos," he said. "She can only use one at a time and can't use them if they're covered."

The group braced themselves, ready to pounce on their foe. I had to admit, leaning forward on my recliner, it was a great plan. I wished I had time to make popcorn.

Simon closed his eyes and activated his space-time formula. He concentrated on the memory of that tingling feeling that stemmed from Sirabetta's altered form.

Keeping that sensation in mind, Simon narrowed his attention so he was more intent on space than time. He imagined a thin, limitless rope extended between him and Sirabetta, using that one spot on the path as ground zero for it.

Then, with all the intensity he could gather in mind and body, he yanked the rope.

Nothing happened.

A few minutes passed.

Still nothing.

A few more minutes passed.

By now, the nothing was getting quite good at its job. It seemed smug somehow.

Flangelo shifted from emu to human. "Can we assume this isn't how it's supposed to work?"

Simon frowned. "I don't understand. I felt it. I felt the connection and I pulled on it. It should have worked!"

"Hey, it's a new technique," Alysha said. "It's not like turning friction on or off. You might need a few tries to get it right."

"Yeah, remember how long it took to get good at plain old gravity?" Owen asked.

"Okay," Simon said. "Give me a few more minutes to work on this." He closed his eyes and pictured what he wanted to do in his mind again. Then he clapped his hands together and rubbed them, exhaled, and opened his eyes. "This time it'll work."

Once again, about fifteen minutes after the first attempt, Simon pictured the rope of space-time, the distance it covered, and then the pulling. He visualized the air ripping open and Sirabetta falling through it, only to plop onto the ice patch and into their trap.

The nothing did its equivalent of saying *nyeah-nyeah* as Sirabetta, rather stubbornly, I thought, persisted in not appearing.

"Maybe I need more rest," Simon said. "Maybe I should reread that section of the Book. Get more clues on how to do this." He reached into his backpack for the Book.

And that's when everything exploded.

CHAPTER 43

BRUTALITY AND JUSTICE FOR ALL

The air in the middle of the group burst apart with a deafening *boom*, flinging them in all directions. Most of their falls were cushioned by the giant mushrooms lining the path.

Simon, positioned far from mushrooms or friends, wasn't so lucky. He was launched up into the trees, smacking through dozens of branches before disappearing from sight. Moments later, he could be heard crashing down, branch by branch, and then striking the ground with a wrenching thud somewhere deep in the forest.

"This place brings back memories." Thirteen-year-old Sirabetta strutted down the path toward them. She wore a jet-black wet suit that let her show off the assortment of perfectly formed tattoos on her arms and legs—gone were the days where she had to hide them. She was also soaking wet, which made the wet suit a practical choice of clothing.

And she wasn't alone. Preto, Krissantha, and Aleadra—similarly drenched—walked behind her as she approached the scattered Physics and Biology members.

Sirabetta didn't bother to hide her triumphant grin as she addressed her stunned enemies. "Funny thing: there I was, thousands of miles away, when I felt this buzzing. Like an alarm in my head and body, telling me *exactly* where Simon Bloom was."

I groaned as I realized that Simon hadn't worked his formula properly. Instead of teleporting Sirabetta, he had only managed to alert her.

"A quick Gateway trip, a soaking from the Union's trusty rainstorm, and here we were. Only fifteen minutes, door to door. Back to good ol' Dunkerhook Woods."

She scanned the faces of the fallen. "Hmm. Was my attack too rough for poor Bloom?" She looked off into the forest. "I'll scrape him off the ground when we're done with you all." She rubbed her hands together. "I've been looking forward to this."

Kender, protected by his shell, was the least affected by the blast. He'd been knocked down but rose and stood between his enemies and his friends. "So you're the famous Sirabetta. You don't look so tough."

"Really?" Sirabetta asked. Five feet tall and slender, Sir gave a sweet smile to the seven-foot-plus, massively armored man. She thrust an arm out and pointed to a silver tattoo. It was one of her favorite weapons—from the Order of Astronomy.

"Does this help?" she asked and read the tattoo aloud. It glowed brightly and a pulsating, grapefruit-size ball of silvery light shot from her outstretched hand. The searing globe was made of the same stuff as a star: it was superhot and devastatingly powerful. It streaked through the woods, covering the twenty feet to Kender in a second, and detonated in a burst of silver-white fire across his right side.

Kender was sent spinning up and back through the air before striking some trees with a loud crash. He rose to his feet unsteadily; the part of the shell covering his right side had been destroyed.

"I guess I'm out of practice," Sirabetta said. "The next one'll do the trick." She hesitated; one more star-ball would probably kill him. Was she ready to get blood on her hands? Then she reminded herself that these hands were just part of the misery these people had heaped onto her. *Yes*, she thought darkly. *It's time for them to die.*

Before she could act, the tall, bearded one heaved himself up to his knees and spat a cloud of tiny dots that enveloped her. Sirabetta shrieked with disgust as she saw they were mushrooms and with pain from the sting of them latching onto her flesh. The multiple fungi began growing instantly, gaining length and depth with every passing second.

They weren't fast enough, though. Sirabetta quickly regained her composure and read from a blue tattoo on one arm; the tattoo glowed brightly and a burst of intense heat incinerated all the mushrooms on her.

"A giant bug-man and a mushroom-spitter," she said with a snort. "Is this the band of warriors trying to keep me from my destiny?"

Preto and Krissantha laughed while Aleadra looked on stone-faced. "Before you get overconfident . . . the others are recovering, too."

Sirabetta looked over; the skinny bird-man, Flangelo, and the short, velocity-wielding boy, Owen, were rising. She didn't know the two women with them, but she recognized the girl, Alysha, stirring beside them.

"Not a problem," Sirabetta said, her voice almost maniacally cheery.

"No," Alysha snarled. "It's a problem." She threw a handful of sparking metal pieces on and in front of Sirabetta; they exploded and raised a huge cloud of dirt.

Sirabetta coughed and waved her hands to clear the air, but she was laughing. "Stupid, stupid, stupid, Lite Brite. Did you forget I'm electricity proof?" She pointed to a glowing half-yellow, half-green tattoo on her left shin; it was a biochemical tattoo she'd chosen for complete insulation.

"Forget? No. Care? Nope," Alysha rasped. "Ever hear of a distraction?"

As Sirabetta and her allies finished waving away the dust and debris from the attack, they found a surprise. Though the redheaded woman was still sprawled on the ground and Simon had not returned, most of their opponents had gotten to their feet.

"I remember how tricky and persistent you were," Sirabetta said. "This time, no more asking for what I want. No more offers of surrender."

"No problem," Owen said through gritted teeth.

Sirbetta snapped her fingers at her allies. "Get them."

Aleadra stood to the side, folding her arms, as if she was just going to observe. But Preto reacted right away, changing into his half-man, half-manta ray form and gliding on wing-like fins toward his enemies. Flangelo shifted into emu form and stepped in front of him, letting out an emu roar and fluttering his tiny, flightless wings. Preto let out a keening wail and swooped at the large bird.

They collided, and Flangelo was thrown back by the more massive, faster-moving attacker. He got to his feet quickly and let out a booming challenge in emu language: the equivalent of telling Preto his mother smelled funny.

Preto swiped one of his wings at Flangelo's head; Flangelo ducked under it, but Preto lashed out with his tail and yanked Flangelo off his feet.

Kender rushed to attack Preto, but Krissantha blocked him.

"I warned you before," she said. She swiftly darted to his side and grabbed his armored leg while activating her hydrogen bond–formula. The chitin that made up Kender's exoskeleton started to dissolve, exposing his flesh-and-blood leg underneath. His human leg was much shorter, so Kender had to balance on his still-armored leg to keep from falling.

Kender swung an armored fist at her, but Krissantha was too quick. She ducked under the attack and tapped his arm. That part of his shell began to crumble, too. He had minutes—at most—before his armor was gone. Then she would start in on his body.

Cassaro spat a cloud of spores at Krissantha, but her formula made them disintegrate upon touching her. Aleadra nodded silently, still just watching.

Owen used velocity to launch numerous metal rods at Krissantha and Preto, but Sirabetta used her air pressure formula to knock the missiles off into the woods. Then Owen used his power to send Sirabetta zooming toward the nearest thick tree, which brought a frown to Aleadra's face.

There was no need for her to take action—Sirabetta had a counter for Owen's attack. She read a blue tattoo and grunted from the sudden stop as the formula, based on balancing energies of motion, opposed Owen's.

"Did you forget that I can resist your silly formula?" she shouted while hovering.

Owen smirked and used velocity to launch four rusted toasters at her. "No, but did *you* forget that you can use only one tattoo at a time?"

Bobbing in mid-air, Sirabetta fired a quartet of glowing star-balls in succession, destroying the flying appliances one-by-one.

Owen's jaw dropped. "You used two tattoos at once!" he moaned.

"That's right," Sirabetta said. "I got an upgrade when I had my tattoos replaced."

Owen didn't respond, he just disappeared from sight.

Aleadra wrinkled her nose. "Someone's been learning octopus-camouflage. That won't do at all." She wiggled her fingers, and Owen suddenly became partially visible. He looked down and gulped; stripes of visibility ran up and down his body, making him all too easy to spot.

Sirabetta read another tattoo, generating a beach ball–size globe of multicolored light in front of Owen. He used his velocity control to fling it into the woods, but the damage was done; the boy blinked furiously, his vision surely filled with spots.

Alysha, meanwhile, flared her nostrils and jet propelled over to Krissantha, one outstretched hand crackling with electricity. "Hang on, Kender, I'm coming!"

"Another octopus trait . . . jet propulsion through your nose, hmm?" Aleadra said. "How creative. But tell me, do you have any allergies?" She wiggled her fingers.

Alysha's shocking touch was inches from Krissantha when she suddenly scrunched her face up. "Oh n—" was all she managed to say before she let loose a huge sneeze that sent her flying ten feet backward. "You think that's going to st—?" And then another sneeze ripped out, shooting her off into another direction.

"There's little about Biology that I can't manipulate, child," Aleadra said.

"Try Physics," Loisana said, at last recovered enough to fight. She turned the moisture in the air to water and doused Aleadra. Then she froze the water, encasing Aleadra in ever-thickening ice. Loisana then turned to Krissantha, changing the dirt beneath her to its liquid form—like quicksand, but faster-acting. Krissantha sank fast, clutching uselessly at the liquefied ground.

Kender gasped with relief that Krissantha's attack had stopped; almost his entire exoskeleton had been stripped away. He'd need time to rest before he could grow another one, but there seemed little chance of that.

Preto turned at the sound of Krissantha's and Aleadra's screams, giving Flangelo–emu an opening. The giant bird sprang up and sent a spinning kick to Preto's midsection, knocking the wind out of the larger being. Flangelo followed up with a hard smack of his beak into Preto's forehead. The half–man, half–manta staggered back.

Flangelo spun around, ready to finish Preto off with a kick to the head, but Sirabetta was faster. She shot a fiery star–ball at him; though the emu jumped back to avoid getting blown up, the star–ball exploded underneath him and catapulted him backward. Loisana quickly changed water vapor to water around Flangelo, probably dousing him to make sure his feathers weren't on fire.

While Loisana was distracted, Sirabetta used her heat-generating tattoo to thaw the frozen Aleadra, and Preto pulled Krissantha out of the ultraquicksand. Sirabetta used her air pressure tattoo to cause an explosion between Loisana and Flangelo, knocking both out.

Owen used velocity to smack Krissantha into Preto, distracting Preto and stunning Krissantha.

"Enough of your tricks," Sirabetta said to Owen. She wavered in midair before she could strike, though. "What's . . . happening . . . to . . . me . . . ?" she moaned. She felt a crushing weariness wash over her, making her slowly sink to the path.

Aleadra fixed Targa with a look. "Using epinephrine? We can't have that, can we?" she muttered. She wiggled her fingers, redirecting Targa's formula onto Owen, who slumped forward with exhaustion. Sirabetta sprang to her feet, her strength restored.

Cassaro spat a cloud of spores at Aleadra, but with a slash of her hand she deflected them onto Targa. Targa shrieked and started smacking at the tiny fungi now clinging to her while Cassaro's jaw dropped in surprise.

Preto used one of his fin-wings to slam Cassaro to the dirt, unconscious, then turned and did the same to the unarmored Kender.

"Who's left?" Sirabetta asked with glee. This was more fun than she'd hoped.

Owen struggled to stay awake, but his heart rate kept slowing until he finally sank to the dirt with a whimper and passed out.

Alysha, out of sight among the trees, let out another sneeze and a pained groan as she crashed through some bushes. Aleadra wiggled her fingers, and Alysha's next sneeze was huge, smacking her into a massive tree trunk. She flopped to the ground, out cold.

"Then there was one," Sirabetta said, pointing to Targa. "Battle's over, sweetie."

Targa was frantically tearing at Cassaro's mini mushrooms. She looked up at the enemies opposing her and backed away, her big blue eyes growing larger with fear.

Preto moved in from one direction and Krissantha came from another. But Preto wailed as he was suddenly jerked into the air by an unseen force. Krissantha shrieked as she was dragged forward, her feet leaving grooves in the dirt. Aleadra wrinkled her nose and started to look around before she too was grabbed by something invisible.

Sirabetta had time to open her mouth in protest before she felt crushing pressure wrapped around her body like a giant snake. She knew who it must be—Bloom, ambushing her with some strange gravity attack. She managed to activate the formula that gave her power over kinetic and potential energy—the same one that let her resist Owen's velocity—and used it to break free of the boy's grip.

Aleadra strained to pull that unseeable something away

from her neck. "It's like an octopus, but different," she gasped. "I can barely resist it. Help me, Sara Beth!"

The unseen force smashed Preto into a tree, and he collapsed, unconscious. It also slammed Krissantha face-first into the dirt, leaving her crumpled in a heap.

Aleadra tried to speak, but she could only manage strangling sounds; her clothes rumpled, as if something—or several somethings—were constricting around her. With Krissantha and Preto out of the way, perhaps the attack on her grew stronger—it was clearly getting past her defenses.

Sirabetta floated down to Targa. "Are *you* helping Bloom do this?" She turned to stare at Aleadra's suffering. "Leave her alone!" Sirabetta shouted, using air pressure to knock Targa out.

If anything, the assault on Aleadra became fiercer—she was lifted into the air, where she twisted and writhed.

"No," a cold, angry young voice said. "She's hurt enough people today." Branches snapped and cracked as coils of gravity made room for Simon Bloom to leap up from the heart of the forest. He landed in the center of the path, probably using his gravity powers to slam into and shake the ground as if a giant had struck it. His clothes were torn and his face scratched, but Simon Bloom stood straight with clear confidence.

"How dramatic," Sirabetta sneered. "Now release her and face me, Bloom."

Aleadra wriggled helplessly above as Simon and Sirabetta circled each other.

"So you can gang up on me?" Simon said. "I don't think so."

Sirabetta shifted from hateful glare at Simon to worried look at Aleadra. "Put her down!" she yelled, her voice cracking with concern.

"Sure—as soon as we can settle this one-on-one."

Sirabetta was filled with horror as Aleadra stopped struggling and slumped forward. With a flick of his eyes, Simon flung her to the ground, hard . . . and she did not move. "Mother!" Sirabetta screamed, running to her.

"Mother?" Simon said, his fierce expression slipping. "Aleadra is your mother?"

"What, your spying Narrator didn't know something?" Sirabetta spat as she cradled the former Keeper's head. "Alive," she whispered. "She's still alive."

"Of course she's alive," Simon said, sounding indignant.

Sirabetta stood and clenched her hands into fists as she stared down the path at Simon. "You're going to pay, Bloom," she growled. "For standing in my way, for ruining my life, and for daring to harm my mother."

Simon pointed at his friends spread out on the ground, also unconscious, and his expression hardened. "If she helped you do that," he snarled, "then she got justice. And that's what you'll get, too."

Even the Breeze stopped blowing as Sirabetta cracked her knuckles, and Simon rolled his neck and shoulders. As they both prepared to unleash powers beyond imagination.

CHAPTER 44

THE NIGHT THEY DROVE OLD DUNKERHOOK DOWN

Sirabetta activated a blue tattoo on one arm, launching herself up into the air. At the same time, Simon soared upward with a twist of gravity.

They maneuvered quickly but carefully, swooping and ducking under and around branches, and circling huge tree trunks. This hide-and-seek led them out into the clearing or, rather, high above it. Suddenly they faced each other across open air.

"No more dancing, Simon," Sirabetta snarled.

Simon changed his gravitational pull so he could hover. He lashed out with a gravity arm, snatched Sirabetta, and whipped her at the nearest tree. With visible effort, she tore free of his grip and flew back to her place.

"Did you forget?" she said. "Gravity—your favorite toy—

doesn't work on me. Here's a new toy for you." She fired a ball of star-stuff at him; it sizzled the air as it flew.

Simon gasped. Like Owen, he was shocked that Sirabetta could now use more than one tattoo at a time. He didn't hesitate, though; he'd gotten used to thinking on his feet (or, as now, in midair). And he didn't need much thought to set his gravity arms in motion.

Simon grabbed the searing ball in a coil of gravity. Stars, after all, were as subject to gravity as anything else in the universe. He whipped it around and slung it back at her. "No," he yelled. "You keep it!"

Sirabetta cursed under her breath and barely managed to send another star-ball at this one in time to destroy it. The backlash of force and flame staggered her in the air, knocking her backward.

"Impressive, Bloom. Too bad you're not so slick with space-time. Maybe your friends wouldn't be lying in a pile in the dirt. It's a pity they trusted *you* as a leader."

Simon gritted his teeth. He had made a mistake with space-time, yes, but he wasn't going to allow guilt to wash over him, or self-doubt to distract him. Not this time—not ever again, if he could help it. It was courage and confidence—tempered with caution—that made a good leader. And whether he wanted to be or not, that's what Simon was.

Sirabetta fired off a series of six of the burning globes at Simon, but he used gravity arms to flick the first two star-balls aside, sending them deep into the woods. They blew apart a pair of distant treetops, setting them ablaze. He snagged the other four out of the air and sent them soaring back at Sirabetta. She bobbed and weaved to avoid them, singeing her leg on the fiery tail of one that came too close. They exploded beyond her, destroying several massive trees and igniting many others.

Sirabetta looked at the devastation behind her and smirked. "Wrecking your beloved woods?" she said. "I can help." She pointed to a yellow tattoo—her deforestation control—and, with a wink, activated it. Her formula cut through the bases of the trunks of the biggest trees around the clearing, eating away at the wood.

The sight of Dunkerhook being torn apart wounded Simon, but rather than show it, he went for Sirabetta's soft spot. "Aren't you afraid you'll hit your mommy?"

"You don't get to speak about her!" Sirabetta screamed. She set off air pressure explosions on the far sides of the trees, toppling them toward Simon. He narrowly avoided the enormous columns of dying wood. She hurled another barrage of star-balls at him, one after another in rapid succession. There were too many for him to grab and throw back without getting hit.

But this was not the same Simon Bloom who had been confounded by how to fight the mammoths—at last he understood and accepted what he was capable of. He could shape gravity to his will with his extra arms . . . and gravity was the same stuff that could crush buildings and move planets.

Simon quickly used his gravity-coils to grab large pieces of broken trees and swing them like gigantic baseball bats. "I. Am. Getting. Sick. Of. You. Lady!" he shouted, punctuating each word with another swing. Each impact between wood and star-ball resulted in a terrible, forest-shaking explosion and a shower of wooden shrapnel across the entire area.

Sirabetta used her heat and deforestation tattoos to annihilate the shards that flew at her, while Simon spoke a gravity-reverse that flung the pieces away. Both fighters sustained small cuts and burns from the chunks of wood that slipped past their defenses or ricocheted off trees behind them.

After several minutes, the clearing fell quiet. Sirabetta and Simon floated idly, squinting to see through the smoky air. Both panted; Sirabetta was feeling the strain from her heavy tattoo activity, and Simon was growing weary from his constant formula use. They looked around and saw considerably fewer trees in Dunkerhook Woods than there'd been before.

"Is this what chess players call a stalemate?" Sirabetta asked.

"I don't know—never played chess," Simon said, stone-faced and gruff-voiced.

"Can I convince you to give up?" Sirabetta asked. "What if I promised to let you go? I only want the Book, Bloom."

"The Book stays with me. I won't give in," Simon said. "Not ever."

"So heroic," she growled. "Or is it stubborn? Either way, you're a fool." She directed an air pressure burst at him, but

Simon wrapped a gravitational field around the rapidly expanding air, compressing it back to the way it was.

Sirabetta sighed, sweat pouring down her face. "Well, *that* didn't work, did it?"

Simon breathed heavily and smiled. "Nope. Tattoos still hurt to use, huh?"

"Nothing I can't handle."

"You know, *you* can give up," Simon said. "Surrender, have the tattoos taken off, stop trying to kill people, go for counseling."

"Yeah, right!" she spat. "After what I suffered, all the unfair treatment I got, I deserve this victory! And when I'm done, it'll be a better world for the Union and the Outsiders."

They bobbed silently on the air in the ruins of the forest, floating lower to the ground in their weariness. Both breathed deeply as the Breeze blew away the acrid smell of charred wood and ashed greenery. They drifted close enough to talk quietly.

"I'm sorry," Simon said, "but that's the dumbest thing I've ever heard. I think you want power and you want revenge and you're probably a little crazy."

Though Simon's words were harsh, his tone was gentle; he wasn't even mad at Sirabetta anymore. He felt bad for her, just from knowing only a sliver of what had happened in her past.

"You're probably right," Sirabetta said. Her voice was calm, almost serene, perhaps finally moving past her rage. "But I've come too far to stop now." She sighed. "I know you're just a kid. Powerful, but a kid nonetheless. You don't have the killer instinct. Even after all you've done to me, I wish it didn't have to end like this. Truly." She took a deep breath. "But it does."

Sirabetta chose another blue formula: activating it unleashed waves of fierce heat that reached Simon in a split second.

Simon screamed as the air around him burst aflame and he was blasted by the heat. The Book fell through his disintegrating backpack and to the forest floor. Sirabetta saw this and her eyes lit up; she need only swoop down and grab it. But that moment of distraction proved disastrous.

See, the heat she generated was caused by a type of radiation: infrared light. And light could be affected by gravity, too. It took a lot of gravitation—much more than needed to lift a mammoth—but with the right inspiration, Simon had near-infinite gravitational control at his disposal.

The agony he felt from the heat caused his body's natural epinephrine to surge, giving him the same effect as from a boost of Targa's formula. And Simon, desperate to undo this scorching attack, unleashed a mighty gravitational warp.

It was focused on the burning air and radiating heat, extinguishing the fire that engulfed him and the woods around him. It also bent the waves of heat, twisting them along the intricate web of gravity and sending them raging back to their source. Back to Sirabetta.

She had no way to defend herself against such an assault,

and she screamed at the sizzling air as it surrounded her. She turned off her tattoo, cutting the source of the heat in time to save herself from all but a slight singeing, but Simon wasn't done.

His pain and anger pushed him to a level of gravitational force that he couldn't control, and it all slammed into Sirabetta. The tattoo that let her resist previous attacks could not match this, and she was dragged down to the forest floor.

Simon formed a gravity bubble around Sirabetta, drawing in dirt and stone and wood and air, and compressing it all ever more tightly until it risked crushing her.

For a fraction of a second, even the light waves curved and distorted, blurring Sirabetta's appearance, but then the strain burst Simon's control. Consciousness fled him and he fell to the forest floor.

He landed hard about ten feet from where Sirabetta lay, bruised and battered, amid a pile of forest wreckage. Neither combatant moved. In between them, its cover closed and sealed shut, sat undamaged the *Teacher's Edition of Physics*.

Long moments passed, and amid the ruins of Dunkerhook Woods, there was silence once again.

CHAPTER 45

TWO FOR THE PRICE OF ONE

Thanks to his octopus resilience, Simon stirred first. The fall had hurt, though, and the burns from Sirabetta's attack were painful, too. His hair was partially burned off, and his skin was seared. He was not a pretty sight.

Simon took a few deep breaths and then rasped the formula for space–time, aiming it at himself. It reversed his injuries, taking his molecules back in time several minutes until right before Sirabetta's heat attack. His hair, clothing, and backpack reformed, too, as if they had never been burned. Thanks to the space–time warp, they hadn't.

It was a highly localized way of affecting time, though. He didn't move in space; he remained there on the ground instead of reappearing back in midair. Also, the Book did not reappear in Simon's backpack as it had been before; it stayed on the forest floor between Simon and Sirbetta. Apparently, the only space-time shifts that could affect the Book were its own.

Simon was weary from his exertions, and he couldn't use space-time to undo that—using space-time was a draining effort in itself. Plus, he still bore the sting of all the cuts and bruises he'd gotten during the bulk of the fight; he'd only reversed time up to the point of the heat attack. That had been tiring enough for him.

Sirabetta groaned and stirred. She shifted some of the debris around her and coughed at the smoke she'd inhaled. She sat up and saw Simon, just ten feet away, staring at her. Then she saw the Book on the ground and gasped. She reached out for it with one hand—the hand that was tattooed with the multicolored mark of the Board of Administration. It was the most crucial of all her tattoos; it allowed her to force the Book to work for her.

The tattoo worked best with physical contact; if she could get hold of the Book, she could do whatever she wished with it. But she was too weak to walk or even crawl, so she tugged at it with the tattoo's limited influence.

Simon was too tired to use gravity yet. He called to the Book, trying to use his Keeper-link to pull it back to him. The Book trembled, trapped between two summonings. At just five feet away, with the Book out of Simon's possession,

Sirabetta's tattoo gave her just enough of a hold to cause another stalemate.

Simon wracked his brain for what to do. He thought of space-time, the very same formula that had turned Sirabetta from a thirty-something into a thirteen-year-old. He could try reversing what he did last time, and restore Sirabetta to her true age; perhaps twenty years of growth would stretch out her new tattoos and make then unusable. But, then again, they might still work, and she'd have an adult's physical strength, too.

Better yet, if he made her much older—perhaps elderly— the tattoos would be unreadable on her wrinkled skin, and she would also be physically weaker. It was worth trying.

Simon spoke the words for space-time, aiming it at Sirabetta while hoping he was using it properly.

Maybe it was that—Simon not knowing how to control the formula in this way. Or perhaps it was Sirabetta's and Simon's split mastery over the Book that so distorted the effect. It probably had at least a little to do with the space-time connection between Simon and Sirabetta. And it certainly didn't help that Simon was so tired. But whatever the cause, the effect was . . . dramatic.

The sound of air ripping dominated that part of the forest. A dusty smell spread through the area, but that, like the air ripping, was part of the normal unpleasantness of space-time bending.

A blue glow surrounded Sirabetta. "No!" she wailed. "Not again!" Her entire body rippled like water in the wind, and then she grew. She aged. From thirteen to thirty-three in seconds. There was a tearing sound, and she grabbed at her wet suit, desperate to keep it covering her now more womanly body.

"I'm back," Sirabetta shouted triumphantly. "No more acne! No more puberty! No more getting treated like a kid!" She looked down and grinned; though her tattoos had stretched a bit with her changed age, they were still intact.

But then, as Simon gaped, her body rippled again and returned to thirteen. "NO!" she screamed. "This is not fair!" The wet suit, though torn or stretched in a few key places, was now the right size again. She clenched her fists. "You've done this to me for the last time!"

She extended a hand toward him and looked down at a tattoo, but she froze, with lips pursed on the first syllable. Her skin was wavering again and, before her startled eyes, returned to age thirty-three once more. She clutched at the wet suit. "Oh, you have got to be kidding," she rasped, her voice too spent to yell anymore.

Simon gulped. "What's going on?" he asked.

"Like you don't know," she said. "Like this isn't some sick joke of yours. I've had enough of you, Simon Bloom. I'll fix this myself once I have the Book!" She pointed her hand at him and chose a different tattoo.

Simon was too weak to use gravity, octopus-style or not,

but he knew he had to stop her. He reacted with instincts he didn't know he had—another octopus attribute—and spat something vile and viscous from his mouth.

A puddle of jet-black fluid shot through the air at Sirabetta. She screamed hoarsely as the liquid struck her, coating her face and arm in octopus ink. "Ahhh! What is this?" she shrieked.

Simon was too busy trying to get ink off of his tongue to answer; he felt like he'd gargled with water paint.

Sirabetta swiped at the liquid clinging to her, then gave up and turned to her other arm. Simon prepared to let loose with another ink attack, but he paused. He didn't understand what had happened: Sirabetta was surrounded by a blue glow and wasn't moving. Not even blinking or breathing. Had he done something without realizing it?

He was too puzzled and tired to think; he just waited numbly for something to happen. At the sound of laughter, he looked around; it was definitely not from Sirabetta.

"It's okay, you can relax," a deep male voice said between chuckles. "I'm sorry, I should have done something sooner, but I *had* to see that again. It's been a while since the first time, and I was too surprised to really appreciate it then. Want a breath mint?"

Simon whirled his head around and stared at the source of the voice: a young man in his twenties or late teens. And he looked so familiar.

"You're thinking I look familiar right now, aren't you?" the young man asked. "And you're wondering if you need to try and whip up one of your patented gravity–coils to take care of me. Don't worry, I'm a friend. The best friend you'll ever have."

"Who are you?" Simon asked, though on some level part of him knew. He thought he knew, but he couldn't believe it was even possible.

"It is possible, and it is true," the young man said.

"Are you reading my mind?" Simon asked.

"Nah," the young man answered. "I just remember what I was thinking; I remember it vividly, 'cause it was the weirdest thing I'd ever seen in twelve years of life. And considering I was Keeper of the Order of Physics then, that's saying something."

"Um . . . what?" was the best Simon could think of to say.

"Oh, man. I'm you. I'm Simon Bloom. Simon Bloom from the future, to be exact."

"Oh," Simon said. "Thanks for clearing that up." And then he passed out.

CHAPTER 46

DON'T SHOOT THE MESSENGER . . . ESPECIALLY IF IT'S YOU

Simon was jarred awake by a strange, unpleasant buzzing. "What?" he shouted, sitting up with a jolt.

"Sorry to wake you," the young man said. "I don't have much time. Don't worry, you'll have a chance to rest soon. Before things get really crazy."

"You—" Simon stammered. "You said you're me!"

The young man gave a gentle smile. "I *am* you. I know it's hard to believe; trust me, I know *exactly* how you feel." He frowned. "Though I could have sworn I was a little taller at that age. Hmmm. Maybe it's time you laid off the soda and started drinking milk, huh?"

Simon just stared. Then he remembered Sirabetta. "What about—?"

The young man (for the sake of easier narrating, I'll call

him Future Simon) waved a hand casually. "Oh, don't worry about her. She's frozen in time now. It's a complicated trick; it'll take you a while to get the hang of it."

"And what . . . ?"

"What do you do with her?" Future Simon said. "Ah, that's where things get sticky. First, take this." He handed Simon a bottle of water and a breath mint. "It'll help get the taste of octopus ink out. Seriously—ugh." Future Simon nodded as Simon swished fresh water around in his mouth and spat it out.

"Second, I want to compliment you; this was a tough day. A tough week. You've had to deal with a lot, and you did great. I'm proud of you, Simon."

Simon nodded. "Thanks. But if you're really me, aren't you just complimenting yourself?"

"Hey, learn to take a kind word, okay? I guess I was uptight when I was you."

"Uptight? Are you kidding me? This is the most bizarre thing I've ever seen!"

Future Simon shrugged. "Just you wait." He glanced at his watch. "Not much time left; you did this by accident and have no idea how to keep the time passage open."

"Can't you just . . . I don't know, come here—"

"Come here on my own? Nah, it doesn't work like that."

"But why? If you're the future me . . . you *must* know how to do this per—"

"Perfectly?"

"Could you stop finishing my sentences for me? It's annoying."

Future Simon smiled. "Sorry; I just remember this all so well. My Future-me did that, and it bugged me, too, but we're running out of time and you're too frazzled to make good use of it."

"Okay," Simon said. "So why can't you come back?"

"Time travel isn't easy to do, but it might also be dangerous. We're not exactly sure if changing the past can mess up the future, but why risk it? It's better for you to handle it; move forward, not look back."

"Is this really the time to sound like a fortune cookie? Fine. So what am I supposed to do?"

"Just listen for a few minutes. You did great here. Don't worry about the woods." He looked around and whistled. "Though . . . wow. Nice mess. It'll be fine; the woods will fix itself. Eventually."

Simon nodded, relieved. The destruction around him was awful.

"When I disappear, my time-stop on Sirabetta will wear off, and you'll have to take over; a simple thump on the head from a gravity-arm will do the trick. After that, it'll be harder to keep control of her; she's a feisty one."

"No kidding."

"But as long as her tattoos are covered, she can't use 'em. The ink'll work in a pinch, but there are better methods. And as long as you're within about eight feet or so of her, she'll stop shifting back and forth between old and young. She'll stay thirteen. I'm warning you, she's not going to be happy about this." He chuckled. "She's going to be a handful."

"Wait," Simon said, rising to sitting position. "Why am *I* going to have to take care of her? I'm just going to turn her over to the Council and then to the Board, right?"

Future Simon shook his head. "Sorry, pal. That's the most important thing I have to tell you. All those renegades you've fought . . . they're nothing. They're pawns. Even Sirabetta has no idea what she's really involved in. The Board of Administration is the true danger."

"What?"

"Yeah. They're behind everything. Not all of them, but enough that they're a real threat to the whole Union. The whole universe. But especially you, right now. You have to take care of Sirabetta on your own. Well, you and your friends, of course."

"What? Why? How?"

"Think about it," Future Simon said. "Where did Sirabetta go after Bio to get work on her tattoos done?"

"Greygor said Chemistry, to see a mad scientist Order member named LaCurru."

Future Simon nodded. "So what should you do to get rid of those tattoos?"

"If it's up to us, not the Board . . . I guess I'd take her to Chemistry, have their Keeper—Olvero, I think—help us find LaCurru or some other way to remove them."

"There you go," Future Simon said. "It won't be easy." He looked away, his face and shoulders sagging. "But be strong. The fate of the universe is on your shoulders and all that." He shivered. "The burden gets heavy at times, but we can handle it."

"Wait!" Simon yelped. "What is this about the Board? I thought they were the good guys. The ones who kept this all together!"

"I—" Future Simon shook his head. "I can't tell you about that. You'll have to find out on your own."

"But why? I need all the help I can get, and you know everything about this!"

Future Simon looked miserable as he shook his head. "Sorry, but my Future-me never told me when I was you, that is, your age. Understand?"

"Nobody could understand that!" Simon moaned.

Future Simon chuckled. "I remember saying that. So funny." He held up a hand. "And I remember getting mad at Future-me for laughing at something so serious. But it's like I said before: we can't risk ruining the future by changing the past. We're pretty sure that you can't, thanks to something called a causality loop. Interfering in the past only causes the proper future to happen."

Simon shook his head. "You must know I have no idea what you're talking about."

"It's like all those Greek tragedies you'll get around to reading in school. An oracle tells someone that something bad's going to happen. The person changes their whole life to keep that bad thing from happening but, in trying to change it, actually causes it to happen."

"But I'm not Greek!" Simon shouted.

Future Simon sighed. "Sorry, man. Can't do it." He reached down and helped Simon to his feet. "Don't forget that," he said, gesturing to the Book.

Simon mentally summoned the Book, and with Sirabetta no longer competing with him, it leaped right into his out-stretched hand. He felt something odd through his mental connection with the Book.

"The Book's acting funny around you," Simon said. "What's going on?"

Future Simon smiled. "That falls safely under the 'can't-tell-you' heading."

"Great. So glad you stopped by. Is there *anything* else you can tell me?"

Future Simon looked up into the sky. "Hey, Greygor. Re-member to plant your feet to fight the spins, okay, buddy?" He looked back at Simon. "As for you, keep a firm grip on the Book, and Sirabetta's BOA tattoo on her palm won't work. But don't let her touch it. And . . ." He shook his head. "Nope, I think that's all I can tell you."

"Please, you've got to tell me more," Simon said. "The fate of the universe is a lot for a twelve-year-old."

"It is," Future Simon said, "but you're no ordinary twelve-year-old. Look at what you've accomplished! You're the

Keeper of the Order of Physics, you've stopped all sorts of villains, and you've mastered incredible abilities from Biology, too. You're using your abilities in ways that the other Keepers never dreamed of, and you're just getting started! You'll do fine, Simon."

Simon paused and thought about what he said. He'd come so far in just a few days. Maybe he could handle this. But still . . . "Can you at least give me a better hint? A few small clues? Greygor broke the rules to help us out, and that turned out fine."

Future Simon looked away. "You're really being a pain, did you know that? Fine. I guess I can tell you a couple of small things to help you out."

Suddenly, the air around Future Simon started to distort. "Oh, right," Future Simon said. "I just remembered—*this* is why my Future Simon never told *me* more. Sorry, Simon . . . and good luck!"

The air tore open again, making that awful ripping noise as Future Simon was sucked through the hole and off to his future existence.

Simon stared off after him and realized something; Future Simon had said he *"was* Keeper of the Order of Physics *then"* in the past tense. As if he wasn't anymore. What did that mean?

He remembered something else and whipped his head around toward Sirabetta as she suddenly found herself back in the normal timestream.

For her, no time had passed since she had wiped away some ink and was preparing to use another attack tattoo. She was thus shocked to find Simon gone from where he'd been and, instead, standing several feet away, holding the Book.

"What the—?" was all she managed to say before the dusty stink of space-time bending sent her into a coughing and sneezing fit.

Simon marshaled his energy and, as Future Simon suggested, formed a small gravity arm to conk Sirabetta on the head and knock her out. He then took a deep breath as a strong gust of the Breeze blew around him, filling him with renewed vigor. Soon he felt strong enough to wrap a gravity coil around Sirabetta and lift her up. Though she was still unconscious, her body kept shifting back and forth from thirteen to thirty-three every minute or so.

He made sure his gravity-grip was tight enough to keep her arms and legs pinned and to keep her wet suit from falling off. He made her body hover above him; luckily, the ink clinging to her face and arm was caught in the gravity field, keeping it from dripping. Simon kept her three feet above him and, as Future Simon had said, she stopped her age jumping and remained thirteen.

Great, he thought. *Keeping a crazy supervillain within eight feet of me is going to suck. Not to mention her being a girl . . . going to the bathroom's going to be tricky.*

With Sirabetta floating above him like a girl-shaped balloon, Simon rushed through the wreckage of Dunkerhook

Woods in search of his friends. He was relieved to find them standing around the still-unconscious Krissantha, Preto, and Aleadra. Targa was focusing her adrenaline control on them, lowering their heart rates enough to keep them from reviving. Alysha was nearby, ready to zap them if they stirred, and the others were on full alert to back them up.

"You're all awake!" Simon shouted, running toward them. "You're okay!"

"'Okay' is a relative term," Flangelo said.

Indeed, as Simon got close enough he saw just how battered they all looked. Seeing Simon's face crinkle with concern, Alysha mustered a smile. "I'm bruised, I'm exhausted, and my clothes are a mess. But at least it's over."

"About that," Simon said, clearing his throat. "I've got some bad news."

CHAPTER 47

The More Immediate Future

Simon had to repeat his story several times as his friends struggled to understand what had happened.

They didn't doubt his explanation of his battle with Sirabetta; the evidence was all around them. More than half of the trees and bushes of Dunkerhook Woods had been torn to pieces or badly burned during the struggle. Fortunately, the fight had been far enough away to leave his friends unharmed.

They weren't too surprised by his ink-spitting ability; it fit in with his octopus-powers-theme. As for what Simon learned about Aleadra . . .

"Sirabetta's mom?" Alysha said. "That's pretty lame. I mean, cut the cord, lady! Let your daughter fight her own battles."

The part they had trouble grasping was that whole Future

Simon bit. He showed them the way Sirabetta now changed back and forth in age when too far from him, which only added to their amazement. Even considering the week they'd had, it was a pretty abnormal thing to witness.

"Normal?" Simon asked. "No offense, but we've left normal far behind."

"True, true," an aged man's voice said. "Normal and even strange are left by the wayside when you deal with space-time."

"Ralfagon!" Simon, Alysha, Owen, and Loisana shouted at the same time.

Targa leaned in toward Flangelo. "Is that their grandpa or something?" she whispered.

"Grandpa?" Eldonna said, ambling along just behind Ralfagon. "Have *you* got a lot to learn."

Simon introduced everyone, and Targa gave Ralfagon a respectful apology. Her dealings with Aleadra had taught her not to take any ex–Keeper lightly.

"No offense taken," Ralfagon said. "Now, young Simon, it seems you've been busy with your new role as Keeper." He gazed around the wreckage of the woods. "I think we have to work on your self–control, though."

Simon and his friends took turns describing their adventures thus far, ending with Simon once again explaining what Future Simon had told him.

"Ah. What a frightening warning from your future self . . . most alarming, really." He rubbed his chin.

"How did you know to come find us here?" Alysha asked.

"You'd be amazed just how much noise your little scuffle made for ears that are attuned to hear it," Ralfagon said. "I'd have been here sooner, but the sound gave me quite the headache. Wound up programming the Gateway to the wrong setting."

Eldonna sighed. "We ended up in Amsterdam, where the Order of Physics used to meet centuries ago."

"Yes. That place certainly has changed," Ralfagon said. "Not that I was in the Order back then. I don't think so, at least," he added.

"So what do we do now?" Simon asked.

Ralfagon frowned. "Simon, I'm afraid that is up to you; you are the Keeper of the Book of Physics, the holder of astounding Biology powers, and the captor of one very ill-tempered, age–changing villainess." He gestured to Sirabetta. "I trust in your skills and your wisdom."

"Hmmm. You've redecorated since I've been here last." Everyone turned to see Gilio and his own Book.

"Gilio?" Ralfagon said in surprise. "How fortunate that you showed up!" He put a hand to his head. "Wait, I didn't call you, did I?"

"We could definitely use some first aid," Simon said.

Gilio grinned as he gave Ralfagon a friendly embrace. "I didn't think your Book called me here for my advice on tree care, Bloom."

Alysha rolled her eyes. "Everyone's a comedian, today," she muttered.

"The Book?" Simon and Ralfagon said at the same time, while the *Teacher's Edition of Physics* floated and flashed blue in greeting to the *Teacher's Edition of Biology*, which flashed green in response.

"Ralfagon, you wouldn't believe the things Simon has been achieving with that Book," Gilio said. "Not to mention my own. Beyond anything I've ever heard of."

Simon smiled and looked away, uncomfortable with the praise.

Alysha rubbed her back. "Didn't someone mention healing?" she asked.

"As you can see, you're definitely needed here," Eldonna said to Gilio.

Gilio smiled widely and gave a showy bow to Eldonna, who blushed. He used one of his formulas to sedate the captured villains completely, and then he tended to the injured while Simon and his friends relayed all that had happened.

"I wish I could do something for the woods," Gilio said as he surveyed the devastation. "But that would take far more energy than I have right now." He frowned at the unconscious Aleadra. "She was my Keeper," he said with a sigh. "A good friend and adviser." He shook his head. "Sad."

"Worse, what do we do with them?" Simon asked. "We can't hand them over to the Board of Administration."

"No, we certainly can't," Gilio said. "And frankly, I'm not

sure if it's safe to take them prisoner in the domain of Biology. There might be more traitors in the Order. And who knows what other tricks Aleadra has up her sleeves."

"I'll bet the BOA freed the traitors we already turned over to them," Owen said.

Ralfagon patted Simon on the shoulder, ducking under the still-unconscious, still-gravity-wrapped Sirabetta bobbing in the air above him. "My boy, you've got your work cut out for you. But I will do all I can to help you."

"You know we're in," Alysha said.

"Yeah, to the Order of Chemistry or wherever," Owen said.

Kender frowned. "This is turning out to be a lot more dangerous than I thought," he said. "I almost died. We all did."

"If the Board is behind Sirabetta, nothing's going to be safe," Simon said.

Targa folded her arms. "So what's the plan?"

"If someone can keep an eye on these bad guys," Simon said while gesturing at Krissantha, Preto, and Aleadra, "I'd say the next step is Chemistry. Alysha, Owen, and I are supposedly away on a school trip for at least a few more days, so we can go. We'll get these tattoos off Sirabetta before she kills someone. Maybe get some info out of her along the way. After that, who knows? We'll have to figure it out as we go along."

Standing there in the shattered remains of Dunkerhook Woods, they put together the beginnings of a plan. The world as they all knew it had changed, and it could be a long time before things got back to normal.

But at last Simon knew he could handle this. His friends and he were up to the challenge; they were stronger, wiser, and more resourceful than just a few short—actually, they felt very long—days ago.

And no matter what the future held, Simon Bloom knew he was ready to lead them.

PLANT MY FEET, INDEED

I sighed as the image of Dunkerhook Woods faded away and the green light went out. This Chronicle of Simon Bloom was over.

I was staggered by how much Simon and his friends had faced, and by how much lay ahead. I wondered if they'd visit again before going to the Order of Chemistry.

I turned away from my Viewing Screen and recalled something Sirabetta said. She mentioned having me "taken care of." And she'd said it in a tone that did not imply a nice muffin basket. What could she have meant? Hopefully, her current difficulties would keep her too busy to come after me.

There was a knock at the door. Was it Simon and his pals already? As I opened the door, my smile dropped. "Willoughby Wanderby?"

He aimed his formula at me, spinning me violently into

my living room. Luckily, I struck my reclining chair, which was padded enough to keep me from harm.

Wanderby stomped into my living room. "So you're the spy helping those fools fight us. I have a message for you from Sir. It will involve a bit of dying, though."

"Er, how much is a bit?" I asked.

Wanderby gestured and I spun again, this time crashing into the sofa. Once more a rather soft landing, but I was running out of comfy spots to bounce off of.

"How did you find me?" I asked as I rose to my feet. I hoped to get him talking until Simon and his friends could come to my rescue.

"No more secrets for you, Narrator," Wanderby snarled.

My Narrator abilities kicked in; they'd been working all along, but my terror had kept me from noticing. Now I realized exactly what I needed to know: after waking up from Simon's bug attack in the jungle, Wanderby fled the Biology domain by a prearranged escape route and got in touch with his mysterious contact. Then Sirabetta got word to him to deal with me. Apparently she was quite put out by my narrating her activities.

Everyone's a critic.

Now Wanderby intended to eliminate me, ambush the kids, and free Sirabetta.

I grabbed the first thing in reach and held it out in front of me as a shield. Unfortunately, it was a sofa cushion, which Wanderby spun away from me.

 349

Very well, I thought. If I was to, as they say, "go out like that," I'd do so fighting. I planted my slippered feet firmly on my carpet and raised my fists in a boxing stance. It wasn't a particularly effective stance—I have no idea how to box—but the message was there. I would battle this ruffian until the end.

About five seconds, I reckoned. Ten if I was lucky.

Wanderby again gestured, but this time I didn't spin off into something with a loud crash. Instead, I felt a tingling in my feet.

"What?" he shouted. "How did you do that?"

"Me?" I asked, clueless. "Perhaps you're too tired to use your formula?"

Wanderby flicked a hand at the kitchen, and my top-of-the-line refrigerator (stainless steel, built-in ice maker) spun into—and through—the cupboards across from it.

"That was uncalled for!" I shouted. "What did my kitchen ever do to you?"

Wanderby tried his formula on me again, and again I did not budge. There was only that tingle.

"So you've found a way to resist my formula," the fleshy man bellowed. "I'll have to do this the old-fashioned way." He raised his fists which, I couldn't help but notice, were larger and more menacing than my own.

"Oh, that's quite enough of that," a clipped British voice said.

Wanderby and I both turned to my doorway through which, to my delight, Miss Fanstrom was striding.

"Mr. Wanderby, I must ask that you stop harassing my Narrator," she said.

"Miss Fanstrom?" Wanderby asked. "Why do you keep showing up at moments like these?"

"All part of the job, Mr. Wanderby."

Wanderby aimed his formula at Miss Fanstrom, but like me, she was unaffected.

"Your job? As principal?" he asked in clear confusion.

"No," she said as her magnificent column of hair stretched out and walloped him across the jaw. "Keeper." Once, twice, three times, her hair struck until he sank to the carpet, unmoving.

"I didn't want to do that," Miss Fanstrom said. "It's dreadfully tedious to have the same villain defeated the same way in two different Chronicles. But that's the problem with history, I suppose."

"What's that?" I asked.

"Oh, you know," Miss Fanstrom said. "It repeats itself."

"Ah," I said. And then I utterly failed to come up with anything else to add.

"It's good that you planted your feet," Miss Fanstrom said. Seeing my confusion, she pointed to my feet. "Those are standard-issue Historical Society Narrator slippers, Mr. Geryson. With feet planted, you can't be moved in them, not

even by Mr. Bloom's gravity-coils. Of course, he could probably lift the floor up with you."

I glanced down and wiggled my toes inside my slippers.
"Really?"

"Tut tut, Mr. Geryson. Haven't you read your handbook?"

I blinked, remembering I'd only read about how to get
free movies on my Viewing Screen between Chronicles. I certainly hadn't seen anything about slippers.

"Clearly," she said, "you should take it now." She pointed
to my bookcase. "It's there, between an old television direc-
tory and a rather worn Harry Potter novel."

Once I'd found it, Miss Fanstrom nodded, her hair im-
mobile. "Come on, we don't have all day. We've got to put Mr.
Wanderby in proper custody, seal your apartment off, and get
on with our role in all this."

"Our . . . role?"

"Oh, Mr. Geryson. Have you not been paying attention?"

I nodded, shook my head, and finally shrugged. I was still
trying to digest the fact that Willoughby Wanderby had come
here—*here*—and attacked me.

"That's precisely my point," Miss Fanstrom said. "The rules
are crumbling in the face of all this change. Upheaval, really.
Terribly hard to do a good Chronicle in the midst of that, I
assure you. And with the Board of Administration involved?"

"It's true, then?" I asked.

"You saw it there, straight from the lips of our dear Mr.

Bloom the Older. I've suspected things were amiss, but now I have confirmation. And we must not be idle."

"We mustn't?"

"No, and that should please you. Weren't you whinging about wanting to lend a hand to your friends?" She gestured to the Viewing Screen. "Quickly now, gather a travel bag. Only the essentials . . . but include your handbook and your portable Viewing Screen. Whatever else happens, you're still a Narrator."

"Oh, certainly," I said, still trying to process all this.

"And don't forget to bring a tin of that delicious vanilla mint tea you've got," Miss Fanstrom continued. "Simply delightful."

"No . . . rather, yes, or . . . let me just change clothes, first," I stammered.

"Absolutely not!" Miss Fanstrom said. "Those slippers and that standard–issue Historical Society Narrator bathrobe are marvels when you're facing danger. Which is almost certainly what lies ahead of us."

"Is that right?" I asked with a gulp.

Miss Fanstrom nodded. "I'm afraid so. The entire universe is in its greatest danger yet, Mr. Geryson. Together, you and I are going to help save it." She paused and steepled her fingers together. "Under the circumstances," she said, "perhaps I'd best start calling you Greygor."

GLOSSARY FOR THE WORLD OF
THE TEACHER'S EDITIONS

(In case you're too lazy to use a dictionary or encyclopedia—though, let's be honest, those are much more reliable than this.)

Active Transport The way a cell takes in or gets rid of objects (food, waste, messages–in–the–bottles). So instead of opening a mouth to eat, the cell creates a special bubble (called a vesicle) around the food and lets that in. Sadly, this makes it quite difficult for cells to chew gum.

Atom The smallest part of matter. (Okay, that's not true. It's made of smaller parts–neutrons, protons, and electrons, some of which are made of even smaller parts–but the atom is the smallest you can divide matter without using an atom smasher or a nuclear explosion or something.)

Bioluminescence This is when a living thing has an inner glow—literally. It has a natural way of giving off its own light without needing batteries or an electrical outlet.

Capacitance Certain objects can conduct an electrical charge, and some of the conductors can store and release that charge. These capacitors are in electric circuits, among other places, and are exactly the wrong kind of thing to stick your tongue into.

Chromatophore Pigment–containing cells. Octopi and certain other animals can change their skin color and skin texture thanks to these nifty things. So octopi are one of the few types of animals that cannot only look blue but actual *feel* blue.

DNA (Stands for deoxyribonucleic acid, a word as hard to say as it is to spell.) Every cell of every living creature has a copy of its DNA—molecules filled with a code that defines what that creature will look like inside and out. (At least before it eats lunch or goes shopping.)

Double Helix DNA molecules look like this—two curled lines intertwining like a spiral staircase. Except this staircase has all the information of life on its steps . . . so you'd better hope nobody trips as they walk up or down.

Drag A special kind of friction between an object and a gas (such as air) or a liquid (such as water) around it. The more drag there is, the slower the object moves, which is quite a drag, if you'll forgive the really lame pun.

Epinephrine Sometimes called adrenaline. This is the stuff that your body uses to get you prepared for danger so you can fight or, if you're not feeling too tough, run away. (A good pair of sneakers helps, too.)

Exoskeleton Some animals—such as insects, arachnids, and crustaceans—have their skeletons on the outside (as opposed to on the inside, called *endoskeleton*, like humans do). Exoskeletons give these critters extra protection and strength; they also provide an extra crunch if they're squished.

Friction Whenever two objects are touching, there's friction between them. The more friction there is, the harder it is to move them. When the two objects are in motion, it's called kinetic friction; when they're not moving (like you with your butt on the chair while you read this), it's called static friction.

Gene Not to be confused with jeans, these are found on DNA molecules; each gene has a code on it, and that code causes a specific trait or attribute. (For example, you might have a gene that makes you look good in jeans.)

Gravity/G There's a really good reason you don't just go flying off into space every time you take a step, and it's not the grippy soles on your new shoes. It's the force of gravitation, which is the attraction between two objects. The more mass something has, the more it pulls on other objects around it. So everything on Earth is pulled down toward the Earth's core, where most of its mass is. (It's believed that gravitation is linked to the space–time continuum—more massive objects curve space–time around them. Maybe if you eat a big enough lunch, you'll be able to affect space–time.)

Ion When an atom gains or loses an electron, it gains an electric charge (not to be confused with a credit card charge). That atom is now either a positive or negative ion.

Mass The amount of matter (solid, liquid, or gas) in something. More mass doesn't necessarily mean the thing must be big—a refrigerator box is bigger than the refrigerator that came in it, but trust me, the refrigerator is a lot harder to lift.

Megafauna This is the name for any type of really big animal, especially ones that went extinct. You may want to try to pet some of them, but beware: even if some megafauna won't try to eat you, they might accidentally squash you.

Myopia Nearsightedness—you can see things up-close just fine, but the farther away they get, the more blurry they get. So if you're myopic and you've just fallen off a cliff, you'll get an increasingly better view of the ground as you come closer to splatting into it.

Norepinephrine This is related to epinephrine (as the name sort of gives away); it makes the mind more alert to match the body's increased readiness for fighting, running away, or playing a particularly exciting game of chess.

Phase Change This is a shift between the different states of matter—solid, liquid, gas, or plasma, which is sort of the unofficial fourth state. The change occurs with heat: ice melts into water; water evaporates into gas–or cold: gas condenses into water; water freezes into ice. It's an especially important process when you leave the ice cream out of the freezer.

Plasma Not to be confused with plasma in blood . . . this is the unofficial fourth state of matter. Extreme heat can strip away electrons from a gas, turning them into ions. The result, plasma, can be a pretty lightshow (like the aurora borealis) or an explosive, dangerous substance like that found in lightning or stars. (You know, like the sun, that big, hot thing way up in the daytime sky.)

Pseudopod Translates to "false foot" . . . and that's what it is. Amoebas have 'em, forming them from their bloblike bodies as a way to move around. But they're not real feet, so amoebas have no need for wearing sneakers on them when they want to play soccer.

Space-Time This is the combination of space and time—the where and the when of things—which are believed to be connected as a whole. The combo is known as the space–time continuum, and you're in it right now. (Say hello to the nice continuum.)

Spore This is the way certain living things—such as fungi or plants that don't have seeds—reproduce. So some of these spores, which would look like tiny dots to humans (if we can see them at all), are really bouncing baby mushrooms. They'd be cute if they weren't so gross.

Terminal Velocity This is a fun rule of physics that only applies when in an atmosphere. It's the speed at which something falling can't accelerate any faster because of friction with the air. That may sound like a good thing but trust me: if you're falling and reaching terminal velocity, your landing will still hurt. A lot.

Velocity This is the speed and direction of something. If you're not moving, you have no speed or direction. If you're falling out of an airplane, your speed is really fast and your direction, unfortunately for you, is down. (Hope you remembered a parachute or a really, really soft cushion.)

Vesicle This is a container–like a sac or a bubble—used to bring things into and out of cells during active transport. Think of it as a special type of gift-wrapping.

Acknowledgments

This is my second published novel but my first sequel—an exhilarating and frightening thing to craft that, in many ways, was more daunting than book one. While I got to thank many before, there are others who must be noted. (And if I leave anyone out, please forgive me.)

First, thanks again to my family for their love, support, and advice (even if I didn't always heed it): my dad, Sheldon, as an extra PR agent; my sister, Michele, getting her school to welcome me; my mom, Karen; and Grandma Elsie, and cousins, aunts, and uncles telling everyone they know about my book . . . thank you all. (And please, don't stop!)

Next, I want to send bottomless appreciation to specific people: Damon Ross, who, on top of connections and shared knowledge, gave me reading to sustain me. My agent, Nancy Gallt, who provided calming guidance when I was at my most crazed. Stephanie Owens Lurie, my wonderful publisher at Dutton, who ushered *The Gravity Keeper* through its final stages and then took the time to be my oh-so-patient (and tolerant) editor for *The Octopus Effect*. It couldn't have been easy to take on a hyper, oft-neurotic author stumbling through a complicated sequel, but she did so with grace, skill, and smiles . . . this book benefited immensely from her work. Debbie Kovacs of Walden Media, for her support, insights, and my Venezuelan birthday. Thanks also for PR magic from Samantha Del'Olio and Nicole White, and excellent innovations and effort from everyone at Penguin and Walden Media. I can't express how grateful I am to you all for helping me get Simon Bloom into the hands and hearts of others. While I applaud every single member of the Penguin sales force, a special cheer must go to Todd Jones, whose enthusiasm for my book moved me and so many booksellers.

Huge thanks go to everyone at The Gotham Group, especially my managers—Ellen Goldsmith-Vein, Lindsay Williams, and Eddie Gamarra—for their amazing work in steering a big pile o' pages into a bright 'n' shiny movie deal. Plus, of course, Peter Nichols for his deal-making wizardry, and Melissa for putting up with me as she slogged through that fierce contract. Deep appreciation goes to producers Gary Ross, Allison Thomas, and Naketha Mattocks at Larger Than Life, and to Jeffrey Kirschenbaum at Universal—thanks for seeing so much potential in my work.

All my friends were so encouraging and helpful and I love you all for it. I have to single out some who truly went above and beyond in spreading the word and book: Jo, Rahul, Ric, Jaime, Sarah and Zack, Rebecca W, and Dan B and Yael. Thanks also to Mike W for science tips and the bunny, and to Stephan for his generous and brilliant website work. And big hugs to Laura A and Amanda Y, whose passion for Simon Bloom helped shape its fate. I'd like to raise a glass to the mighty LAYAs—the LA Young Adult authors—who gave me sharp advice, potent laughs, and understanding shoulders on which to lean. (And a spotlight on the amazing Lisa Yee, who brought me into the group.) Once again, thanks to Lucia and Insomnia Café for being my second office and my sanctuary. There were many friends who listened to me whine and kept me sane, but I'd especially like to thank Garrett, Tara, Grace, Ronen, Robert M, Raj and Lora, Keary, Farrell, and Michael L. A separate, massive thanks goes to Yaniv Bar-Cohen, MD, for being a first reader, story adviser, scientific pointer-outer, photographer, videographer, and, of course, a great friend.

I'm no scientist, and so I heartily cheer my science consultants: Wendy and Larry Woolf, and Leigh Goldstein; this book wouldn't have worked so smoothly without their aid. An extra nod goes to rocket scientist Yosi Bar-Cohen, who got me to realize just how cool octopi are.

Finally, I'd like to express my respect and admiration to everyone out there who works so hard to bring books to people, especially young people. To the teachers, librarians, and booksellers who care enough to nurture and nudge, and to authors like Douglas Adams (always Douglas Adams), Terry Pratchett, Lemony Snicket, and every other writer who inspires others to read (and me to write). And finally, thanks to all of you—young and old—who've enjoyed Simon Bloom and shared your reactions with me. I'll keep writing 'em if you keep reading 'em!